WISHING FOR A STAR

ANA BALEN

Published by Ana Balen
Wishing for a star
Zagreb, 2018

ISBN: 978-953-48139-0-4

ISBN: 978-953-48139-1-1

Edited by: Hot Tree Editing
https://www.facebook.com/HotTreeEditing/
Cover design by: JM Walker with Just write. Creations
https://www.facebook.com/justwrite.creations/
Formatted by: JM Walker

For Šimun

PROLOGUE

ONCE UPON A time, there was a little girl. Like all little girls, she was a treasure to her parents, their little princess. Her beauty was perfect—blonde hair with big ringlets, big curious blue eyes, and pink chubby cheeks. She was excited about the world, wanted to know everything had a million and one questions, and even more answers.

One night, while falling asleep in her mother's loving arms, out of the blue, she asked, "Mommy, do you know where I was before you were my mommy?"

"No, baby, I don't," her mom answered, curious about where this was coming from. "Do you?"

"Of course I do," the little girl scoffed, because how could anyone dare to ask her if she knew the answer to a question. "I was a little star in the sky, and I watched and looked, and I saw you. So I decided you would be my mommy. I climbed down from the sky and came to you. I wanted you to be my mommy and nobody else."

"Thank you, baby," said Mommy, her voice thick with tears and full of wonder for she didn't expect such an answer. "I love you."

"I love you too, Mommy," said the little girl, already half asleep.

That night, the little girl stayed asleep all night long in her mother's loving arms, while her mom cried tears of happiness, love, and, above all, gratitude for such a lovely and precious baby girl.

That was twenty years ago. The little girl grew up to be a lovely and precious young woman. She still has the beautiful blonde hair and the big, curious blue eyes. She's still very excited about the world and is still inquisitive, with a million questions and even more answers. She is my sister.

And as the time has its doing, she doesn't remember that night or the words she said. But our mom does. She's told the story a million times over, and every time, there is a glint in her eye. And every night, right before bed, there is a smile on her face. No matter what's going on in her life, she is always grateful—grateful there was a star in the sky she once wished upon, and as that wish came true, that star became hers.

CHAPTER ONE

"*YOU NEED TO understand something. Our children will not have usual names. They have to have something extraordinary, just like their mother," he says with such conviction I almost believe I'm pregnant at that very moment, while I watch his warm green eyes.*

"What the hell are you talking about? Are you crazy?" I ask, trying to get up, but as he's lying on top of me, his weight becomes heavier and his arms wrap around me like steel, preventing me from running.

His lips meet mine—not a kiss, just a touch. "Yeah, babe. Crazy," he mumbles. "I'm crazy 'bout you. You should know that by now." The truth of that statement shines brightly in his eyes.

"We've been seeing each other for only two months, and you're here babbling about kids? Yeah, no, I'm not going there." But my heart is in my throat, drumming with excitement, and there is a goofy smile on my face.

And then I see it. The picture he painted. The dream I would give everything to come true. Even if we've been together for such a short time, in my soul I know. I know he's the one for me. He's going to be the very essence of me and the father of my children.

Have you ever had a moment when you just knew the life you had was going to change completely? That one moment in which you knew nothing would ever be the same again? I've had those moments three times in my short life—well, if you consider twenty-nine years a short time.

First was when I met my husband, Sam.

Second, the day we got married.

And the third time?

Right now.

Only this time, there are no butterflies in my belly. My whole body isn't shaking with barely controlled excitement, and I don't have a smile on my face so big that if I didn't have ears I would swallow my head.

Instead, this time, my stomach has decided to take a trip and explore my feet, but that's not far enough, so it said, "Fuck it" and went right out of the building, leaving me hollow. My head is swimming, and the expression on my face is nowhere near a smile. Nothing in this moment is funny.

My name is Danielle Hunt, and this is the moment when my life will turn and take me on the ride through hell.

"I'm sorry, Danielle." Hearing those words in that soft voice filled with regret, everything in me just stops. My eyes go from looking at the doctor sitting in front of me to his right side, where a picture is hanging on the wall.

I want to go to it, take it off the wall, and smash it into a million pieces until it's destroyed.

For the last ten years, I've come to this office for regular checkups. It's a nice office, a standard one with a desk and chair. There's a big plant in the left corner and a couch on the right side of the room. On the walls hang the normal diplomas, some framed articles—probably written by the doctor—and generic art, the kind that's mass-produced. You can find it in every office where the occupant has no interest or time to pick something unique.

But then there is that picture.

In it is a woman in her most magnificent state.

A pregnant woman.

She's dressed in a pink T-shirt and is standing in front of a white background, caught in midcaress of her unborn child. But the most striking thing in the picture is the woman's face, as she wears a look of serenity.

I want that.

I want to have that expression on my face, to have that big belly as I carry my child. But most of all, I want to give that to my husband.

And now I never will.

It's during this thought I feel my nose start to tingle and tears pool at the bottom of my eyes. But I don't let them fall. Taking a big breath and squashing the desire to destroy that picture, then curl up on the floor and cry, I move my eyes back to the doctor to give him a slight nod.

I fear if I do anything else, like, say, open my mouth to reply, I will somehow manage to introduce my face to the beige carpet on the floor, even though I'm currently sitting down.

"Do you have any questions?" the doctor asks, and I feel a hand on my thigh squeeze.

Looking to my left, as always, my breathing stops for a second. It stops without failure.

It's because, after all my wandering, after all the assholes I met, and after buckets of tears spilled into wine and icecream while complaining to my friends, six years ago, I found *him*.

The love of my life.

My husband. Sam.

Dressed in jeans, a black T-shirt, and his boots on his feet, he sits beside me, his eyes looking firmly forward. And even though he's sitting down, it's plain to see he's a huge man. Tall, broad-shouldered, his thigh is almost as wide as my torso. He's my bear of a man, made completely out of muscle. Those eyes, the color of grass after the rain, are always full of love for me, and now, they don't even spare me a glance.

He's the most beautiful man I've ever seen. He keeps his midnight black hair clipped short, since it's curly. If he let it grow longer, he would sport something that resembles an afro on a head held high, since he's secure in the knowledge he made all the right decisions in his life. The mistakes made have been corrected, and the lessons lurking in them have been learned. But now, that head comes down as he bows it.

Seeing that, something deep inside me cracks, sending pain so strong and so sharp it's a miracle my heart keeps beating.

I always know what's going on inside his head.

But now, I'm terrified, because, for the first time, that's not the case. And I don't know what to make of this. For some reason, fear starts creeping into my heart. Fear of what, I don't know. But, as it's inching deeper and deeper with each second, I make a silent promise I'll do everything in my power to not let it break me, that I will make our dreams come true. On this thought, I move my eyes back to the doctor.

"When can we start?" I finally manage to push words out of my mouth.

"Since this is out of my area of expertise, I would like to recommend you go to Dr. Sanders," he answers, reaching across the desk with a file in his hand. "These are all of your medical records. I took the liberty of contacting Dr. Sanders, and she is expecting your call. So, if you decide to take this step, you're all set up from my end." He nods like he's congratulating himself on being so prepared.

Yeah, good job, Doctor. You prepared some papers.

Automatically, I lift my arms and take the file. Managing a small smile, I murmur, "Thank you."

"C'mon, babe. Let's go." I hear the deep voice I love so much as I feel two strong arms come around me.

But I don't move. I can't. My eyes are once again drawn to that picture. I want that. I want it so much my insides hurt.

"Up, baby," he whispers in my ear.

Still in a daze, I let him lead me out of the room, but that image is burned into my mind.

That freaking picture.

That beautiful image of a pregnant lady. And in my mind's eye, seeing that picture, the tears finally come, making everything blurry as I let them fall silently down my cheeks.

"Would you please say something?" I beg as we drive to my parents' house.

I don't know why I do this to myself. Don't get me wrong, I love my parents. But I know once today's news comes out of my mouth, my dad will get that faraway look in his eyes, like he's contemplating the meaning of life. I think he's really only remembering the last game he watched and is analyzing every play that was made, just so he doesn't have to say anything. My mom will fall apart. Every time there's even the smallest glitch in life, I end up being the one who has to console her.

I remember when I had to get my appendix removed. After the surgery, I was in so much pain, but my mom stood in the doorway and cried her eyes out, saying how sorry she was that she couldn't be with me when I was in the OR—like she could have helped me more than the doctors did. Even if by some miracle she was allowed to come in, she would've probably done a face-plant in my open stomach—and that she couldn't take the pain away. She was so brokenhearted that I forced myself to get out of bed to give her a hug, despite all the pain I was in. On my graduation day, she cried about how life goes by so fast, remembering how we were running around the house in diapers just yesterday. So, of course, I was the one who spent half an hour trying to convince her I wasn't going to move halfway across the world—although at that moment I had been considering it. After an ugly breakup, I came to her for some love and for her to tell me I'm the prettiest girl in the whole wide world and that anyone who ended up with me would be the lucky one. You know, mom stuff. But somehow, *she* was the one who cried on *my* shoulder! My sister broke her leg doing something stupid. I really don't remember what it was. Mom cried again—yep, you guessed it—in my arms.

Every single time, she sobbed, "Why, God? What did I ever do wrong?" You would think the world was ending with how much she cried.

After I would manage to calm her down, after all the pain she felt on our behalf would run its course through her, she would become the most dedicated and loving mom in the world. Often calling to checkup on us and see if we needed her in any way.

And somehow, I think this is going to be the worst of all. No, I'm sure, because in this moment, I feel like the world *is* ending. At least, life as we know it. So my mom's reaction is anyone's guess. Her responses are made out of love for us; the rational side of me knows that. But once… just once… I wish she would be the one holding me while I cry. And right this second, while we drive to their house, I am once again able to fool myself into thinking she won't break apart.

"What's there to say, Dani?" Sam asks, eyes firmly on the road.

"I don't know. Something!" I press, trying to get some kind of reaction out of him. "You haven't said a word since we left the office. I need to know what's going on inside your head. What are you thinking? What do you have to say about all of this?"

"Babe, relax. Everything is going to be fine."

"You can't just tell me to relax!" I wave my hands around like there's a bee inside the car. "We can't get pregnant. Through the entire length of our relationship, we've talked about having kids. And now that I can't give you one, all you've got to say to me is 'relax.' Are you crazy?"

"Crazy about you, babe. Always crazy about you." He places his hand on my knee and squeezes. "Besides, no one said we can't have kids. We'll just have them the hard way. It's our way. We do everything the hard way." He finally looks at me and winks.

"Don't be all cute and funny now. You haven't said anything, and it's starting to freak me out more than I already am." But the smile on my face is a dead giveaway he's succeeding in calming me just a little bit.

He doesn't say anything, just takes my hand in his and places it on his thigh, squeezing. And even though his words and his seemingly easy acceptance of our new situation is managing to relax me, I take a page right out of my mom's book and start chanting inside my head.

Oh, God.

Oh, God.

Oh my fucking God.

And the whole time, all I see is that damn picture.

CHAPTER TWO

"*I DON'T KNOW what, but there's something sad in her eyes," he said, turning to look at her. "But I'll do everything I can to make her smile."*

Walking those four steps that are separating us, he comes to me and leans close, so close our noses are touching. "I'm going to change your life, you just wait and see." Turning, he saunters off like he hasn't just rocked the foundations of my perfectly organized universe.

I love coming to my parents' house. Sure, Sam and I got married four years ago, and as I got older, I was my mom's shoulder to cry on. But every time I set foot in their house, I become their little girl. Nothing can touch me here. I am safe from the world.

Through my teen years, I couldn't wait to get out of the here and live my life by my own set of rules—since we all know parents just don't get it and they cramp our style. And when the time came for me to leave the nest and spread my wings, I was out of here in a second. I love Sam and our life, but every once in a while, I just want to go back. Go back to when there was no job, no bills, no money issues, and no adult responsibilities to be had. Only for a brief moment, I just want to once again be my daddy's princess and my mommy's pride and joy.

No one told me that once you're out, you're out. There's no coming back. Yeah, you can come to visit as much as you want, and maybe you'll feel the same way I do, like you're going back in time to that magical place. But if there are problems in your life, they'll still follow you there.

Coming up their driveway, I know today is the day when no amount of their love can keep the monsters at bay. They are dead set on coming in.

As Sam shuts down the car, my hand in his tightens. "Let's sit here a little bit."

"Baby, we have to go in. They'll see us sitting here."

"Yeah, okay." I turn to look him in the eye. "But if you abandon me once my mom starts ranting, I'll kick your ass." Finishing my statement, I give him a sweet smile.

"You're crazy, Dani." He chuckles.

"As you always say, my love, about you. I'm crazy about you," I tell him, leaning in and giving him a kiss.

Getting out of the car, I look at my childhood home. A few years ago, Mom decided they should paint the house. "White is boring," she said, and made my dad paint it light blue. Not my first choice of color for the house, but what do I know?

Coming to the door, I don't knock, just go in. "Hey, we're here!"

"Hey, guys." I hear my dad's voice coming from the family room to my right, and sure enough, when I look that way, I see him sitting in his chair watching TV. It's a big room, with bookshelves my mom filled with family pictures, various knickknacks, and some of her books. Since I introduced her to the Kindle, she stopped buying actual books, declaring it gave her more space for her treasures. It drives my dad insane, since he can't put a limit to her buying more stories. My entire life, she encouraged me to read, read everything and anything I could put my hands on, and that way I would always have something to talk about, no matter who I'm with.

There's also a coffee table in front of dad's chair and a huge sectional brown leather sofa that is so comfy if you lie down for a minute, it's guaranteed you'll fall asleep. Heaven.

"What are you doing home?" I ask, coming up to him. My dad has worked construction all his life, so it goes without saying he is solid. Getting up from his throne, he gives me a gentle smile, and then his arms close around me, for a brief moment giving me the illusion of a time long gone by, reducing me to five years old. As the top of my head comes up to his chin, it's like a wall is hugging me. Sam's hugs aside, the best hugs come from my dad. I'm a lucky girl.

"Your mom told me about today's appointment," he explains.

Three years ago, my mom put her foot down and demanded my dad retire. He was a busy man who always had to work on something. He claims, if he stops working, he'll go crazy, so they made a compromise. My dad cut back his hours significantly, but he still goes to work most days. If he isn't working on a job, he finds something to work on around the house or goes fishing. Drives my mom nuts. It isn't the retirement she had planned for. But I think he's doing it just so he can avoid going with my mom to all her various events, like an antique fair, or book clubs, or whatever is on the schedule for that month.

"And what's the verdict? When am I becoming a grandpa?" he asks, and I can hear hope in his voice that my answer will be something along the lines of "eight to nine months."

I knew I shouldn't have told her anything. Knew it the second the words left my mouth, but as always, I needed somebody to talk to. It's usually Marcy, my best friend since we met the first day of college and my partner in crime. Although those "crimes" were actually almost always at her initiative. My sister, Jules, is also part of my support system. That day, it was my mom, since I hadn't told Marcy or Jules anything yet. I was so anxious I wasn't thinking, and I told her today was our appointment with my OB. Thankfully, I hadn't told her the reason why—that we'd been trying for some time to get pregnant and it wasn't working. It was supposed to be just a regular checkup, since it hasn't yet been a year since we started trying, but deep inside I knew something like this would happen. Month after month, when my period came, or when the test came up negative, my mind more frequently went to the possibility of how maybe we can't get pregnant for some reason. But I pushed that thoughts away, telling myself it hasn't been a year and to not make assumptions. After making the appointment for a checkup, my nerves got the better of me, and I couldn't stop my hands from shaking. The hollow feeling in the pit of my stomach was the main reason for seeking someone to talk to. As luck would have it, it was my mom. If I told her my fears, she would still be in tears, and it was three days ago.

"Where's mom?" Seeing his hopeful look and knowing in a few minutes I'm going to squash it with one sentence is killing me inside.

Oh, God.

"Dani, what's wrong?" he demands, his voice rising.

"Dad, let's find—"I don't have a chance to finish my sentence.

"Hey, honey." My mom's melodic voice comes from behind me. I always liked her voice, thought it was beautiful. She's constantly singing while cooking and cleaning.

11

"Mom," I breathe, rushing to her, tears already falling down my face.

She's melodramatic and nosy, always asking where I've been, who I saw, and what we talked about. When she doesn't get answers, she gets angry, claiming she only wants to know because she worries about me. She drives me up the wall, and we fight every other day, but she's my mom. She is the person I ask for advice. She's the one who always cleaned and kissed my boo-boos, the one who cried and laughed with me, no matter what life threw at us, and now I need her. I need my mom.

Finally finding some comfort in her arms, I let the morning's events go through my mind, once again that picture coming into focus. I'll never have that. How am I going to tell my parents that, essentially, Sam and I can't have kids? How am I going to see my friends get pregnant, have their babies, and get everything I always wanted?

My tears have become body-rocking sobs. It's like all the pain and anguish is trying to come out in one fell swoop.

"Come on, baby. Sit down," Sam whispers in my ear, taking me from my mom's arms and transferring me into his. I vaguely hear their murmurs as Sam deposits me on the sofa, but he positions me so close to him I'm basically sitting on his lap.

"Will somebody tell us what the hell is going on?" my dad growls.

Swallowing my tears, I look at him and then my mom. Her posture is rigid, and her brown eyes hold pain. She knows. I don't understand how; maybe it's that mother's instinct or just seeing her child crying her heart out. But she knows what I'm going to say will change us all forever.

"I… I can't… I can't get pr-pregnant," I finish on a wail.

My declaration is met with complete and utter silence. It's like time has stopped. My dad is half seated, half standing, his muscles twitching like they want to move but he's restraining them. The look on his face is one of utter devastation.

He was hopeful not even five minutes ago, and now there's no trace of that hope left. I'm almost scared to look at my mom.

Her eyes are wide open, and her mouth is opening and closing like a fish, moving her lips so quickly they actually make a sound. Looking back at my dad, I can see he's now seated himself and his trademark faraway look has set in. Oh, God, I can't stand this. Even though Sam's arms are around me, trying to give me strength, I feel like I've disappointed my parents beyond repair. They've been begging for a grandkid since practically the moment we said our vows. So, I cast my eyes downward like a little girl who got caught doing something she wasn't supposed to.

"Oh, God," my mom whispers. "Oh, my poor baby."

The statement sends a jolt of surprise through me, since it was the last thing I expected. I was sure she would start asking God and the universe "Why? What the hell did I do wrong in my previous life?" You know, the usual.

For the next couple of minutes, time stands still as I watch my mom's tears fall down her face, quickly gaining momentum. First, there are just a few of them, but after five seconds, it's like a dam in her broke and they're coming so fast all I can see are two wet lines on her cheeks, the tears dripping from her chin.

I knew it would come as a shock. Hell, it came as one for me too, and I knew something was wrong, since we've been trying for a baby for almost eight months and nothing happened. Not even a maybe. I was sure it was some kind of hormonal imbalance and I would get some medication and we'd be off on our merry way. After the initial shock and pain seared its path through me, the fear of how to tell my parents set in. They were going to be disappointed, and I hated disappointing them. How could they not be, since they had grandchild fever for four straight years?

When we were driving to the house, on some basic level, I had tried to prepare myself for their reaction. I figured Dad wouldn't say a word and Mom would rant to everybody and nobody in particular about how life isn't fair, how she's probably paying for her mistakes from her previous life, and how somebody most likely put a curse on her—her norm. And after I managed to calm my mom down, Dad would say some wise words and then life would go on. Albeit, slightly changed, but it would go on.

Did that happen?

Nope.

I got complete and utter silence for fifteen minutes straight.

Fifteen minutes.

If Sam weren't running his hand up and down my side, I would think time indeed stopped, leaving us frozen for all eternity. Turns out, we're trying to imitate our family photograph.

After clearing his throat, my dad asks, "What did the doctor say?"

"That it's highly unlikely I will get pregnant, and if it somehow did happen, it would be dangerous and the pregnancy wouldn't survive, since it can't go to my uterus and would be stuck in one of the tubes. Also, I have some cysts on my ovaries, so there's a big possibility that I don't have ovulation every month, if at all." I try to explain it as simply as possible, not wanting to confuse him with medical terms. I'm confused by them enough.

"And how does he know that? Should we get a second opinion?"

"He did an ultrasound and put some dye in me to see if the fluid will go as it's supposed to. It didn't," I reply. "And no, Dad, no second opinion is needed. I've been going to Dr. White for ten years. I trust him." My voice is firm. "Besides, he already referred us to another doctor. He said that IVF procedures are out of his field of expertise."

"IVF?" my mom whispers. As I said, my mom is loud; her opinion is always heard, so this whispering business has me on edge.

"Invitro fertilization, Mom," I clarify.

"I don't understand. You said you can't get pregnant."

"I can't. At least not the normal way," I tell her, my fingers making quotation marks when I say the word normal. "As I explained to Dad, there are some cysts on my ovaries, and Dr. White isn't sure if I have regular ovulation. Even if I did, my tubes aren't road-friendly, which means, if I get pregnant on my own, the embryo most likely wouldn't make it through the tube and into the uterus, and they would have to terminate the pregnancy before the tube burst. It's dangerous since the woman can develop sepsis when that happens and the pregnancy is never carried out to term.It would be very dangerous for me to conceive without some help."

"Okay." She's *still* whispering.

"What I want to know is will you give us a grandchild?" my dad asks.

At that question, I freeze. I don't know what to tell him. I want to shout "Yes!" but at this point, there's a possibility the answer in no.

"Absolutely," Sam states. To my surprise, there's zero doubt in his voice.

"All right then," Dad says as he stands and goes out of the room in the direction of his office.

As I watch his retreating back, I'm not prepared for my mom's loud "Oh my God!" and it startles me so much I jump a little. "Why is this happening to me? What did I ever do wrong?"

Here we go. Right back on track. This is the mom I love and know how to handle.

"Mom, calm down. Nobody is doing anything to you. And you definitely haven't done anything wrong." I dive right in to the calming-my-mom routine. Truthfully, it's a relief she's behaving this way, because it means she will get it out of her system and then go back to being my supportive mom.

"Haven't done anything wrong? Then why is it you have this problem? Because I know down to my bones you haven't done a single thing to deserve this. And neither did Sam."

It's my turn to act like a fish.

"Okay, kids, here's the deal." Dad comes back and, thankfully, interrupts the moment, so I'm not required to reply to my mom's statement. I have no idea what to say. Those words warmed me so much I started to sweat. "These are all our worldly possessions. You tell that new doctor of yours that we want the best. *Best of the best.* And if he isn't what we require, then you leave that office and we'll find what we're looking for. Nothing, and I do mean *nothing*, will stand in my way of being a grandpa. I'll sell every last damn thing I own if I have to. Did you hear me?" he asks, as he throws a bunch of papers on the coffee table.

Sam grunts like someone punched him in the stomach. "That won't be necessary, Tim. But thank you, nonetheless."

Dad looks at Sam like he just told him the sun is blue and the sky is yellow. After a moment, though, he nods in his direction and says, "You're a good man, Sam. And I know she's your wife now, but for the last twenty-nine years, she's been my little girl, and nothing will ever change that. So, if it's needed, the money's yours."

All I can do is stare at my parents wide-eyed with my mouth hanging open. Everybody loves their parents—unless they're truly awful people—and think the world of them. But at this precise moment, I come to realize how awesome mine are. God, but I love them.

"Now, enough of this conversation. It's time for lunch." Dad tries to close down the topic. In his mind, it's simple. If you have a problem, find a solution. No exceptions. He's found one for now, and if the circumstances change, so will the solution.

"I need to call your sister," Mom says to me.

Before I even utter a word, Dad looks at Mom and tells her, "For the love of God, please don't call that girl of mine. I've got no patience for her love problems."

Uh-oh.

"I don't know what you're talking about. Besides, she's waiting to hear about Dani's appointment." Mom tries to act innocent.

"Please stop acting like you don't know. Why do you think I'm blind is beyond me." Dad is having none of it. "You think I don't know about her hotshot lawyer? It's like history's repeating itself. Dani used to tell me that she and Sam were just *friends.* When every time someone mentioned his name, she had stars in her eyes. When did people start to call it being friends? Thought you could fool me!" He ends his lecture, muttering the last part with his chin tilted down.

I look at Sam, only to see he has a smug look on his face. Bastard. I'll kick him first thing when we get home. He deserves it.

"We were just friends at the beginning, Dad," I defend, leaving the part with benefits out. No one's dad should know that piece of information.

"Yeah, right."

"Mom, don't call Jules. I'll talk to her later. And where are you going?" I ask Sam's back.

"I'm hungry!" he calls as he goes into the kitchen, his voice vibrating from holding the laughter in.

It's after lunch, and we are having coffee. My mom made cake, preparing for the celebration of my nonexistent pregnancy. They were sure that was the reason for my checkup. Every time I go to the doctor, even for a cold, they somehow convince themselves I'm expecting. Dad is back on his throne, and Sam's arms are back around me, holding me close like he's afraid I'll shatter if he lets me go. I look up from my cup and to the right, finding my mom seated next to me. She looks deep into my eyes, the pain there still fresh and the wound still bleeding. "It's going to be okay," she says. Leaning toward me, her eyes go gentle, made that way by the memory of a night long ago. "You're going to get your star." Her hand lands on my cheek, and her thumb collects the tears that had started to roll down. "It's going to be okay, baby," she whispers. All

I can do is nod. I don't feel as confident as the people in this room, but I drink in all their love, in it finding the strength to hope.

We're on our way home when my phone starts ringing. "Damn, not even fifteen minutes out the door and she already called her," I mutter, reaching into my bag and fishing for my phone. "Hey, Jules."

"Honey," my sister breathes into my ear. "How are you feeling?"

"I honestly don't know. But from your question, I gather you're all up to speed."

"Yeah, you know Cathy Steward. As soon as the door closed, she called me, and for the first time, I'm glad she did, since you would tell me next week. And that's the earliest estimation."

That's true. Every time I have a problem, I go inside my head and run the worst-case scenario over and over. Only then am I ready to talk about what is bugging me and do something about it. She knows me all too well. Funny thing is, I'm glad Mom called her too.

"Yeah" is all I say.

"What happened?"

"I don't want to talk about it right now." I close the subject down. I'm drained physically and emotionally for the day. "FYI, Dad knows about your lawyer."

"Which one?" she immediately asks.

For any normal person, that would be a weird question, but not for my sister. She's a magnet for trouble. Problem is her troubles always end up in a broken heart. Hers, to be precise. She lives in Denver and works as a legal secretary. Her newest trouble is she's in love with her boss but dating a guy who is his archnemesis, or something like that. She could have any guy she wants. At five foot three, curves in all the right places, blonde hair down to the middle of her back, and big blue eyes, she's a knockout. Why she constantly puts herself in these situations is a mystery.

"Don't know." I'm looking through the side window, seeing nothing and focusing on my sister's voice. I miss her so much.

"It doesn't matter. I'm thinking about breaking up with James."

Uh-oh.

"What? Why?"

"We'll talk soon, honey. I have to go. Say hi to Sam for me. Bye." And she hangs up, not waiting for me to reply.

"Shit." I hiss as I shove my phone back into my bag.

"What?" Sam asks from beside me.

"Shit's about to hit the fan with Jules. She's thinking about breaking up with James."

"When are you needed in Denver?" He chuckles, knowing how this goes. She'll get her heart broken, I'll go and cuss the ass out with her, and then she'll leave him and the circle will once again begin. She deserves to be happy, to find her Sam. She has to stop pining for her boss, as it's never going to happen, and finally go out with her heart as open as her eyes, and not find the morons of the world, but a guy who will love her for her.

"Don't know yet." I sigh.

"Babe, when were you gonna tell me about the stars in your eyes?"

"Never. You weren't supposed to know that," I reply, feeling the heat in my cheeks. Why I'm embarrassed, I don't know. Maybe it's because of the way our relationship started.

Sam's answer is to laugh. And hearing his laugh gives me a brief reprieve from the sadness and fear that had taken up residence in me this morning. I'm looking to the side, hiding my face from him because I know the melancholy awaits and my face shows it.

Past

For being the day that celebrates your birth, I wasn't having much fun at my birthday party. Sure, the whole gang was there, and we were in a bar. There wasn't a single seat available, the dance floor was full, and alcohol was running like a stream into people's mouths. The air was humid from all the sweating, and after five minutes in, my skin was sticky. The meticulously straightened hair started to curl at the edges, and the makeup started to run down girls' faces. But it was plain to see everybody was having a blast. And still, all I wanted was to go home, take a bath, and curl up in my bed with my newest book boyfriend. Standing in a corner in a crowded bar was not how I envisioned a good time. Not anymore, at least.

Maybe Marcy was right. Maybe I was feeling down because of my most recent breakup, even though I broke up with him. It wasn't that Chris wasn't a good guy or that we didn't have fun together. It was that he wanted to have too much of it. At twenty-two, I worked my ass off during the day at my job and didn't have much desire to go out every single night to bars and drink myself into oblivion hanging out with his buds. Sure, an occasional drink sounded just fine, desirable even, but during the week, I tended to be in bed at 10:30 p.m. I mean c'mon. I get up at 6:00 a.m. Give me a break. And shame on me, wanting to spend some alone time with my boyfriend, or, God forbid, go out on a date. Who did I think I was, demanding such things?

"We're too young to settle into a routine," Chris had said. "Now is the time to go out and do stupid shit. Get drunk every night, or go out of town on a whim and have an adventure just because you want to. There will be a time to shrink our worlds to such mundane tasks as jobs, paying the bills, marriage, and kids. I mean, babe, we still have a little bit of time before we have to get serious and do the adult thing. And it'll go away before you know it" was Chris's way of explaining his desire to go out and party every night. The sad part was… he was twenty-six. His time had come. So, a year after our relationship started, and six months of living together, it was time to cut him loose. The sad-slash-funny thing was… I missed the kick-ass apartment more than I did him. Go figure.

I was so far inside my head and managed to tune everything out that when "Hey!" was shouted in my ear, I nearly jumped out of my skin. Mentally preparing to rip the head off the person who dared to come near me and scare the bejesus out of me, I turned my head to the right and froze.

Staring back at me were the greenest eyes I'd ever seen. They were meadow green, and for a moment, I could actually smell the fragrance of the fresh cut grass and picture a hot summer day. Tearing my eyes from his, I ran them over the person who frightened me.

He was tall. Like, really tall. Maybe six-two. He was towering over me, and if there hadn't been a smile on his face lighting our dark corner, I would've been scared shitless right about now. But because of that smile, those eyes, and something that was entirely him, I wasn't scared, but excited. He was wearing a black T-shirt that molded to his chest, revealing a perfect pair of pecks. His jeans were faded so much they could pass as white, and they were so tight around his powerful thighs that saliva pooled in my mouth. On his feet, he had a black pair of boots.

Running my eyes upward, I could see he had big hands. A little bit of grease caught at the edges of his fingernails. Normally, that would gross me out, but on him, for some reason, it was perfect. It said he worked with his hands, and I imagined he knew how to work well. Big biceps and solid shoulders. Throughout the length of his arms, he had hills and valleys indicating the beginning and the end of each muscle. Yum!

"Uh… hey," I said, finally looking at his face. He had black hair, clipped short at the sides, longish at the top, revealing his hair was curly, because it stood up like there was a ton of product in it. Yet it didn't have that extravagant and artificial shine that resembled glass. Flat nose, and a strong jaw on which there was a five o'clock shadow gracing its perfection. Seeing all that was him, my belly hollowed out and my knees started to feel like jelly. I had to distractedly lean against the wall.

Just pretend like nothing's happened, Dani.

"Like what you see?" He smirked.

Busted!

His voice was rich and decadent, like the most expensive chocolate, but at that precise moment, he had a hint of amusement in it. Okay, not just a hint. There was a lot of it, but I decided to ignore it.

"Huh?" I played dumb. That was always the best course of action in my experience.

"I asked, do you like what you see? Oh, and I'm Sam," he introduced himself, tilting his head upward, like it was some great accomplishment. But, then again, what did I know? Maybe it was. I didn't know the guy. Even though, with every second, I wanted to more and more.

Heat hit my cheeks for some unfathomable reason—I stopped blushing when I was eighteen, right around the time I punched my V-card. Must've been the alcohol! I averted my eyes, but they got caught on the big purple bow adorning his neck. A bow that in my perusal of his body, and almost trance-like fixation on his muscles, I completely missed.

"Um… Sam?" I started, once again being drawn to his green eyes. "Why is there a bow on your neck?"

Just as his smirk turned into a smile, gracing me with the sight of his white teeth, Marcy came our way. "Good, you two already met!"

I averted my eyes as quickly as a virgin turned her eyes from a sex scene in a movie, causing Sam's smile to grow to impossible levels and my blush to rise to the temperature of lava.

Seeing Marcy's blonde curls bouncing around her head like we were at a rave, her whole body vibrating like a Maltese on crack, and the twinkle in her brown eyes shining told me she said bye-bye to sobriety and was firmly in All is Merry and Pink La-La Land. Soon, she would be talking to unicorns. Trust me, I've seen it happen. The most fun we had together, she was walking her pet unicorn with us. I'd never seen it, but for her, it was there. That girl was one ball of sunshine. Nothing could bring her down, not even the final phase in her drunkenness, which was soon to come—worshiping the great white porcelain god. Even puking her guts out, she'd reminisce the great time she had with her unicorn. Makes me wonder where they live when she doesn't see or need them.

"Yeah," Sam said.

"Sooo... happy birthday, Dani!" Marcy exclaimed, pointing her arms Sam's way like he was something on display and she was the girl whose only purpose in life was to showcase prizes.

"You've already congratulated me, honey, but thank you," I replied, a small, indulgent smile playing at my mouth.

"No, I know I have, but I didn't give your present. As I said, it will come later, and now he did." She squealed, clapping her hands.

"Who did?"

"Your present, silly."

"Huh?" Now I was confused, which happened a lot in Marcy's company.

"Ta-daaa!" she singsonged, once again pointing her hands Sam's way. This time, they were jazzhands, so I knew she meant business.

Oh shit!

What had she done now? What bright idea came to her?

I didn't have to wait long for an explanation.

"Don't freak out! But remember that hot guy I was telling you about, Jen's boyfriend's brother, and that we all hung out sometimes? Well, that's Sam. And a week ago, I was freaking out over what to give you for your birthday, and also how I was concerned you dove into your work and went all serious on us—like, no fun in your life... at all. Also, I kind of told them you needed a good tumble in bed. Through all that, an idea came to me, so I asked Sam if he would give you the sex. And like the good friend he is, he said yes!" Again, she squealed.

"What?" I was completely horrified. "And what do you mean you 'kind of told them'? It sounds to me like you broadcasted my personal life to everyone in hearing distance."

"Babe, it's been six months since you dumped the douche." She tried to calm me down. But what she didn't realize was that wasn't possible. "I know you. It'll take at least a year to get you going again. You yourself told me that for the last four months of the relationship, there hadn't been any sex, and now you've been single for six. And still, nothing. Do I want that for my girl? No! No way! So, I took matters into my own hands and secured you some." If the smile on her face was any indication, she was pretty pleased with herself.

"Marcy!" I was appalled. Sam, the guy, completely stopped existing. I refused to acknowledge him. "You're very sweet in some weird way, but—" I didn't get the chance to finish.

"No buts. You're young, Dani. You just turned twenty-three. Not fifty, for God's sake. Live a little and have fun." She turned to Sam. "As for you, make sure my girl has a fun, wild night. And keep her safe. If something happens to her, you'll answer to me." She tried to make it a threat, but remember: Maltese on crack. "Now off you go." She shooed us, but it was she who turned to leave. I was sure I would never, ever move from this spot. I was actively trying to make myself one with the wall.

"Oh, and Dani?" She called me like my attention was elsewhere, a sneaky smile forming on her lips. "I want all the details." And with that, she was gone.

"You ready?" Sam asked.

"For what?" I yelled. Oh, God. First, I was checking him out and got called on it, and then I was blushing like I was sitting on a furnace. Now, I thought all the color drained from my face and I resembled a girl from that movie where she came out of the TV and killed people. And the cherry on top? I just yelled in the guy's face. Could I embarrass myself anymore? And why I was concerned about embarrassing myself after what Marcy pulled was beyond me. I knew I should have stayed home. But did I listen to me? Nooo! I listened to Marcy, and as always, she put me in an impossible situation.

"For whatever you want to do to with me." He chuckled.

"What if I told you I want a long, hot bubble bath?"

"Works for me," he answered, taking my hand in his. His was big and strong, and immediately, I pictured it all over my body, causing a delicious shiver to run through me.

I tried to break his hold, but it only became stronger. "Alone!"

"Maybe you don't get it, sweetheart, but you're not gonna spend this night alone. Tonight, I'm all yours, for whatever you want to do with me. But, bottom line, you most definitely won't be alone," he said as he pulled me closer to him.

His scent invaded my nostrils, causing my stomach to bottom out, and my knees lost the ability to hold me up when he pulled me off my new friend, the wall. What did he use? Pheromones?

Jesus!

Clearing my throat, I tried to sound as firm as I was. "Yes, I will. Spend the night alone, that is."

Chuckling, he said, "We'll see." With that, he turned and, using the hold he had on me, he dragged me out of the bar. And for some reason, I didn't protest much.

CHAPTER THREE

"**WHAT DO YOU** want to be when you grow up?" I ask while playing with his fingers.

We're lying on a blanket in a park, watching clouds sail through the sky. Everyone left after the football game was over, going home for a shower or lazing in front of a TV. But it's such a beautiful Sunday afternoon that we decided to have a little picnic.

"I am all grown up." He sounds offended. "I can show you if you'd like." He winks and starts to roll onto my body, determined to show me.

"You know what I mean," I say, pushing at his shoulder. "What is your life's dream?"

"You're gonna laugh," he responds, and starts looking at the field like he's trying to watch the grass grow.

Now I'm curious. He won't meet my eyes. "Tell me, please," I push.

"I want to be a grandfather," he answers, still not looking in my direction.

"What?" I laugh. That's such a strange answer.

"Told you you were gonna laugh," he grumbles and finally meets my eyes. There's raw honesty in his, and eagerness for me to understand and, above all, accept. What he doesn't know yet is there's nothing I won't understand or try to accept from him. "Hear me out. See, everyone wants something materialistic: a beautiful house, an awesome car, or a glorious career that makes them a lot of money. And there is nothing wrong with that. I just..." He sighs. "I dream to be old. To be a man who's an awesome husband and lived a full life. To know I was good enough father that, one day, my kids will come and see me, bringing their own children regularly, and not just on holidays. I want to spoil my grandkids. Sneak them *candy. You know? I'm aware I ask for a lot, but I want a beautiful life. And I'm prepared to work for it until that day comes."* He looks at me shyly.

"Yeah, that sounds wonderful," I breathe, falling for him just a little bit more.

Since I was a little girl, I liked to live in my imagination. I used to play with my toys and make up their world. Around the time I turned twelve, my mom came to me and gave me a book. I don't remember which one it was, but I still remember her words.

"Read, Dani. It will expand your vocabulary and you'll always have something to talk about with anybody. Books are a universal language."

From that moment on, my imagination took on a life on its own. Then life itself happened, and I stopped imagining and started planning. I actively envisioned every step I would make, but every night when I was tucked in my bed, just before sleep took me over, my imagination would come back, showing me a life I didn't dare to dream. A life full of love and laughter and, above all, someone to share it with.

On the night of my twenty-third birthday, I met Sam. My imagination came back almost instantly. I daydreamed about what our lives would look like. How Sam would look as he got older. Where we would live, how our house would be set up. Our vacations, anniversaries, birthdays, and plain old boring days. As the time went by, my daydreams became plans. Not set in stone, but they were there.

One thing that was constantly present was the fact we were going to have children. We would sit in the yard when we would be old and gray, and we'd watch our grandchildren play, sneaking them candies and spoiling them rotten, making Sam's wish come true.

That was why, when I first stepped into the spare bedroom of our house, I immediately could see what it was meant for. With dark hardwood floors, big windows—from it you could gaze at the clouds sailing by or, at night, count the stars in the sky—and cream walls, it was perfect for a nursery. I could just imagine what our life would look like, and most of all, I could envision a rocking chair in the corner and a crib in the middle of the room.

For the last six years, I never once lost sight of my dream.

And for the last three, every time I set foot in the room, for which I hoped would turn into a nursery, I could see it all.

Until now.

In its place stands the image from the doctor's office. That picture. Only now, it doesn't have any color, since that will never be me.

Standing in the spare bedroom, for the life of me, I can't pull up that dream. It's gone. Every time I try to call it back to me, the image comes, and with it a pain so stark it's like someone is pulling all my insides out.

A week has passed since we heard that terrible news, and for the last week, every night, I find myself standing in this room and trying to bring my dream back to me. It's useless. Something broke inside me that day, and it killed my vision of a blissful future.

"There you are." Turning around, I see Sam leaning against the doorway. He hasn't come in since. I know why. I told him about my plans for this room, about what our future will look like. We spent countless hours daydreaming and planning together. And when I described the crib I envisioned in the middle of the room, he said the moment that plus sign appears on that white stick, he's going to build me one. Just as I want it, until the last detail. And now, all that is gone. "What are you doing?"

Ignoring his question, I turn back and once again look at the sky. "Have I ever told you the story about the stars?" I know I have. I just want him to open up about what's going on inside his head. He hasn't said a word about it.

Sighing, he finally comes inside. Hearing his footsteps echoing on the floor, coming my way, brings me such relief my whole body sags. "Yeah," he says, as he puts his arms around me and his chin on top of my head. I love when he holds me like this. It almost never fails to make me feel loved and safe, and it always bring to the forefront of my mind all the reasons why I love him more and more as the days go by. By taking my weight against his body, I know he is trying to take all my troubles away. My problems are his, and vice versa. He's declaring we're a team. Just the two of us against the world. Tonight, I can still feel his love. It's so strong it actually causes goose bumps to rise on my arms and a delicate little shiver to go through my body.

But tonight he fails to take my troubles away. Somehow, I feel alone. He hasn't said a word about what the future holds for us. Will we go through with the IVF? Will we go with the adoption route? Or will we give up entirely?

The fact he keeps shutting me out causes a feeling I'm not used to when it comes to Sam. It's anger, and each day that goes by without him saying a word, acting like all is merry and bright, the feeling intensifies. Coming to the point it rolls in my stomach like boiling hot lava. Because of my husband and his mute ways, I have a permanent case of heartburn.

Unwilling to start a fight just yet, I ignore the heartburn and the ever-growing doubt for our future, and instead of doing what my whole body wants me to—to tear away from his arms—I simply burrow closer to him. "Do you think our star is up there?"

"Absolutely," he replies, like before, no trace of doubt in his tone.

Unable to look at them any longer, I close my eyes. "Then why won't it come to us?"

"It will when it's ready."

"You sound so sure," I mumble as I turn my head and open my eyes to look at my husband. The love shining through, the look he's giving me has enough force to push away the anger, fear, and doubt I've been feeling lately.

He was the best reckless decision I ever made. There's not a day he doesn't somehow remind meof it. The best part—he doesn't even know he's doing it.

Putting one of his hands at the nape of my neck, he brings our foreheads together. "That's because I *am* sure. Us not having kids? That's just not possible, baby. And any kid who's blessed to have you as their mom is going to be a lucky one." His hand on my neck squeezes. "I'm just glad it's me who's going to witness it all," he says and kisses my forehead.

"Thank you, love," I say, feeling the tension completely leave my body, and I sag against him.

"Don't thank me, baby. You're the one who's gonna have to be the bad cop in this marriage and parenting gig. I'm going to be the cool dad and will get to do all kinds of fun stuff with them."

At his statement, I laugh so hard there are tears coming down my face. "Oh, God," I moan, my stomach hurting from all the laughter. "If you honestly think that's true, you're crazy."

"Crazy about you, babe." He slaps my ass, taking a step away from me. "You ready for bed?"

I don't answer. Instead, I just go in the direction of the door, still chuckling to myself. "Oh, and Sam?" I call to him as I step into the hallway. "If we have a boy, you're the one who's got to do all the *fun* stuff. Talking about girls, sex, and all the changes in his body when he hits puberty. I'm not coming anywhere near those particular conversations."

The look on his face brings a new wave of hilarity. And as I turn around, I have to once again dry my face from tears. It's so good to be laughing again. I feel like it's been years since I did that, when in truth it's been just a week.

***

Sam

That night, holding his wife in his arms and lying in their bed, Sam looked at the sky through the window.

He watched the stars and he remembered.

The first time he saw her.

She smelled like a flower. He watched as her lips tipped up in the tiniest smile while looking across the room at her friend Marcy. She was clearly in her head, thinking of something, but as she traced her friend across the bar, her smile widened, and he knew she wasn't even aware of it. And he remembered thinking her lips couldn't be real. No one had lips like that. The top one was the perfect Cupid's bow. It was like someone drew it. That was until her eyes looked intohis after he scared her by shouting in her ear. He became stupefied the moment he saw them. Not because of their color or shape or any of that.

It was the pain he saw in them.

Sadness.

Grief.

He never did find out why they were sad and why so much hurt radiated from just her stare, he could feel it piercing his skin. But in that moment, he vowed to himself he'd do anything in his power to erase that sorrow from her eyes. He wanted to see joy in them. Nothing but joy. As he made a fucking fool of himself going along with her friend's plan—making himself a fucking stallion for the night for this girl—he saw curiosity enter them as she tilted her head, and he felt a grin slowly stretching his face, so he winked and tried his damnedest to charm her panties off her, while that bow in her favorite color made his neck itch.

When Marcy first came at him with her request, his first reaction was to shut her down. He couldn't understand how someone could possibly do that to her friend. But she came again, and he shut her down once more. When she came to him the third time, he thought, *Why the hell not?* He was single, and if he could make some girl's birthday one she would always remember, he was glad to do it—even if she was shy or ugly or had something wrong with her that her friend had to find and beg someone to fuck her.

What he didn't expect was *her.*

She was gorgeous. The most beautiful thing he'd ever seen. At the first sight of her from a distance, he felt his gut squeeze. When he came closer, he had to fight his cock from getting hard. And when he took her to his place and saw the trust she had in him, and no sign of pain and sadness, his chest ached and he felt like something clampedaround his heart.

Game fucking over.

She was his.

On their first official date, he asked her what she wanted most in the world. She said it was the stars. He didn't ask, but he had a feeling it wasn't materialistic.

He was right.

It took a year for her to tell him the story about her little sister and her whispers at bedtime. That was the second most beautiful thing he ever heard. The first was the sound of Dani's laugh.

That night of her birthday party, before their first kiss as a couple, he looked closely into her eyes. Pain was there again, but the sadness was gone. And in that moment, he knew his girl was lonely. She surrounded herself with friends and family, but she still felt alone.

She won't be lonely any more, he assured himself.

Two years later, it was their wedding day.

It was sunny, it was warm, and all the crap that made for a good wedding.

His main focus was Dani, as always.

She was beautiful.

Breathtaking.

But most importantly where her chocolate eyes.

They were warm, light.

It took a moment, but he finally saw it.

Joy.

He did it. There was joy in them and nothing else. That was the day she promised him fifty years.

But now, again, the pain and sadness were back. He knew they would be. What he didn't expect was that she would close herself off completely and he wouldn't be able to reach her. Tonight, they were in their bed, and like almost every night, they made love. He was big enough of a man to say it was making love. It was. Because it was with Dani. But what happened was something that hadn't until then. Dani wasn't into it, and for the first time, she faked it. Initially, it was a blow to his ego, but as he held her afterward, he came to realize it didn't have to do with anything he did wrong. It was that damn pain in her eyes that was blocking her and slowly taking her from him.

His wife wished for a star, and he would do everything in his power to give it to her. To make that dream of hers come true. He knew the force behind her longing were his words confessed years ago. But it became her dream. And he would see it come true. In time, he would eradicate the pain and sadness from her eyes once more, and nothing would ever touch her again.

CHAPTER
FOUR

"*THE FIRST TIME we were together, I didn't plan on having sex with you. I thought I would make you smile, tease you a little, maybe kiss you. But then, I couldn't help myself, because you were you, and I fell...*" He takes a big breath and looks at me. "*And every day, I think I can't fall anymore. But I come home, and there you are, being you. And every day, I fall in love with you harder.*"

I'm in the bathroom, drying my hair. After our shower, Sam left me to do my thing while he went out for coffee—another little something he does that shows me how lucky I am to have him in my life. It's a small thing; I'm sure most people don't even register it when their loved ones do it, taking it for granted even. But for me, it's huge. It's one small gesture among the many big ones that tells me how much he loves me. Every morning, he makes me coffee, sometimes bringing a cup to me. Other times, I stumble to the kitchen, still half asleep, following the rich fragrance.

Seeing him coming into the bathroom holding my mug, I smile at him and shut off the blow-dryer. "Thanks," I say, feeling light and happy. Maybe it's because of our sweet end of the evening yesterday, or maybe it's because of the shower we shared earlier, or because it's Sunday. Yesterday was the first time I ever faked it with Sam, but I told myself it was just because I was tired and mentally drained from the things happening in our lives. I shut the door firmly on worrying about it. It's probably a combination of all those, but I don't care. Today, I feel like my old self, finally coming out of my trance. "So what's the plan for today?"

Even though Sundays are a lazy day, that's not the case for us. Okay, not every Sunday. Sure, there are times we'll veg out in front of the TV and cuddle on the couch, but most of the time, we go out and do something.

"For me, I'm not sure yet. I'll probably be out in the yard doing something. But you've got a date."

He winks at me, pulling himself toward the vanity and bringing me between his legs. "Hmmm… only if he's hot," I say, coming to stand before him and putting my hands on his chest.

"Only the best for my girl," he answers, grinning. "But it's a she, not a he."

"Ohhh… kinky." I wiggle my brows up and down. I love bantering with him. At first, when someone hears us, they think we're insane, joking around about having an affair or a lover. Now, they just roll their eyes at us.

All joking aside, I'm a 100percent certain that will never happen, that Sam will never cheat on me. He would rather cut his own arm off. As for me, well, there's no one but Sam. I can't even bring myself to try and picture it, let alone do it. "Who is she? Please, don't tell me it's my mom. I'm not in the mood for her drama," I groan, rolling my eyes.

"Marcy," he says, putting his arms around me.

"What? I don't have anything planned with her today."

"I know. I called her."

Uh-oh.

"What? Why?" I ask, confused.

"Because you need your girls." His arms around me tighten, preventing me from taking a step back and out of his grip.

"You told her?" I breathe, anger and betrayal burning through me. It's not that I want to keep our situation a secret. There's no reason to; I'm not ashamed. And I tell Marcy pretty much everything that goes on in my life. We don't have secrets. It's just that Sam and I haven't discussed what we're going to do, so I decided not to tell anyone outside of our family, and we haven't even told Sam's parents yet. For him to call Marcy and talk to her, it's the ultimate blow. He won't talk to me about it, but obviously will with anyone else.

"No, baby. I just called and said I plan to do some work today and don't want you to be all cooped up in the house waiting for me." He tries to calm the storm brewing inside me. "Dani, you need to tell her. You can't keep things inside."

Taking a huge step back, I tear away from his arms. Finally letting the anger out, I raise my finger and put it lightly back on Sam's chest. "You know what I need?" I ask, sarcasm dripping from my voice. "What I need is for my husband to finally start addressing the elephant in the room. To tell me what the hell is going through *his* mind. What I need is to discuss what the hell you want us to do. Do I make the appointment, or should we discuss other options? Or, God forbid, give up altogether?"

My chest is heaving from how worked up I am, and my finger goes from lightly lying on his chest to pushing with enough strength that my fingernail leaves a mark on him. Putting my hands on my waist, I take a huge breath. "What I don't need is for you to assure me one second that yes, we will have a baby, and the next, act like all is bright and merry in the world. What I don't need is for you to ignore my questions and attempts for conversation. And what I definitely don't need is for you to decide when the right time is for me to tell my best friend that I *can't have a baby*!" I end my rant on a shout.

As he stands there staring at me and saying nothing, I realize that even though I just spilled everything that's been on my mind for the last few days, it doesn't change a thing. The anger is still simmering in me. And now, on top of it, there's a slight disappointment, because he's still mute. He's looking at me like I lost my mind. I sure as hell feel like I did. Not being able to look at him for one more second, I avert my eyes.

"I'll see you later," I mumble as I turn from him, intent on leaving.

"Where are you going?" he asks, standing from the vanity.

"On a damn date," I reply, and leave without looking back at him.

How dare he? Who the hell is he to decide when I tell my friends, when he's the one who keeps evading the topic? He's the one who insists that everything will be fine but refuses to do something. Slamming the door behind me, I'm able to take a huge breath, dispel the last of my anger, and finally breathe. I'm not used to feeling like this. I'm not an angry person. If something is bothering me, I like to talk about it and resolve the issue. Sure, I might dwell on it a little bit and retreat inside my head, but all these years with Sam have taught me that the sooner you fix something, the sooner you can move on from it. We had our share of fights because of my tendency to lock myself up tight. And now I'm standing in front of a wall that just won't budge. The wall that, for the first time, Sam has put in my path. It's like he resents me.

Oh, God.

Is that it? Is he blaming me? I am the reason for us not having a baby, and all those months of trying, he was the one who assured me that everything would be fine. But did he really mean it? Or was he just resigning himself to the inevitable. Maybe deep down inside, he's giving up on me, on us.

Shit.

Not for one second have I stopped to think about what he might feel. I was so wrapped up in all the negative pregnancy tests and disappointment after disappointment to ask him how he was. And then that horrible news came....

What will I do? How will I break through that goddamned wall of his?

"Please, don't give up on us," I pray aloud as I start the car, sending one last look to the house. For whatever reason, Sam wants me out of the house today, and I have to give him some space. I'll give him today, but after I get home, we have some serious shit to talk about. It's time to get some things straight and decide what we'll do. But for now, I have a date to go on.

***

Going off to college was a huge change for me. I wasn't ready. Every kid I knew was without a doubt excited and counting the days for that moment when they'd finally be free. Free of parents breathing down their necks, free of rules that high school brought, and just free of all those authority figures that kept imposing themselves in their lives. Every one of those kids was ready to party. And I was sure I was one of them. Ready to take everything the world had to offer.

I loved my life at home. As long as I didn't break my parents' rules and obeyed my curfew, I had free rein of what I wanted to do in my spare time. I was able to go to parties, hang out with my friends, and once I turned sixteen, go out on dates. I didn't have to sneak around for anything. Once, I went home drunk, and there wasn't any yelling and lecturing from my parents. As always, my mom waited for me to get home, and as soon as she saw the state I was in, she simply sent me to bed. The kicker was the next morning, the loud—and I mean *loud*—music woke me up. It was pure, living hell. I thought my head would split in two. The air surrounding my head hurt. Hearing the drums in the song my mom put on, I had a feeling the drummer was drumming on my head and simultaneously inside my skull and not recorded it in the studio using the instrument. My dad came banging on my door and walked in my room with a big smile on his face like the proudest father there ever was, and he told me that Mom made a special breakfast for me, considering the hangover I must've had. Feeling relieved there wasn't going to be any yelling and apparently any repercussions, I calmly walked into the kitchen only to see a big bouquet of purple gerbera daisies on the breakfast bar. My favorite. There was a card tucked into them. On the card, there was a note.

Congratulations, Dani!
You came home drunk.
Welcome to hell.

Love,
Mom and Dad

The relief I had? It was gone in an instant. I slowly lifted my eyes to look at my mom just in time for her to slide the plate brimming with food toward me.

"Eat up, honey," she said, not once looking at me. "You're going to need your strength."

Looking down at the plate, I saw the horror that was on it. I could actually feel the small amount of color in my cheeks draining from them. Pancakes, ham, and eggs. Usually, I loved food, and food loved me. I could eat what I wanted and never gain weight—unfortunately, that little magic said bye-bye over the years, unfortunately—but, at that moment, the smell alone was making me sick. The urge to puke my guts out was overwhelming.

"I know you want to run to the bathroom and worship that white toilet of ours, but you're going to sit your perky little ass on that stool and eat your breakfast. And I do mean every last bit of it. Then you're going to sip your way through that glass of water. And then, and only then, I will grant your overwhelming desire for this big cup of strong, fresh coffee, and these two little pain pills." As she was delivering that speech, my mom's voice had gone from sweet to a downright scary movie voice. The whole time she was talking to me, she had a smile on her face, but I could see in her eyes there was a battle between amusement of my current condition, anger from what I'd done, and disappointment. What hurt me the most was the disappointment. She was trying to conceal it, but my dad? Not so much. His face was stark.

With nothing else to do, I did as I was told and sat myself on that stool and swallowed down the bile that crept up my throat at the sight. Every bite I took was torture. Halfway through, the food tried to rebel and make a break for it, but I managed to keep it down. That was the point the tears came.

"I'm sorry," I croaked through my tears, the silent sobs shaking and bucking my body.

"What was that?" my mom asked all brightly, but you could see it was an act.

"I'm sorry."

"Have you had enough?" she asked, motioning to my plate. I nodded, keeping my head down. "Look at me, Dani." As I did, my dad put his arm sideways around me. "Do not ever do that again. Do not ever come to this house drunk out of your mind. And especially on your own. I do not want to know how you came home. What I want for you to promise right now is if you get drunk again or if you ever need us, call. Call, honey, and we will come to get you. And there'll be no consequences," she said.

After that, things changed. My chores increased, my allowance becoming dependent on those chores being done. They said I should look at my allowance as getting paid, since I obviously considered myself an adult. The fact I got home drunk told them that. The hell they welcomed me into was not being able to take a nap at all that day, which my body begged me to do, and the music stayed loud all day long. That was it. Sure, they made fun of me now and again, telling all their friends about it. But I never came home drunk again. I don't know why, but it was probably because of despoilment, which ruled the house that day.

So, going off to college was a scary thing for me.

I knew I was safe at home, that every mistake I made wasn't that big. As long as I didn't lie to my parents, they would have my back. I could come home to them with everything and they would either help me or simply be there for me. And now all of a sudden, I was to be responsible for myself and my actions without a safety net.

With my plans for the future and what my college experience would be, I was ready to spread my wings and go on an adventure—not ever realizing there was no coming back. Of course, life threw me a curveball.

Marcy Crane.

She was my roommate. I'm not ashamed to admit she scared me a little. There was this petite girl with pink hair and big, almond-shaped brown eyes. A lot of people say almond-shaped eyes are sad ones. She is the exception on that rule. It was stunning how those eyes shined with such joy and eagerness to take what life had to offer. Her bubbly personality was contagious. You had to be in a good mood when you were in her presence—that was the power of it. Unfortunately, our senior year, it dimmed a little when her mom died from breast cancer. But, miraculously, she pulled through and came back strong.

Being roommates, we became close friends. Every once and again, she would pull me off the track my plans put me in for some much-needed fun. We were together through thick and thin. She cried and ate icecream with me when that jerk decided to teach me a lesson that "pretty girls should be careful and blow on yogurt for them not to get burned." These words should have raised a red flag as soon as he uttered them, but for some reason, they didn't. Well, taught me a lesson, he did. When I got a bad grade, she was the one who brought tequila and helped me drink my troubles away, only to push me to be better the next day. We went through all her phases together, and colored her hair.

Luckily, she's now settled on dark brown, which suits her the most.

When her mom died, I was the one who packed us up to go to the funeral, and I was the one who brought her back when she was taking too much time. And of course, she was the one who ultimately gave me Sam. He started as a joke, as her wish for me to let my hair down and enjoy life. Neither of us could have even imagined what would come out of it. If I didn't know Sam was my soul mate, I would seriously be concerned and think life screwed me over by giving me one in a female form.

***

Still reeling from the fight with Sam—if you could even call it a fight; Sam would've had to participate in it to be a fight, not stay completely mute—I park the car in Marcy's driveway. Shutting down the engine, I expel a huge breath and try to calm myself down. Since I'm not quite ready to tell Marcy about the new developments in our lives, I better be prepared to give an Oscar-winning performance of joy and happiness so she won't be able to see right through me.

Taking one last cleansing breath, which does very little to calm me, I enter Marcy's house. "Honey, I'm home!" I yell as my greeting.

"Finally, baby, I've got your wine right here at the ready" is her way of welcoming me. We do this all the time, and it's never less funny.

I love Marcy's house. When she bought it a year ago, I seriously considered moving in with her; it's that beautiful. But she wouldn't let me bring Sam with me. She said she's not ready to live with a guy just yet, so I had to stay at home.

With an open concept, you can see from the door to the kitchen, which is where she is. And this time, she does have wine at the ready. But my appreciation of her home is not what has me standing in place. No, it's the three people sitting at her round table, looking at me.

Uh-oh.

It looks like Marcy's fed up with me being MIA for the last few days and decided to drag out what is bothering me. And she brought reinforcements.

Shit.

This will be more difficult than I thought.

"Sorry, babe, but I'm not drinking today. I'm driving," I say as I come in and join the girls at her round glass dining room table. "Besides, isn't it a little too early? Even for us?"

"Hello to you too, Dani," Brooke says on my left.

"Sorry, guys. Hey. I was lost in contemplating, once again, if it is humanly possible to steal someone's house without them noticing," I lie to them, going for the long-lasting joke between us, and earning a few chuckles.

"If it is, let me know. This kitchen alone would be worth it," Kate replies, eyeing the dark brown cabinets and white quartz countertops. Best of all is the huge, kick-ass island and stainless steel fridge.

"Enough with you all getting hot and bothered over my house. It's not porn, for Christ's sake!" Marcy chastises us, even though she's got a little satisfied smile playing on her lips. "Tell us, Dani, how are you? Everything okay?"

At her question, panic grips my insides. "About what?" I ask, feeling on edge, because I'm just not ready to share the news, especially with all of them.

"Well, school started two weeks ago. How're the kids?"

Oh, thank God.

As relief swamps me, I think about my kids. I teach preschool. There's nothing as fun and gratifying as helping shape little minds. Also, unfortunately, they can be exhausting little monsters, so by the end of the semester, I'm left feeling drained of all energy. They just suck it out of me.

I never thought about someday being a mother and having a family—that is, until Sam. Even though I envisioned my future and every step I needed to take to get it, I didn't count on them. Then again, I didn't count on someone like Sam to enter my life and turn my world upside down either. I knew I wanted to spend my life with someone, but actually planning for kids never crossed my mind. If they came, great. If not, that was also okay.

As Sam and I got together and then got married, it still didn't provoke the need in me to start planning. I had him, and that was all I needed. Sometime after that, I started dreaming, but that was about it. I didn't feel like I was ready to become a mother, and that's definitely something you need to be ready for. Or so I thought.

Every day, I get to work with young minds. One of my favorite things to do is ask them a thought-provoking question. Something like, what is love, or what does heaven look like, or even who is going to be our next president? It's not to change their opinion. It's just to see how their minds work. The things they come up with are both fascinating and hilarious. Most of all, it's always honest. They could make you stop and reflect, or they could have you doubled over in laughter, crouching down and holding your stomach with tears streaming down your face; you just never know. And as I asked these questions, I started to wonder what my child would one day answer. What he or she would like and even look like. As time went by, that wonder turned out to wanting to know, and eventually, that turned into a desire to have our child. When the news about my problem came, the desire had already morphed into longing, which, the moment my brain processed the words coming out of the doctor's mouth, turned rapidly into *need.* Somehow, being a mother and a wife turned out to be my dream. And I needed my dream to come true. But more, I need Sam's dream of being a grandfather one day, of us sitting together and sneaking candy to our grandchildren, to come true. He deserved that, and I have to make it happen.

"Oh, things are great. Next week, we'll have our first big discussion. I just have to figure out what to ask them."

"I'm pregnant!" Amy suddenly blurts.

Hearing those words, everything in me just stops. I feel my blood turn cold and pinpricks take over my whole body. There is an unfamiliar sensation in the pit of my belly, turning the heavenly taste of coffee sour. While the girls jump up and down congratulating Amy on her very much unexpected news, I'm rooted to my seat, unable to move as jealousy and rage take over. My vision blurs from tears, my hands start to shake, and I am afraid I'll throw up on Marcy's table.

Past

What the hell am I doing here?

How I allowed myself to trust a complete stranger and go home with him was beyond me. I mean, sure, he was Marcy's friend. And on the way to his place, he did stop and drag me into a store to buy anything I wanted to drink and eat "so you can be sure I won't drug you or some other shit," pushing the stuff into my hands so I'd know it was safe. It went a long distance to equally freak me out and calm me down that he would do such a thing.

The minute we entered his place, the smell assaulted me. The odor every bachelor pad had. It screamed "dirty socks await!" Surprisingly, smell aside, the place was clean. A few T-shirts thrown across the chair in the kitchen-slash-dining room, a huge TV mounted on the wall opposite the couch and an armchair, and from behind it there were countless cables snaking out in every direction, the vast amount leading to the two consoles on the coffee table. What was most surprising was a plant by the big window that was alive.

"That's our pet," Sam said when he saw me looking at the plant.

"Excuse me?"

"The plant. It's our pet. Hugo."

"How can a plant be a pet? It's not doing anything and you can't cuddle it," I asked in confusion.

"Sure you can. See?" he insisted, and sure enough, he pressed his cheek to one of the huge leaves. I just stood there watching him, not believing the sight before me. Marcy sure did pick one of her own kind. Figured.

"So, how serious were you about that bath of yours?" he asked as he came to stand beside me.

"Deadly." I turned to look at him. Maybe he was a little coo-coo in the head, but he sure was pretty to look at. Not that I would tell him that. "It's the first thing I'm doing once I get home." That was, if my mom didn't assault me with questions right after I walked in. Lucky me, I was twenty-three and once again living at my parents' house. I finally got over the shock college gave me and the wakeup call to be a serious adult, and the first chance I got, I was running back to Mommy and Daddy to save me from the big bad wolf that was life in general.

"Okay," he said and took the stuff from my hands only to dump it on the brimming table. "Sit, relax, and I'll be back in a second." After issuing his order, he turned and disappeared into one of the rooms.

Confused, I did as I was told and waited to see what was going to happen next. Not five minutes later, he came back, only this time he was shirtless. The sight of his tan skin covering his pecs and sculpted abs like the finest silk, made my mouth water. I knew I was blushing once again, if the smirk on his face was anything to go by. Thankfully, he didn't know my panties were soaking wet and I had to rapidly clench my thighs together to alleviate the nagging ache between my legs.

Taking my hands in his, he pulled me up to my feet and took me into the mysterious room that turned out to be a bathroom. The first thing I saw were the bubbles. The second, the candles flickering their light across the white tiled walls.

"What's this?" I whispered, afraid if I talked in my normal voice the perfection before me would disappear.

"It's your bath. You said you wanted one, and since it's your birthday, I gave you one. Also, I said we could do whatever you want, but I promise to be perfect gentleman and leave you alone while you enjoy it. I won't make you share." All I could do was stand there and gape at him like he was some mystical creature come to life. He couldn't be real, could he? "Stop looking at me like that," he growled. It was a warning for what I wasn't sure, but I wanted to find out. "Dani, please stop looking at me like that or I will...." He didn't finish.

"You'll what?" I asked, bracing myself.

He didn't answer. Instead, he put his hand on the back of my neck, hauled me to him, and kissed me.

As his tongue entered my mouth, introducing it to mine and asking it to come out to play, something in me broke. I decided, just this once, to be a twenty-three-year-old and do something crazy. I decided to take all he was offering me and, in turn, give all of me to him just for this one moment in time.

With that decision in place, my hands started to roam, traveling from his abs, up toward his chest, touching the finest silk that was his skin on their path. When I brought my hands around his neck, one instantly dove into his thick hair and the other explored the muscles of his upper back. I fused my body to his, squishing my heavy breasts against his chest. His answer was to groan, and my knees lost all their strength. His hands caressed my body, from my neck all the way down to my butt, like he couldn't decide where to land. They finally came to the bottom of my shirt, and in the next second, it was on the floor, giving him a little room to maneuver.

"Fuck," he rumbled, looking down at me. "You could have told me that you needed help undressing for your bath, baby." He pulled my bra off and took my nipple into his mouth.

I was lost. My head spun from the glorious feel of Sam playing with my nipples. I didn't know what was up and what was down. All I knew was Sam and his hands and mouth were all over my body, wreaking havoc on my sanity.

Sometime afterward—I think I actually lost consciousness from the amount of pleasure Sam gave me—I realized my shoes and clothes had joined the floor to have their own party with my shirt and bra, plus Sam's jeans, and I was on top of them. Sam's hands were stroking up and down my legs, with him kneeling at the tips of my toes, and with every caress upward, he pushed my legs open a little. Sending a quick glance at my face, checked my reaction. A fresh wave of goosebumps raced along my skin in anticipation of him reaching the finish line. Finally, losing my patience, I opened my legs all the way, giving him a prime view of my core.

The sound that came from him when I did that was a painful moan. "What do you want?" he asked.

"Everything," I breathed.

"Doesn't that hurt?" he suddenly asked.

"What?" I was confused. Yes, it did hurt, but the pain was exquisite. After a moment, when I was able to focus again, I realized that his hand had stopped moving. Looking at him, I saw his head was tilted and he was staring at something.

"That," he prompted, as he retrieved the shoe I was lying on.

"The only thing that hurts is the fact your tongue isn't stroking my clit," I snapped. I was done. I decided I wanted it all that night, and I was getting it all.

"Is that so?" he asked, raising his eyebrow and throwing the shoe across the floor.

"Yes." I was back to breathing heavily, not getting enough oxygen in my lungs, the look on his face making my insides burn for him.

"Well, then...." He leaned to my ear, his breath whispering along the sensitive skin on my neck. "Let's do something to relieve that pain," he murmured. Moving down my body, he placed small kisses and bites along the path. As he brought his face between my legs, he flashed me a satisfied little grin, right before his tongue made contact.

The first stroke of that wicked tongue of his was a promise of a good time. The second, even better. By the third, I was climbing. And when he sucked, simultaneously entering me with his finger, I soared up, only to crash in brilliant colors, feeling on top of the world. Every muscle twitched, my skin tingling and my head spinning like never before.

"Damn, you're beautiful when you come."

"Shut up and fuck me. I want more of you," I demanded breathlessly, the orgasm that he gave me still coursing through me.

"Well, since it is your birthday, your every wish will be granted," he whispered with a smile, coming to hover over me.

"Enough of the banter for now," I said, taking him in my hand and guiding him to me. He was big and wide, and as I helped him enter me for the first time, I felt every inch as he stretched me. Then he did as I asked. He fucked me. It was hard, it was long, and above all else, it was glorious. I never knew I could feel like this. It was the best I ever experienced, and I didn't think it could get any better. Until it did.

As his hard thrust became faster and harder, he put his hand between us and found my sweet spot. His finger rolled against my hardened nub, taking me to heights I'd never achieved before, and on the fall, making me scream with ecstasy.

I always rolled my eyes when I read in one of my books a heroine's declaration that the hero ruined her for all other males. But at that moment, I had my eyes wide open and knew it was true. It could happen. Because, feeling him gently gliding in and out, coming down from his own peak, Sam had just done it to me.

Afterward, I was in my bath, but I wasn't alone. Sitting between his legs, his hands massaging my shoulders and his lips peppering kisses along my neck, I realized I was in trouble. I just fell in love with the guy who was supposed to be a one-night stand. And worst of all, it was a pity fuck on his side. My friend had to beg him to fuck me as my birthday present. It wasn't the sex that made me fall; it was the bath he was sitting in right then with me. All the while, wearing that purple bow around his neck. I did play with my present after all.

CHAPTER FIVE

"*I* DO BELIEVE *in God, but not in church. For me, church is just an institution, a place where someone has the right to tell me what is wrong or right and how to live my life. And then they go and do the opposite of what they're preaching,"* *he answered my question, and I can see he's bracing himself for my reaction.*

"Hmmm... interesting," I say.

"What, you don't agree?" he asks.

"I wouldn't say that. But still... it's the house of God."

"No, it's not. It's just a building. Earth is the house of God. He is the creator of it, isn't He? The faith teaches us that God is everywhere around us and is with us at all times. So why is that building, that institution, His only house? I refuse to believe that," *he explains and leaving me speechless.*

Coming to my destination, I shut down the car. After successfully pulling my shit together, I managed to fake joy for my friend and her bright but unexpected and definitely unplanned future. After jumping up and down for her—because what else do woman do when there's news like this?—and toasting with orange juice, we had a three-hour-long discussion about everything baby, from names to nurseries.

Emotionally drained, I excused myself and decided to go home, but once inside the car, my mind had another idea and took me to this place.

Just outside the town's limits, on the lone road in the middle of the field stands this beautiful church. Made entirely out of wood, the building has been in this spot for over two hundred years. In the evenings, when the lights shine on it, it looks like it's right out of a fairytale. Even though the wind finds its way through the planks of the walls, it never fails to bring warmth to me. Something about it warms me up inside. I love this church. I can spend hours just sitting inside, watching the pictures painted on the wood walls. Their colors remain bright after all this time, still somehow feeling alive.

I'm not an overly religious person, but there is something about this old beauty. I don't go to mass every day, or even on Sundays. I believe God is always with us and there when you want to talk to Him. But this church has a special place in my heart.

Walking up to it, I feel nothing but cold.

Every step I take on this gravel walkway to the entrance is heavier and heavier, the weight building on my shoulders. Until finally, I enter the church. I have a feeling that if it was one more step to the door, the weight would have crushed me and I would've fallen to my knees, unable to get up anymore. I don't look up as I walk to the bench and take a seat. I don't look at the images that are painted on the walls. And for the first time, I feel the wind breezing through the planks, the cold penetrating my clothes and flesh, right down to my bones. All I can do is think, *Why me?*

What have I done wrong?

I was a good girl. I followed my parents' rules, respected my elders. I've never changed partners like socks and always take care of myself. I go to checkups twice a year. How this shit snuck up on me is beyond me.

What have I done to be punished like this?

That's what it feels like. Like I'm being punished. And not being able to have a child, to give my husband that child, to start a family? That is the cruelest punishment of them all.

I know every human on this earth has their cross to bear, but I don't deserve this. This isn't supposed to be my cross.

I was a good girl, goddammit!

Looking up, I gaze around the church, not seeing anything, until my eyes stop at the altar. The colors surrounding it are a various shade of red, orange, and yellow. The white tablecloth on the altar glows in comparison to the colors of the wood painted behind it. This place used to bring me peace; it used to fill me with contentment. Now, it offers nothing.

"I'm angry with You! I'm angry, and I don't want to be. But You're the one who did this to me. So, I'm angry with You!" And with that, I leave, abandoning a piece of my heart inside.

***

Coming home, I find Sam sprawled on the couch in front of the TV.

"Hey, babe. You have a good time? Everything okay?" he asks, barely sending a glance my way.

"No, Sam. I think it's time we talk," I reply, my voice flat, and go into the kitchen.

"Sam?" he repeats. "What did I do wrong?"

"Nothing, honey, just...." I can't even finish the sentence. As he comes to the kitchen, I look at him—really look at him. His beautiful green eyes have lost their bright light, he has dark circles under them, and I think he has lost some weight. And my heart breaks. What have I done to him? "Nothing, baby, you did nothing wrong. I just think it's time to talk about what's happening to us. To our future."

"What do you mean?"

"What? What do you mean, what do I mean?" Now I'm confused.

"I mean what about our future?"

"It's completely changed. We can't have kids. That is what I mean!" I yell.

"Nothing has changed. Our future is still bright and shiny, as you say. There is nothing to talk about," he declares.

"Well, if you think that, then let me inform you that come Monday morning, I'll be calling Dr. Sanders and getting an appointment. We're going with the IVF."

He doesn't say anything to that, just looks at me for a few seconds, then, turning away, he goes back to his show. And, once again, I'm left alone in this nightmare of our new reality.

Sitting on our back deck and looking over our backyard, I still feel confused. Confused and abandoned. And angry. How can he say nothing has changed? How can he be in such denial?

Everything has changed. Everything we have been working for is now completely gone. Even this deck and yard are proof of that.

I found out what he was doing all day. He was finishing my deck for me. He poured so much love and care into it. Gray, smooth stone, big pots with lemon trees in them. We bought brown, wooden deck furniture, but decided to sand them and repaint them, give them a washed, used look. Comfy, welcome-feeling. Our first project together. We talked about how we would sit in them and watch our kids play in the backyard. A backyard that is nothing but grass. Such green grass that you could feel your eyes drawn to it and rest. It was a work of art.

Everything—the work, the planning, the dreaming—it was filled with such bright light it almost sparkled. Funny, that was only a year ago, and now, for me, it's dull and sad and has a cloak of gray over it. The dream will never come true.

"Here, baby, I made you some tea," I hear Sam say, and turning my head, I see him sitting next to me. I didn't even hear him come out. It's a peace offering, one I'm glad to take.

Reaching for my favorite mug, I ask him, "Does it still sparkle?"

"What, baby?" he asks as he looks to me. "Does what sparkle?"

"Everything. The grass, life, me?" I question, holding my breath and waiting for his answer.

Taking my mug back, he puts it on the table in front of us, and with his free hand, he grabs one of mine, muttering, "Come here."

Standing up, I go to him and straddle his lap. He sighs as his hands travel the length of my arms, his eyes tracking their path, watching goose bumps forming in their wake, until they reach my neck, and putting a little pressure on each side, he asks, "Remember that sunny day, four years ago, when you stood next to me in your pretty white dress and you promised me something? You promised me that you would fulfill my every heart's desire. But, baby, all I wanted is for you to give me fifty years. And when you said I do, you did exactly that."

Opening my mouth, I start to reply, but he shuts me up with a quick kiss. "No, listen to me. You know what I want from life. You know what I dream of. But, what you obviously don't get is, in my dream, when I'm old and gray, you're sitting right next to me. I would rather have fifty years with you and no children, then have fifty children and no you. So, yeah, it sparkles. As long as I have you right here with me, right next to me, the light shines so bright it's blinding." Pushing one of his hands in my hair, he brings me closer. "But, I promise you, babe, we will have our future, our family. There are ways to do that. I just don't want to rush into anything."

"But the doctor said I can't—"

"No, babe, the doctor said it would be difficult," he corrects. "He didn't say it was impossible. So we're going to try, yeah?"

"Yeah," I agree.

"And besides, if our every effort fails, including the IVF—when we decide it's time to go down that road—we still have the option to adopt. I'm not against that. I just want us to try on our own first. Okay?"

"Yeah," I repeat my previous answer. There's hope shining bright after a week of nothing but darkness inside me.

"Good. Now… wanna make out?" he asks but doesn't wait for my answer. He kisses me, and just like always, my mouth instantly opens for him. The kiss is long, wet, and lush. It sends a tingling sensation all over my body. His hand in my hair brings me even closer, while his other hand goes to the front of my neck. He drags it down across my breastbone and to the right, cupping my breast, squeezing it a little.

Grinding down, I moan into his mouth. One of my hands is in his hair, fisting, while the other is across his shoulders, pulling him closer, closer, fusing us together.

"How are you feeling, babe? Good?" he asks. His voice is deeper, huskier.

"Mm-hm" is all I can get out, his hand going south across my tummy to my right thigh, then up and under my skirt. It was only this morning when we last did this, since I had his cock inside me. But now, it feels too damn long ago. I missed it so much I'm wet and ready.

Cupping me and discovering how aroused I am, he growls, "Good enough for a ride?"

"Oh yeah," I breathe, reaching for his zipper. Opening it, his cock springs free and my hand circles him, stroking.

He pushes my panties aside and commands, "Up." And then he's in me, filling me, stretching me. It's so exquisite my back arches, my head goes up, and my mouth opens in a silent scream. His hands span my waist, and he demands, "Ride me."

And I do.

Up and down, I start to tingle all over. His thumb on me, rolling, his words flashing through my brain, I start to feel it coming. Then, it's there. The world explodes in color. I shove my face in his neck and bite.

"Fuck," he moans, and feeling him jerking inside me, I know he found it. Without opening my eyes, I press my forehead to his. The breath that expels from my lungs feels like a hundred pounds, and I literallysag with relief. "Love you, Dani," he whispers.

"I love you too."

"Now, go clean up, and then come back and finish your tea. Meanwhile, I'll order us a pizza."

I don't think. I don't even blink. I just give my husband a peck on the mouth and go do what he said. After what feels like years but has only been days, finally, I feel lighter, freer. Even though our problems are still there and they are still waiting for us, some of that light has come back for a brief time. I just hope it's here to stay.

What I didn't know is we should've been bracing for the hardest ride of our lives.

CHAPTER SIX

"**YOU ARE SO** tiny. I have this urge to pick you up and put you on a mantel somewhere," he says, watching me getting dressed.

"Thanks," I reply, sarcasm dripping from the syllable. "That was a nice way of calling me short. But just remember, perfumes are kept in small bottles."

"Or venom," he finished for me. "No, seriously, I want to pick you up and put you somewhere safe. Where nothing could ever touch you and harm you again."

Every moment I spend with him makes me fall more and more in love. And this moment, this precise moment in time, in this universe, is no different. Soon, I'll stop falling and land. Then what will I do? How will I pick myself up? Or maybe, just maybe, he'll catch me... and put me on that mantel of his.

Our decision of trying to get pregnant on our own ended after Sam found me crying on the bathroom floor with a negative pregnancy test fisted in my hand and pressed against my chest. I called the office and made the first appointment with Dr. Sanders the next morning.

We're in a waiting room, sitting silently in our chairs. For once, it's a nice waiting room—big, airy, and with white walls that had a splash of color here and there. On the wall are advertisement posters, all with women in various stages of pregnancy. Thankfully, none of them are the picture that's followed me awake or asleep for the last two and half months. And then there's a wall behind the reception desk, on which hangs a huge picture frame, one you can buy in almost every store, just a big sheet of glass with cardboard for the back. In it are probably a hundred pictures of newborns and toddlers.

When I ask the nurse at the reception desk what's with all the photos behind her, a huge proud smile spreads on her lips as she replies, "Those are all of our kids. There's more displayed around the clinic, but these were the ones who were most unlikely to have been conceived in the first place."

I'm floored and calmed in an instant. Floored, because of the evidence of success staring me right in the face. And calmed, because here, these people obviously care for what happens with their patients.

It's the most beautiful piece of art I've ever seen. I say art, because that's exactly what it is.

All around us, there are couples with the same or similar problem. We have one thing in common: we all desperately want but are unable to get pregnant without medical help. What's the saddest of all is, for some of us, even medicine can't help. What strikes me most is these are all young people. I talk with some of the other couples while we wait. One woman is only twenty-two. She came for her first appointment three days ago, clutching her husband's hand like a lifeline, eyes as big as deer's in headlights. And the hubby, he stands stoically by her side the whole time they're waiting, like a guard keeping his queen safe. Must be what we all look like when we enter this purgatory for the first time.

I've heard that ten years ago, only older couples were having this type of procedure done. And by older, I mean, forty years and above. Now, there's not one couple above thirty-five. If they're here, it's because they've been trying for at least a year, and so far, even with all the help from the doctors, still nothing. Not even a plus sign on a pee stick, let alone high betaHCG levels. Or, the fact that breaks my heart every time I let myself think about it, pregnancy that ended in miscarriage. I can't even fathom the pain those couples are living with on a daily basis. It paints a terrifying picture, one I hope with all my being isn't our future. I don't think I could go through this more than once. This has become a plague of the century, and it seems like there's nobody who cares except for the loved ones of the couples going through this torture.

At first glance, most people would be frightened of Dr. Sanders. At least, I am. Seeing her dark wine-red hair pulled into a tight bun, the glasses on her face only highlighting her serious expression, and the fact she's wearing a white lab coat, like all doctors do, reduces me to a five-year-old waiting to get a shot and only wanting my mommy. Maybe, if I'm a good girl and don't cry, I'll get a candy afterward.

Sitting across from her at her desk, for a few seconds, she studies the papers there, my anxiety rising even more. But then, the woman looks into my eyes and her face softens, a small smile playing peek-a-boo at her mouth. At that small miracle, I start to relax.

"Hello, I'm Dr. Sanders, but please call me Chloe. We'll be spending enough time together to be on a first-name basis." Her soft voice caresses my ears, soothing me further, and ifthe wall of pictures behind the front desk weren't indication enough, those words and the expression on her face confirmed we chose the right doctor. Somehow, she manages to gain my trust.

"Hi, I'm Dani, and this is Sam," I say, flipping my hand Sam's way. He just grunts, making me wanna smack him upside the head.

"Now, let's get down to business. I've studied your medical history and the results of your previous tests, and while the situation is not ideal, it's not helpless either." Again, she glances at the papers spread out in front of her. "What's missing in all of this are Sam's results, so I would like for you to come in and give us a sample so we can do a sperm count to see if we have some surprises hiding there."

At that, Sam gives another grunt. Looking at him, I can see he's crossed his arms on his chest, and I know, if he were standing, his feet would be planted wide, his muscles tense, painting a picture of superior masculinity.

I try to swallow my laughter, but a giggle burst through. Hearing that, Sam sendsa scowl my way.

Men! How dare we question the power of their swimmers?

I cross my eyes and stick my tongue out at him, only to remember where we are. Feeling the heat in my cheeks, I look at the doctor, who's wearing a wide smile and her shoulders are shaking slightly.

"I see the situation hasn't brought you down, which is excellent. You'll need to keep up the positivity. Also, Dani, I would like for you to repeat your blood work to see your hormone levels, so we can see if they need to be regulated."

"Okay, what else?" I ask, still feeling the burn from my earlier embarrassment.

"That's about it for now. Make all the arrangements with the nurse, and when the results come in, we'll go from there."

And that's it. Our first encounter with the woman who will hopefully give us our baby, and the official start of IVF preparations.

***

A few days after, it's time to get my blood drawn and Sam's swimmers checked. It's a silent ride to the clinic. I don't dare say anything, since his mood deteriorated the moment I reminded him of our plans, and the fact we couldn't have sex because of it.

Since I'm the first one done, I'm sitting in the waiting room, when I see Sam coming my way—brows drawn in, narrowed eyes, the hard line of his mouth. He's in the fighting zone.

Uh-oh.

"Up," he barks at me in a firm tone, one I've never heard come from him before, as he passes in front of me, going in the direction of the exit.

"Shit," I hiss, gathering my stuff and scrambling after him. He's out the door in a second, not even checking if I'm behind him, or, God forbid, slowing down so I can catch up. Every step, he's making me run after him, my anger jacking up another notch.

Fuck him! He's mad? Why? Just because he had to come to the clinic and jerk off? It's not like he doesn't do it on a regular basis. It's just the location changed. Big deal! I'm the one who got stabbed with a needle. Repeatedly! My arms look like a pin cushion or like I'm a junkie.

I don't get why he's acting like this. What, the porn wasn't to his satisfaction? Porn is porn, and anyway he had his phone with him, so he could've just as easily gone online and found something he liked.

As I'm watching his stiff back marching toward the car, I slow my pace. Let him wait for me. Maybe he'll calm down a little.

By the time I get to the car, Sam is already in it and has his head reclining against the headrest while running the palm of his hand up and down his face.

Hmmm… it seems he hasn't calmed down even a little bit. Seeing him like this, I decide to take my time getting into the car, acting like a ninety-year-old lady, knowing it'll piss him of more and he'll spill what's got him into this state.

I can hear him puffing out air as I slowly and with great care lower my ass into the seat, but when I rigidly pull my legs in, that's when he bites out, "Dani."

"Yes, my dear?" I ask, faking innocence and batting my eyelashes at him.

His answering "Jesus" is intermingled with exhaling a huge breath.

"What's wrong?" Now that my anger has completely vanished just as fast as it came, worry is taking its place. He doesn't answer, but he doesn't look at me either. "Sam?"

Still, nothing.

"If you were fantasizing about a hot nurse you saw in there, that's okay. I won't be mad," I lie. Because, seriously, if he did and admits it, I'm gonna kill him. "But just tell me what's wrong. Because you went right by me, not even stopping for the three seconds it would take me to get up, and you barked at me like a dog. And, honey, you do many things, but you don't bark."

"There was no hot nurse, Dani," he says finally. "You wanna know? Sure, I'll tell you. You know how they make it look in the movies?" he asks, but he doesn't give me a chance to answer as he keeps speaking. "That in there was nothing like that. There were five of us, standing in a line one behind another, waiting to get our turn in the room that is the size of a bathroom stall. We all knew what the guy in there was doing, and what we were gonna be doing when we got in there. And, the next thing I know, this guy behind me starts telling me how he and his wife had to get up at 5:00 a.m. to be here and didn't get much sleep, so he was tired and was worried how he'd manage to do his thing in there. I do not need to know those things, not now, not ever! When I got in there, there was no TV, no nothing, except a few old magazines that I would not touch if my life depended on it. You could see they were *well used*. When I got out, that same guy *congratulated* me on how fast I was. Seriously?"

I don't comment on any of it. I'm too busy holding my laughter in. My abs start to hurt from the effort.

"And no, there was no nurse. But there was a cleaning lady, who is probably in her mid-fifties, has bad hair, and probably had her hip replaced for the third time. Her limp is that bad. But did that stop her from walking up and down that hallway and sending us those weird smiles? Nope, it didn't."

By the time he finishes his rant, I'm doubled over from the pain in my stomach, but thankfully, no sound has come out.

"Oh, you poor thing," I coo, rubbing his arm. "If you want, I'll take care of you when we get home, make you forget all about this horrible experience."

"Damn right you will," he grumbles. "And next time I have to go in there, you're going with me."

This time, I do burst out laughing, earning me a scowl from Sam and a growl. I don't have the heart to tell him that I won't be there for him next time, seeing how I'll be in the OR getting my eggs harvested.

But I do take care of him when we get home, and in turn, Sam takes care of me three times. And today, I don't have to fake it.

***

A week later, the results come in. Sam is healthy and ready to go. I, on the other hand, am not. It turns out, my hormones have a party going on inside my body and my testosterone levels are high.

"We'll put you on these high-level pills for one cycle, and hopefully the testosterone will come down," Dr. Sanders says.

So, I start the pills, which in turn send me to the ER.

***

I'm on top, sliding down, filling myself with Sam. The feeling, once again, pure bliss.

A few hours before, after dinner, I was sitting on our deck looking at the night sky. There wasn't a cloud anywhere, giving a perfect view of the moon and the stars. Gazing at them, I was lazily wondering which one was ours and when it would be time for it to come to us, when Sam came out holding a gin and tonic and a beer. We had a few, enjoying each other's company and making tentative plans for the future. But mostly, fantasizing what it would look like. The evening was perfect, the mood mellow. Just what we needed after all the stress lately. Then, we went to the bedroom. Feeling light from the alcohol, my walls slightly coming down, I was restless and in need of something. So, I jumped my husband, and thus the festivities began.

Just as I'm sliding down, my hands traveling across Sam's chest, and leaning slightly closer to his face, there's a sharp pain in the lower part of my abdomen. It's so intense that it forces me to double over, my muscles to contract, and I shove my face into Sam's neck.

"Oh my God," I moan, terrified of what's happening, and at the same time hoping it willgo as quickly as it came.

"Dani?" Sam asks, worry evident in his tone as his arms become steel bands around me. I can feel his body turning to stone.

"I'm fine, baby. We can finish." My voice is small. As soon as I say those words, I find myself not on top of Sam, sprawled across his chest, his cock inside me, but on my back, his angry face looming over me.

"Babe," he bites out.

"Please. Give it to me. It's gone. We can keep going," I beg. And I'm not lying. The sharp pain gone, I feel only a whisper of it, so I'm totally on board to keep going. I don't want our lovely night to end on a bad note.

"I'd give you anything, Dani. Anything. But never, not ever, will I give you something that causes you pain. And that includes me. Call the doctor, get checked, and then you'll get me again." And with that he pulls out, goes to the bathroom to get a washcloth, cleans me up, and calls it a night.

The next morning, the pain is back. Once again, it comes sharply, but after a few deep breaths, it becomes dull but constant. An hour later comes the headache. Just as we're about to leave the house to go to work, I'm ready to stab my own eye so the pressure in my head will go away and the pain will lower. That's it for Sam. He puts me in his car and drives me to the ER, calling Dr. Sanders while on the way. She meets us there. I'm delusional from the pain and can't see very well, so I end up talking to the mirror—thinking I'm talking to the doctor, but speaking so low, nobody can hear or understand me—leaving Sam to answer the questions for me.

Turns out, due to my hormones going back to their normal levels thanks to the pills, some cysts I had started popping. The headache was a migraine, but coupled with all the stress lately, it reached a higher level of pain. I'm put on bed rest for a couple of days. Also, it's demanded of me to relax.

Guess what. It can't be demanded. The worst thing of all, Sam decrees there will be no sex until I'm100 percent. He doesn't specify when he expects that will be.

A month passes and there's been no sex in our household, and I'm horny all the damn time. Thank you very much, hormones.

***

When I finally return to work, the time has come to ask my *big* question. Since I do this two or three times throughout a year, I've decided to go easy.

"What is love?" I ask my kids, and I'm met with silence, not one little arm goes up in the air.

I can actually see the wheels turning in their heads, a faraway look in their eyes as they contemplate the answer. Then, almost as one, they come pouring in.

"Love is when Daddy gives Mommy flowers."

"Love is when you share with somebody."

"Love is when you help somebody."

"Love is when Granddaddy hold Grandma's hand."

Those are just a fraction of the answers. Some make me laugh, same give me hope that we're teaching our young right, but all give me a warm feeling in my chest. But, they're all beautifully simple and, above all, true. They give the answers to the question that would have most adults running for the hills or going into complicated debates, when there is no need. It's simple; love is everything, every good deed, every smile, every breath. But then comes the answer that slays me, almost brings me to my knees.

"Love is my mom."

I don't ask Laurie to elaborate; I know exactly what she means, as do all the kids, if their nodding heads are any clue. After that, I make the kids draw what they think love is, so we can put the pictures on the wall with their answers. All that time, I sit in the corner fighting back the tears and thinking about Laurie's answer. And hoping that some day I will have a child who will, when asked that question, give the same exact answer.

So that's that. Six weeks have gone by in the blink of an eye since I first met Dr. Sanders. Aside from a few meetings with the girls—I still haven't told them—not much has happened. But every day, I feel like I'm losing myself, and I'm in touch with reality less and less. I'm on a rollercoaster of emotions, going from one extreme to the next. One second, I'm angry; the next, it's like nothing happened and I'm fine again. And I'm becoming obsessed with being pregnant and having a child. So much so that nothing else is important anymore. And I'm missing Sam like crazy, but for some reason, I don't have the courage to do anything about it.

CHAPTER
SEVEN

"*W*HAT CAN I *do?" he asks, his arms bringing me closer, letting me burrow deeper into his chest, allowing my tears to leak into his shirt and taking away the hurt. "How can I make it better?"*

"Just hold me. Just love me," I whisper.

"Since there is no me without you, that will never stop. I will always love you." His arms become my sanctuary as he holds me. "Don't let what anyone says or does ever affect you, our decisions, and our lives. Don't listen to them. Only thing that matters is us, us and our child."

I don't think there's a doctor in any field of medicine as disliked as an OB. We all know we need to take care of that area once a year, but when that time comes, we became a nervous wreck. Sitting in that waiting room, with slight interest, I watch the newcomers. They're shaking their legs, biting their manicured nails, with horror written all over their terrified faces as they watch the nurse call out names, hoping against hope it isn't their turn.

Unfortunately, thanks to the last several months, I've become an old pro. So, when the nurse comes out and calls "Hunt!" with a kind smile on her face, I don't even jump. I just calmly get to my feet and follow her to the exam room. Normally, when the doctor comes in, I'm blushing like a virgin watching her first porn and can't even look them in the eye. But now—from having to come to several appointments in the last few weeks—I don't even bat an eyelash. I just call a greeting and spread my legs wide.

"Change in here, make yourself comfortable, and the doctor will be right in," the nurse instructs in that quiet, gentle tone.

Suddenly, my hands start shaking, fear running up and down my spine, and there is a lump forming in my throat. This is it. The last exam and the last blood draw before we get the green light on the hormonal injections that will help my eggs. Didn't I, just a few seconds ago, mentally give myself a pat on the back for exuding such coolness, not even jumping or casting a nervous glance to the nurse? And now, here I am, like a leaf in the wind.

On shaking legs, hoping and praying my knees don't give out, I climb onto the exam table and attempt to get in some kind of comfortable position. Fat chance of that! Whoever invented these tables was clearly not a fan of women. Not being able to find a comfortable position lying down, I decide to sit on the table, swinging my legs forward and back like I'm a kid on a swing, and wait for the doctor.

"Just relax. Everything will be fine," comes that kind voice again.

"Yeah," I whisper, knowing that won't happen, just as there's a light knock on the door and Dr. Sanders comes in.

"Hi, Dani. How are you feeling?" she asks, inspecting me from head to toe.

"Like I'm about to crawl out of my skin," I admit, attempting to smile, but I know all I manage is a weird grimace.

"And how about your emotions? Any fast changes?"

"Yes!" I practically yell. "I thought I was going crazy."

"Nope. That's hormone levels changing. Unfortunately, in about two weeks, you can expect that to go even crazier. It's not uncommon for women in the IVF process to behave irrationally when their emotions are in question." She tries to make me feel better by saying it's normal, but all I hear is that in two weeks, it will go even crazier.

"Does that mean we're good to go?" I ask, hope consuming my whole being.

"Your lab work has come back. The levels are as we want them to be, so if nothing's changed since your last exam, then yes. You're good to go."

Hearing her words, I start to feel the anger that's been present in me on different levels from the beginning of this journey through hell, and tension, seep from my body, making my shoulders slump forward. I look at the floor and tears gather in my eyes. Finally, some good news. I started to believe that every time I walk into this room, I'll get bad news, something that will tilt my already scrambled universe even more.

"Please, lie back on the table, scoot your bum down, and spread your legs," Dr. Sanders instructs, putting my papers down on the little table next to her. "We'll start with the vaginal examination, and then we'll do an ultrasound to see if everything is as it should be for us to start IVF."

I only wish Sam were here today to hear this. He's been here every step of the way, every appointment, and every phone call we've made, and today, when it counts the most, he isn't. I know it's not like she told me I'm pregnant, but to hear we're one step closer to having our baby, our family, after all the ups and downs we've been through, it's the most important news so far. We knew today was probably the big day. But, he had to work. He's been missing too much of it lately. And just because our lives and our world has changed its course and was turned upside down doesn't mean that everyone else's was. Plus, working with your best friend making custom pieces of furniture comes with much more responsibility than a lot of other jobs. Your friend might understand what you're going through, but that doesn't mean you suddenly have all the time in the world. Plus, today they had some big shipment going out and a meeting about a large order, which will essentially bring their company to the next level, so I told him not to come with me today. He deserves his big moment. And he deserves a timeout from our nightmare. So today, Sam's at work, missing this appointment.

"Okay, Dani, we're done for today."

I was so lost in my mind, wishing Sam were here with me, that I managed to stay completely relaxed through the entire exam, not even realizing it started in the first place.

"What's the verdict?" I ask, that hope still going strong, but now that my bubble of thoughts of Sam are pierced, caution is starting to creep inside.

"I expect to hear from you in about two weeks. By then, your protocol will be ready, and we can start. Remember, you have to call us on the first day of your next period," she says with a light tap to my inner thigh.

***

Heading to my car, I decide to call Sam. The happiness and hope still going strong, I'm surprised I haven't started skipping to my car.

"Babe?" he answers on the second ring, clearly waiting for my call.

"I did it," I whisper.

"What?"

"I'm ready to start in two weeks," I keep whispering, for the life of me not managing to speak stronger.

"You mean we're ready?" he asks, once again reminding me we're in this together.

"Yeah, honey. We're ready."

This is met with silence that lasts long enough for me to get to and in my car.

Once I'm in, I lean my forehead against the wheel, my eyes downcast, the vision of my lap swimming, I prompt, "Sam?"

"Here, babe." His voice, like a burlap bag of gravel being emptied on the hard concrete, assaults my ears and sends tears to their silent path down my cheeks.

Keeping our silence, me in the company of my tears and him shuffling that gravel in his throat by clearing it time and again, we share one of the most profound moments of our lives. Knowing I managed the impossible, by beating my body into working right just for a short period of time so we can get to the end of this road, so I can get pregnant and we can have our much-wanted child, not one thing needs to be said.

After some time, it's Sam who breaks the silence. He does it by asking, "What's your plan for the rest of the day?"

"I'm having lunch with the girls."

"Tell them." It's issued as an order.

When I don't say anything, he keeps with the instructions. "Tell them, Dani. I understand the caution, but they're your friends. They'll understand. By staying silent, you're sending the message that it's something we need to be ashamed of, when it's absolutely not. And you know you'll need them. So tell them, babe."

I hate it when he becomes all rational like this. Especially when he's *right* and he knows it. With nothing else to say, I grumble, "Oh, all right."

"They'll have your back," he assures me once more.

"I know. I love you," I reply.

"Love you too." After that, all I get is dead air as he hangs up.

With a huge sigh, I toss my phone in the bag, and I'm off to meet my friends.

***

Coming to the restaurant, I see all three women are here. As usual, I'm the last one to arrive and I'm ten minutes late. Since I'm *always* late, it's not a big surprise to them. It's such a bad habit that, one day, I'll probably be late for my own funeral. Sending a smile their way, I lightly shrug my shoulders in some kind of apology on my way to the table.

I still feel a light tremor in my belly in anticipation of their reaction to my news. But after the phone call with Sam, it's a tiny bit smaller. And besides, every chick knows that as long as you have your girls, that tight circle of good, honest women, nothing in the world can put you down, because they'll be there to pull you up. No matter what.

Walking toward our table and watching them roll their eyes at me—they're used to my tardiness by now and decided to consider it my lovable flaw—or in Marcy's case, discreetly flipping me off, I know in the bottom of my heart I chose my friends well.

Marcy's my closest friend, the one I go to with every little thing that's consuming my mind. For the longest time, we've been a duo. Then when things progressed with Sam, slowly and painfully, we "added" Amy and Brooke as permanent fixtures in our lives. There have been other girls, but since none of them had staying power, and thanks to the fact Sam's friends keep changing girlfriends like socks, things became a little tricky, so we established a trial period, and so far, none of them stuck.

Amy's the sweet one. She's always the peacemaker in the group. The skill is often used on Marcy and me. She reminds me of Princess Jasmine from *Aladdin*, with her *long,* wavy, jet-black hair, and super light brown eyes. Sometimes, when she's out in the sun, they give the illusion you can almost see through them they're so light. Then, there's also her brownish skin. It looks like she has a tan year-round, giving me moments of envy since I could be a walking commercial for milk; that's how pale my skin tone is.

Two weeks before, she brought the first picture of her baby. It was a bittersweet moment for me, and at the end, I didn't know how to feel. On one hand, I was immensely happy for my friend, looking at the picture of a miracle that was happening on a daily basis. Most people lost that knowledge, reducing it to a common occurrence and a sometimes dreaded outcome of a one-night mistake. On the other hand, jealousy and anger play hide-and-seek inside me. One minute, I'm jealous, and the next, I'm angry, but jealousy always wins. In the end, I calm down in the knowledge that we are on the path that will take us to having our baby, and I shove those ugly emotions in the back of my mind.

She's at fourteen weeks now, her bump already showing a little, which is not all that surprising considering Mark's—Sam's best friend and his partner—a giant of a man. The pregnancy was a big shock to them, but one that is highly welcome. Amy even divulged to me that the night she told him she's pregnant, after draining a beer, Mark looked at her for almost half an hour with tears in his eyes and then held her for half an hour more, his big palm covering the lower half of her abdomen.

Brooke's the cynical one. Ash-blonde hair cut in a bob that frames her heart-shaped face perfectly, indigo eyes surrounded with such thick lashes you'd think they aren't natural—which they are, I asked her the first time I met her—and a body even the most popular starlets would envy. She's the smoking hot one of the group. She used to be sweet and outgoing, but the events that took place in the last three years, most of which were her own doing, changed that. She's one of "the sock girls," and she did last longer than the most. When it ended with Nate, she pulled away from us, canceling lunches and hangouts, but we put her right where she belonged, back in our fold.

And then there's Marcy. Marcy is Marcy. She's some kind of weird blend of Amy and Brooke, plus my fairy godmother from *Cinderella*. Sometimes I'm convinced she also has her powers, especially when she was decorating her home. No one is that good at finding all that stuff in dark corners of a store.

Going around the table, I give each of my girls a kiss on the cheek, saying loudly so all can hear, "Hey, ladies. What's new?"

Coming to Marcy and leaning into her to give her a kiss, I'm suddenly stopped when her hand comes to my chin. Moving my face back a bit, she looks deep into my eyes and says in the sternest tone that ever came from her, "I don't know. You tell us."

Wrapping my hand around her wrist, I give her a small nod. The nerves that were lying dormant suddenly awaken.

Pushing her fingers in my cheeks, she again commands, "Now."

"Yes," I whisper, focusing only on her, not that I have much choice. I can see the concern and fear swirling in her eyes. I'm such an idiot. I should have told her right from the start. She has such a strong personality that it's easy to forget what happened with her mom and how scared it left her. She's deathly afraid of losing someone else. And my mood swings and secrecy don't help. I should have remembered there's no fooling her and she would see right through me.

Sitting at the table, I look at all of them, and on each of their faces, there's now fear and concern evident for all to see. Taking a deep breath, I announce, "In about two weeks, Sam and I will start the IVF procedure."

That is met with complete and utter silence. Since there's no comment from any of them, I launch right into my story and confess all the secrets I've kept from them in the past months.

By the end of it, Marcy has a death grip on my hand that's lying on the table, while Amy holds her belly, her face down, but I can see there are tears dripping from her eyes. But Brooke has a weird expression on her face, and halfway through my monolog, she averted her eyes to look over my shoulder.

"So that's it. Two more weeks, and then we start," I finish.

"I don't think you should do it," comes from Brooke.

"What?" I whisper, not believing my ears.

"It's wrong. It's unnatural. God and church are against it. I would never do such a thing," she carries on like I never spoke a word.

"What?" Marcy yells, I can see she's gearing up to get up and probably smack Brooke. "Since when are you such a believer that you're living your life blindly following rules?"

Before those two can get into a verbal—and physical—match, I interrupt them. "You don't know what you're talking about."

"Maybe, but that's my opinion, and you asked for it."

"And it's wrong," Marcy interjects before I can come up with the answer.

"Brooke," Amy whispers, still holding her belly, only now that touch went from gentle and loving to protective. And in that instant, the picture from the doctor's office comes to my mind.

"You don't know what you are talking about," I repeat, saying each word clearly. "This is my choice. And, honey, I didn't ask you for your opinion. I asked you to be here for me, to be my friend. One of my closest friends. You've got no way to prove that my choice is against God's ways, as you put it. I know the last few years were rough on you, and most of that roughness was your own doing. Did I ever tell you that you were wrong? No! All I ever did was give you advice, and that was only when you asked for it, which wasn't much of the time. Then, last year, when you made that colossal mistake, I didn't say a word. I didn't say 'I told you so.' No, I was there afterward when it blew up right in your face, every step of the way, holding your hand, crying with you, and going so far as to make Sam sit down and give you advice and his opinion when you wanted to talk only to him." Brook's face was going paler by the second in fear that I would tell the girls what she did. But I would never do that.

"What happened last year?" Marcy asks.

Ignoring her, I continue, "And maybe, maybe in some way it's wrong what I'm about to do, but picture this. In the near future, you find a man. You find that *one man* for you. The man who gives the world to you, putting it down at your feet, who loves you beyond belief, and then, you find out you can't give him one thing... the thing that's most important to him. A baby. A family. Picture that and tell me... tell me that you would rob him of the opportunity to be a father. To be a dad. To one day hold that precious gift in his arms."

Seeing her opening her mouth, ready to respond, I put my arm up, my palm facing her. "No, actually don't reply right now. Think about it. But not for five seconds or five minutes. Think about it for five hours. Even better, for five days."

Taking a deep breath, I finish, "And I'll give one other thing. And it's not yours to have, because he gives it only to me. He shows it only to me, it's only mine, but I'll give it to you, so maybe you'll be able to understand." It's obvious my words have struck their target, but I continue nevertheless. "Sam is that man. He's the man who'll work himself down to the bone to provide for me. He's the man who'll do anything that's in his power to make my wishes come true. Every morning, there's a fresh cup of coffee sitting next to the sink that he put there, waiting for me when I'm done with my shower. Every night, he blankets me with his body so I'll be as close to him as possible. He's the man who has an arm around my waist or around my shoulders when we walk down the street. He's the man who, when he has something important to say, something that has to sink in, will find a way to make that happen. But, mostly, he lets me go running around with you guys, doing my thing, never complaining about any of the trouble we put ourselves in. Sam's the man who'll walk through the house when I go to bed, in the middle of the night, whenever he thinks it needs to be done, just to check that everything's all right. He's the man who, when we told my parents about IVF, pulled me so close to him I was almost sitting on him. Not because their reaction was anywhere near yours, but because he knew they'd be devastated and I couldn't bear it on my own. And he is the man who comes home to me every night. He's the one who loves me and never fails to show it. And I know, kids or no kids, he would still have me and I would have him. So, you see, he's that man for me. Not because I looked for those traits. No, he's that man *just because he is.*"

"Dani," Amy whispers, but sends a quick glance at Marcy, and I can see she's dumbstruck. I've never shared any of this with her. And, Sam being Sam, they never knew.

"And I know, the day I die, that love won't. I would lie next to him for eternity, knowing I did everything in my power to make his only dream come true. And that's to have grandkids. And that's the way our love would live forever."

Never taking my eyes from Brooke's, I take a sip of water just to let that sink in. Putting the glass back on the table, I instruct, "Now, take your time, as much as you need, and then come find me and tell me. If you had that kind of a man, what would you do?" Staring in her eyes, I can see doubt and indecision swimming in their depths, but I don't care.

Her words and her rejection of me and my choices have managed to wake up the insecurity and doubt that was shoved into the depths of my brain and bring a cloud over me, obliterating my happiness and hope from earlier.

"I have to go," I say as I stand up, not looking at anybody.

"Dani," Brooke calls. "I'm sorry, I didn't mean it like that."

"Yes, honey, you did," I whisper brokenly. Sending a quick wave in their general direction, I walk out of the restaurant and to my car.

***

Driving up the gravel road that leads to the old beauty, I stare at the church. Every creak of stone under the tires of my car sends a shockwave to my heart.

Stopping the car, I shut it down and think about entering the sanctuary, but something keeps me rooted to the seat. I remember the last time I was here. I didn't get the warm feeling I used to have, but instead, I was left cold.

"You're hurting me," I whisper, never taking my eyes off the church. "Everything hurts, and I keep thinking, I keep praying for it to stop. But you're not listening to me."

It's unnatural.

God and church are against it.

Brooke's earlier words travel to my brain for the hundredth time in the past half an hour, leaving devastation in their wake.

"If you think this is the wrong way, if you think this is a sin, then why are you quiet? Why did you let medicine go so far and perfect this field? Why didn't you made us learn from our mistakes?" The tears I held at bay while driving comeback with a vengeance, and my body starts to buck with my attempts of holding them in.

"Is it the wrong thing to do?" I question.

I hate this doubt that's coursing through me. But then I remember Sam. And I remember my parents. And I remember the millions of fantasies and plans for our future. A future that is centered around our child. As the hurt rises in me, I know I have to do everything in my power to stop that before it takes residence in my loved ones. I will not let anybody else feel like this. I will not allow Sam to feel like this.

God and church are against it.

Wiping at my cheeks to remove the wetness that's there, I square my shoulders, and with the last drop of bravery and strength that's left in me, I say, "No. I don't care. I don't care what you think anymore. I will do whatever it takes to give my husband a child. I will do whatever it takes to have a family I want. I'll do what I need to do to get my star." On the last word, my reservoirs are emptied and I break. Because I know I just lied. I could never turn my back on Him.

And I hurt.

***

Sam

"That bitch!" Jules yells Sam's exact thoughts, but when he finally found Dani in her car parked in front of the chapel, and after fifteen minutes of coaxing it out of her, he used a much harsher word.

When he got Marcy's call five days ago, not even two hours after he hung up with Dani, after receiving the good news they were ready for IVF, he knew something was wrong. He just hoped Dani didn't need another trip to the ER. They were in the clear and didn't need one more setback.

No matter what he said or how he threatened her, Marcy remained tight-lipped and wouldn't tell him shit except to try to call his girl, since she was ignoring her calls.

After calling Dani and driving around for almost four hours, there was only one place left. So he turned his truck and went to the church. He knew she struggled with how things were turning around, but that it would drive her to go here, he didn't anticipate.

The sight that greeted him almost brought him to his knees. She sat there in her car. From the outside, he could see her body bucking with sobs. Upon finding her, fear like nothing before started pooling in his gut.

He got in the car, and she didn't even jump. Instead, she remained as she'd been, body bucking, tears running down her face, mumbling under her breath, "Please, please, God. Let me get pregnant. I'll do whatever You want. I'll go to church. I'll stop cussing. Whatever You want. Just, please, please, don't let me do the wrong thing. Don't make me give him up." With that last prayer, she grabbed his arm and started sobbing. She was tearing his heart out, fiber by fiber, leaving him useless to do anything but take her in his arms the best he could in the small space. She shoved her face in his chest and cried there while he tried to find out what happened.

That was the last day he had his girl. She completely shut down, often repeating those awful words the first two days. She ate, she slept, and she spent her days sitting on the couch, staring at the wall. He was at his wit's end and didn't know what in the hell to do. When he tried to touch her, she would gently pull away, offering some bullshit excuse he couldn't hear from the blood rushing in his ears at seeing her reaction. He was reduced to a peck from her beautiful lips, often with her not even looking him in the eyes before or after. She didn't speak anymore, when previously she could talk his ear off describing her day and how her time with her friends went, offering him information he absolutely didn't want or need.

He was losing her, and he didn't know what to do to get her back. So, when Jules called him because Dani wasn't answering her phone anymore, he jumped at the chance for her to come to visit, totally disregarding her bullshit excuse of the time off that came out of the blue. She loved her sister, he knew, but also it was high time to run from the mess she made of her life.

"Bro, you need to do something about this chick," Jules says to him, pulling him out of his thoughts.

Chuckling, he shakes his head just as Dani inserts, "Nobody'll do anything. She'll come around." Hearing her speak sharply, he looks at her, and he can see some of her spark is back. Looking back to Jules with relief, he sees that same relief written all over her face. She didn't miss Dani's pain.

"Anyhow, let's go out tonight. We'll drown in gin and tonic and forget our troubles," Jules tells them in a fake excited voice.

"I don't feel like getting smashed tonight."

"No, you do. And at the end of it, Sam'll carry you to the bed like a knight in shining armor."

"Damn right I will," he tells her before Dani can offer some lame excuse.

"You sure?" Dani asks shyly.

"Babe" is all he says.

"Okay, let me get ready." And with that surprisingly easy acceptance, Dani stands up from the couch that he swears to himself he's gonna burn, going in the direction of the bedroom.

"She's not well," Jules murmurs softly, also looking after Dani.

"No."

"What can we do to get her back?"

"Exactly what you are doing."

Sometime after, he goes in search of his girl. She's taking an unusually long time. He finds her standing in the middle of the room, a stricken expression on her face, looking at the pictures on the nightstand. He knows what she's seeing, and he hopes to God it'll pull her out of her grief and bring her back. For tonight, he's going to get his wife drunk and see if she's still hiding in the darkness.

CHAPTER EIGHT

"**I'M SORRY FOR** today. I wish I could give you what you deserve. I wish I could give you the stars. But I promise you, next year, I'll do better. I'll give you everything you want." He apologizes again for something that isn't his fault.

"It's okay." I try to calm him down one more time, but I know when he gets like this, there's no point.

"God, I love you," he says distractedly, looking at me like I'm some figment of his imagination, completely unaware that this is the first time he's said those words to me, and that from this moment on, nothing else exists for me but him. Only him.

Opening my eyes, I'm instantly assaulted by the bright sunshine, and there's a stabbing pain in them and on its way to my brain, until I close them again. My old friend, the lone drummer, is present in my brain, drumming away, but this time, he brought a gong with him.

Turning my head to escape the light, I see Jules sprawled on the other side of the bed. For some reason, she's covered in tinsel and has a heart drawn on her cheek. Looking beneath the sheet, I see the shape of fingers, big fingers drawn on top of my boobs, and some words there also. It looks like it says *Sam's*. Gingerly moving my body, I try to get out of bed but end up stepping on Marcy. She's lying on the floor in the fetal position, but her hands are clutching a puppy, which is weirdly still, like it's afraid it'll wake her up.

What the hell happened last night? All I can remember is laughing our asses off as we watched Jules sitting in the chair and some guy tattooing her. When that little snippet comes to mind, I bring my hand up so fast that I actually slam it against my nose. Guess I'm not in control of my body just yet. And, yep, right where I thought it would be, around my left wrist is clear saran wrap. If I move it, it will reveal a girl's back as she sits on a swing with her arm extended sideways. Underneath, it says in bold letters **SIS**; another girl and the rest of the word, -**TER**, is on Jules's right wrist.

After finally managing to stumble to the bathroom and take care of business, I go into the kitchen, following my nose and the scent of fresh coffee.

"There's my girl," Sam says quietly, a weird look in his eyes and a small smile on his face. Going directly to him, I snuggle against him and hide my face from the light that seems to be following me just to torture me. Too groggy to process why he stilled, I just snuggle closer.

"What the hell happened?"

"You had fun." He kisses me on the head and then, reaching behind me, gives me my cup. "Here."

"Hmmm… thanks." I try to move away from him so I won't spill the coffee, but suddenly his hand is on the back of my neck, pulling me right back where I was. At this movement, I put my free hand on his abs and look at him. "Is everything okay?"

"It's perfect, baby." There's some emotion going quickly in and out of his eyes that I'm unable to process in my hungover state. "How're you feeling?" He changes the subject.

"Except for the drum competition going strong in my brain and the sunlight trying to blind me, I'm fine." I take a sip of hot brew and, sighing, put my chin on his chest, looking up at him. "Do I want to know what went on last night?" I try one more time.

"Not really," he answers through a smile, his hand lightly kneading my neck, the other going up and down my back. It feels so nice I start purring, making Sam's smile grow wider. "But, keep Marcy away from Nate for some time."

"What did she do?" I ask, dreading the response.

"Not much, just laid into him about how he changed Brooke and she became a bitch, and he needs to do something about it."

"Shit! I'll handle it." I sigh.

"Now, go lie down on the couch and rest. I'll take care of breakfast," he orders.

"Thank you, honey," I say, going to my toes and giving him a kiss. As I lightly run my tongue at the seam of his lips, his whole body turns to stone for a second. The next, my coffee's on the counter after being plucked out of my hand and firmly put there, and he hauls my body into him, deepening the kiss. It's the most intense kiss we've shared since we started this journey, and something in my brain just clicks. At that moment, I vow to myself that I'll find my way back home to my husband.

***

Standing in the bathroom and looking at myself in the mirror, I can't muster the strength to get out and go to Sam.

Yesterday, after getting ready to go out with Jules, I was passing our bed when something caught my eye. That something was the two pictures on my nightstand.

In the first, smaller one, we were at some party, both of us wearing jeans, me in a black corset and black heels. Sam was in a black T-shirt and his boots. He had picked me up, my hair, blonde at the time, cascading down my back and over Sam's arms, our gazes locked. On our faces were radiant smiles.

The second picture was from our wedding day. Sam was in his tux, and I was in my satin wedding gown. We were standing side by side, one of our arms around each other's waist, hand in hand locked around my bouquet, slightly leaning forward, eyes aimed at the camera.

You could see we were tired and had enough of taking pictures. But, still, our smiles?

Radiant.

In that moment, it became obvious I wasn't me anymore. And Sam wasn't Sam. We lost us. And it was all because of me. It's been three weeks since Brooke hurled those awful words at me. Words which managed to change me, started to pull me into the darkness I couldn't fight from. Words, that changed my marriage and made me start abandoning Sam.

We used to talk about everything and nothing, or he would let me go on about stuff that was on my mind in any particular moment. Now, we didn't talk, except for asking about each other's day or some other trivial stuff, and even then there were only a few words exchanged.

Also, before, when we were together, he was always in touching distance, often taking my hand or standing behind my back. Now, I take my hand back or scoot away from him a little before he has a chance to touch me lately. I don't feel worthy of his touch anymore, and I know, in the case of IVF failing, I will lose him to someone who can give him everything. So, in a way, I'm preparing myself.

Sam also became broodier. I often find him staring at nothing, and when I ask what that's about, he just blows me off.

The second change was our sex life.

We had a healthy sex life. Two or three times a week. Sometimes more, sometimes less.

Normal.

It wasn't always explosive, but it was always loving, and Sam always took care of me, whether it was before or after him, and there were occasions when he would take me to the peak multiple times.

But our times together started to come less frequently, and I've realized I was more and more tense.

I kept asking myself if I did things right, if he was enjoying the stuff I did. If he even finds me attractive anymore. I kept winding myself so tight that often I couldn't let go. So, I faked it. A lot.

Of course, Sam picked that shit up and kept reassuring me, but I still couldn't get there.

Hence, the less frequency. And after the showdown with Brooke and my complete meltdown in the church parking lot, it stopped all together.

The realization of what we're becoming broke my heart. And I promise I will do anything in my power to get us back.

This morning, Sam's reaction to my touch and kiss brought everything into focus. It told me I can't put this off for another day. It has to be tonight. I have to show him I'm still me and, despite all that has happened, I'm not gone.

It's funny how one single sentence can make a person's world go upside down. We all know how powerful words are. We all know that sometimes they can do a lot of harm, but I've never had that happen to me. Until Brooke.

Until that moment, I struggled, going from anger to happy and hopeful, and then right back to anger. And finally, for one glorious hour, all that was inside me was optimism. No, not optimism, but *certainty* that we could and would win this. That our star would come to us. And with a few little soft-spoken words, she took all that away from me. All the hope, happiness, even anger was gone. She flipped some switch inside me, leaving me in the forest in the dark, bumping into trees, trying to get back to the light. Trying to get back home. But all I did was go deeper and deeper into the forest, slowly losing myself, and losing Sam.

And now, after all that slapped me in the face, looking at those pictures, and this morning with Sam, it's time. It's time to fight the dark, stop bumping into trees, and find my way home. Only way I know how is to go back to Sam, take us back to the beginning, and let our bodies speak for us.

So, thanks to all that, here I am. Standing in my black nightie, made completely out of lace, its hem brushing the tops of my thighs, while I hide in the bathroom. Feeling like some virgin that's gonna get her some after dreaming of that perfect night all her teen years, when she's finally gonna give her one and only the greatest gift a girl could give. Anticipating candles and rose petals and some romantic song playing in the background. In the end, all she gets is a backseat of the guy's car, some techno beat blasting from the stereo, at which beat he's pumping inside her, while she tries to recover from the most intense bite of pain. Instead of candlelight, there're the sporadic flashes of the other cars' headlights, and instead of rose petals, there's a condom wrapper stuck to her calf. Afterward, he gets fist bumps and high-fives, while she convinces herself that everything's okay. It wasn't all that great, but it was with *him*, so that's all that matters.

I don't want to be like that guy. I don't want to be a promise of something beautiful and magical, and then end up completely disappointing Sam.

I want to give him something he gave me years ago. Something he probably doesn't even remember. I want to give him *me* back. But because of the buzzing nerves, and fear of failure, and that God-awful shame of being the promise of a family, then snatching that away, I'm left immobile, reduced to that fumbling virgin, standing in my bathroom.

Past

We're lying on our sides. Sam has his face buried in my hair, his breath tickling my neck, his arm around my waist. He's spooning me.

The silence surrounding us only complements the moonlight streaming from the window, casting everything in shadow.

I suppose, after our talk, there's not much to be said.

I lied to him tonight. For the first and the last time.

I didn't want to, but from the moment he stepped into the bar I knew something was up, and in the end, I had no choice.

***

Turning my phone to face screen-side-up, I once again check for that text that'll let me know Sam is waiting for me outside. I can hear Marcy's annoyed sigh in reaction to the hundred and tenth time I did this, but I don't care. Usually he's on time, but tonight, for some reason, he's almost half an hour late. And I'm starting to worry.

We've been dancing this dance of ours for four months now. For three of them, I knew I was in big trouble since I did that one thing I wasn't supposed to do. I fell in love. And now, I'm just waiting for everything to blow up in my face. What possessed me to continue to see him after my birthday night, I really don't know. How I could convince myself I could do this friends-with-benefits thing is beyond me. Maybe because we're not friends. There's no communication between us throughout the week, but when Saturday comes, there's a flock of something with wings in my stomach just from getting the text from him asking if we're on for the night.

What we are is acquaintances who meet once a week to have sex.

Today is no different. The text came, I shaved and primed myself to the nines, but now he's not here.

"He'll be here. Don't worry," I hear Marcy say as I turn the phone facing back down so the disappointment doesn't stare right back in my face, mocking me with the blankness of the screen and its lack of messages.

"Hmm...." I hum, glancing through the bar so I don't have to look at her face and see the worry she's carrying in her eyes lately. Worry for me. Of course, I told her about my predicament and my complete unwillingness to break it off with Sam.

Every Sunday, I promise her and myself that I'll end it, and then every Monday, I prolong it for one more week. Right now, I'll end it in a month. I even have the date saved in my phone. I haven't changed it this week, and I'm itching to do it, but Marcy's been eyeing my calendar like a hawk.

"You have to talk to him. Talk or end it." She once again starts to lecture me. I know I surprised her; she meant the request to Sam as a joke, never believing I would go through with it when she introduced me to him on my birthday, but I did. And now, the joke's on me. I'm the one who went and fell in love with the only person I wasn't supposed to.

"I—" I start to assure her I'll end everything with Sam, but the words get stuck in my throat and my breaths become nonexistent when I see him.

He's standing at the door, scanning the room. He's wearing a white T-shirt that resembles a second skin it's so tight, and the person who designed those jeans of his deserves a reward for the best creation there ever was, because they look so freaking great on him. Those green gems of his are like lasers searching for his prey.

"You've got a little bit of saliva dribbling down your chin," Marcy teases.

"Shut up. I don't." But still, my fingers have a mind of their own and lightly touch said chin, seeking any sign of drool.

Right then, his eyes capture mine, a smile slowly stretching his face. He's successfully caught me in his net. The predator got his prey. I'm helpless, completely at his mercy, unable to move a muscle, let alone move my eyes from him.

As he comes our way, I start to fidget. What the hell is he doing? Nobody knows about our little arrangement—nobody but Marcy, that is. And he never comes in to get me. He always sends a text letting me know he's waiting outside, and I go to him. He never comes in when I'm here. So why is he approaching me right now, where all can see?

Just then, from behind me, the shout comes. "Hey, man, glad you made it!" And the spell's broken. He blinks, moving his gaze from me, releasing me from his net. My breath is labored, like I've run up and down stairs five times, or like he's touched me.

Trying to compose myself, I scan the room, and a bucket of ice-cold water's poured on me. Every single eye of every single woman in the bar is on him. And I can't do anything about it. I can't touch him, can't kiss him. I can't stake my claim on this perfect male specimen. I have to stand here and completely ignore him and, what's worse, be completely ignored by him.

"Hello, ladies," comes from beside me, and when I look up, he winks. Those wings start flapping again and my breathing goes wonky. But that's it. He and his friends park themselves right at our table, standing around it for the rest of the night, and it's a mixture of heaven and hell. On one hand, it's heaven, because he's here enjoying his night and I get to witness him in his natural surroundings, hanging out with his friends. On the other, it's hell, because as the night goes on, more and more looks from girls come, some even going so far as to try and approach him and his friends. And the level of my jealousy goes higher, making my skin itch and my hands shake. All I want is to turn and kiss him, put my arms around him, tell the world he's mine. But I can't, since he's not. And he never will be.

***

Later, I'm lying on his bed, my head in his lap. Both of us lost in our heads, not even pretending we're not.

The car ride was completely silent, and it gave me time to think. The whole evening, he didn't say a word to me, and as the seconds ticked by, I was becoming more desperate for some kind of attention from him. But right when I was ready to call it quits for the night and go home, thinking today was going to be the first time I wouldn't spend my Saturday in his bed, the touches came.

At first, they were light, just the skim of his fingers across my back or waist, never breaking the conversation with his friends. I was sure it was just my deep desire for him and the combination of my third gin and tonic that was playing tricks on my brain. But then, those skims became taps on my butt and squeezes of my waist. And when some guy came to stand by me and tried to start a conversation, there was Sam's foot on my own and the finger in the belt loop of my jeans that jerked me his way. My eyes did a quick scan of the people who were standing around us, but it seemed nobody noticed anything. A look at Sam's face revealed he was grinding his jaw. Five minutes after that, he said his goodbyes and I got a text.

We're leaving.

I left after ten minutes, and thus the silent drive started.
"Dani," Sam prompts.
"Hmmm?"
"Are you in love with me?"

At his question, my heart gives one hard beat. So hard, I can actually feel it from the roots of my hair to the tips of my toes. I'm surprised my body didn't move at its force. I wish I could tell him the truth, that yes, I'm in love with him. I have no doubt, but I know that's not what he wants to hear. We agreed we'd leave it simple. Just one night a week. And even though nothing else was discussed, he hadn't reached out to me through the weeks. No calls or texts just to touch base, to hear from me, and I'm too much of a coward to do it myself, when all I want is to spend every second of every day with him.

So I push down the words that are desperately trying to get out, and for the first time, I lie to him. "No."

"I'm sorry, but I can't be in a relationship right now. I have to focus on my business. I have too much on my plate to add a girlfriend to it," he explains.

"Don't worry. I don't want a relationship either. I don't want the complications of it. I want"—I take a deep breath and exhale—"what we have now. I want something like this." I put a hand on my chest to check if my heart is still beating, because it hurt so much to say those words. And now I know. I know he's not gonna be my fairy-tale ending. With one sentence, he killed all hope inside me. There won't be any more prolonging the inevitable, no more of me changing the date when I'll end this game of ours. Because tonight is the last time.

And that's something both of us know.

I want everything he can't or won't offer.

I fell for him. Broke the most important rule in this arrangement we had. And I love him enough to give him what he wants but has left unspoken.

End.

The end of us.

There is only one thing I want to give him more.

Me.

I can't keep doing this anymore. Each weekend, he makes me fall more and more, and pretty soon, I'll be consumed by him. I keep offering myself to him, any and every way he wants, only to get gently rejected with a peck on the cheek when it's time to go home. What's worse is that he's not even aware he's doing it.

So, this is it.

Our last night together.

Our last time.

Everything in me screams those three words that go past so many mouths each day. Which, for some, hold no meaning, but for some, like me, they mean everything, especially now. Lying here in the dark, the only light coming from the moonlight, I can actually see our whole life together. It's a perfect image, one that won't come true.

Battling with myself internally, I'm losing. Because I know.

As soon as he kisses me on the cheek, the craving will start. And as the days go by, at the end of the week, I will need him with the intensity of a person that has come to their limit holding their breath under water. He's that second when you breach the surface and take that huge breath of air. He has become my air. Come Saturday morning, I'll start to count the hours, minutes, even seconds till I'm able to see and feel him again. Until I'm able to finally, *finally* breathe again.

Who would have thought that the one foolish, selfish decision I have made in years would lead me to this? To fall so completely in love that nothing else matters. Nothing but him.

Sam.

It's on this thought that his hand starts moving from where it was placed across my waist and he glides the tips of his fingers slowly—oh so, so slowly—upward, causing my eyes to gradually shut and goose bumps to awaken in their path all over my side and belly. At the same time, on a huge intake of air, he starts lowering his head, his breath tickling my ear as he tips his face to me, catching my hair with his chin, moving it back from my neck, and replacing it with his lips. Not kissing, just lips on skin.

Here we go.

But as devastating as it is, in all the grief that's consuming me, my eyes snap open, because he didn't go for the obvious destinations—or his preferred one, settling that beautiful torture on my breast—but places it right on the spot where my neck and shoulder meet, pulling me deeper into him. It's like he is trying to absorb me. His touch is different. It's slower, lighter. The touch you use when you're introduced to a fragile masterpiece for the first time and you just have to touch it, feel it, hoping against all hope you can somehow take it with you through that one simple touch and carry it always wherever you go.

There it is.

Confirmation.

He's memorizing me. He's taking the only piece of me he will allow himself to. When I want him to take all of me, to make my life burst with color, to sparkle for the rest of my existence, to look into his perfect eyes, he's only taking the memory of me.

Realizing this, pain shoots through me so immense I stop breathing for fear it'll shatter me right here in his arms. He's destroying me in the most beautiful way, and he doesn't even know it.

"Don't," he hisses, giving me a whisper of a kiss on my neck.

"Don't what?" I swallow that ball forming in my throat, once again closing my eyes, submersing me into compete darkness so that all I can feel is him surrounding me.

"Don't think. Forget." His lips form a path from the base of my neck to the top.

"Forget what?"

"Everything, anything. Just be with me right now."

If he only knew.

I'm at that point where I don't know how to live without him anymore. But the funny thing is I had my chance to tell him and I lied. I don't know how to tell him how I feel. An echo in my brain becomes louder and louder by the second, screaming those three little words. They're so easy to tell, so easy to be pushed aside, reduced to nothing, but they mean everything. I'm no longer formed by blood, muscles, and bones, but only from my love for him, and he'll never know. I'll never tell him. When this night comes to an end, it'll be the end of us. I'll go home, carrying the imprint of his lips on my cheek as a final goodbye.

My brain is telling me this is one last, final time; my heart is shouting it's not, that I'll be here next Saturday. I know which one I want to win, but I also know which one *must* win.

"I am."

Moving my hands from their prayer position under my face, I reach behind me to settle it across his waist, my palm on the small of his back, pulling him deeper into me. I'm not strong enough to turn and face him. Not just yet.

It's like I pushed a start button. His hands go up on their fingertips and start roaming lightly all across my body. Still whisper soft, still gentle.

Loving.

The whole world dissolves. I don't know how he manages it. To make me forget everything. Everything but him. All the pain, all the regret of not being honest, just disappears. In a whole other life, we would have and do everything, but in this one, all we have is this.

One hand on the base of my throat, the other squeezing my breast, he pushes us into a sitting position, his long legs caging me in.

"I need you, Dani."

"You have me." *All of me,* I think to myself.

He once again squeezes me, and then the hand that's on the base of my throat goes slowly down my breastbone to the center of my chest so he can push me down on my back.

"So beautiful," I hear murmured while his head begins its slow journey down my body. His lips feather-soft, his breath only a fathom of a breeze, raising goose bumps in its wake.

There's not an inch of skin that's not being touched, kissed, or licked by him. By the time he reaches the center of me, I'm like a rubber band, stretched to its full capacity, ready to snap. I can't settle my hands. They're going from his hair and shoulders to tearing the sheets from the bed. And right when they go back to their path from hair to shoulder, he bites my wrist.

"Still" is what I manage to decipher from the animalistic noise he emanates when he moves my hands back to the bed.

Pushing my legs wide open, we both take a deep breath. He releases his; I lose mine when he licks me from my entrance to clit.

"Relax, baby, and let me take you any way I can."

I do as he says, and I'm lost. Lost to the world. The only thing that's in my head is Sam and those three words that don't want to come out and be introduced to the reality of us.

Every time.

Every single, glorious time he does this, I'm surprised by his skill.

And every single time, that surprise quickly turns into pain so exquisite nothing can compare. Nothing, except the feel of Sam inside me.

"God," I whimper, my hands once again going to his head, burrowing my fingers in his hair. I don't know if I want to pull him off me or shove him deeper.

Just as my body starts to perform a perfect arch, he tosses my legs over his shoulders, his hands going to my ass, and he lifts, burying his face deeper.

He's like a man who got his last dinner, savoring it but at the same time devouring his favorite dish. Every stroke of his tongue is gentle, and after every one, he releases a little hum. But every bite of his teeth, every suck of his mouth, reveals desperation beyond measure.

Getting closer to the edge of bliss, I moan, "Sam." Right then, I lose his mouth. "No!" I wail.

"Not without me," he growls, and he enters me in one, slow, *long* move.

Oh, God, the feel of him. That gorgeous feeling of being so full of him. Of, in one significant moment in time, being one with him.

"Move, honey," I plead.

"Look at me," he demands in his hoarse voice. And when I do, that's when he starts to move. Slow, slow, slowly.

"Faster," I beg.

"Not yet, baby."

Just as I think I'll die if he doesn't go any faster, our bodies slick from sweat, I dig my nails in his back to keep purchase on his body, that's when he starts to go faster, harder. Once again on the fast track to the Promised Land, I start to close my eyes, when he commands, "Look at me, Dani." My eyes open wide again instantly. And finally, I see.

I see what he's doing. He's making love to me.

He's memorizing me.

He's saying goodbye.

And right at that moment, I experience both the most intense pain of my life as my heart breaks in a million pieces and the most powerful orgasm. The power of everything makes me close my eyes, not able to look into his any longer.

Through it, his strokes become even harder, deeper. I can feel his harsh breath on my neck, hear his grunts in my ear from where he shoved his face.

Taking my legs behind my knees, he pulls them higher on his waist and thrusts one, two, three more times. On the third, he goes completely still inside me.

All that can be heard is our labored breaths as we lay completely still, our bodies sticking to each other.

In that moment, I think to myself, *Goodbye, my love.*

CHAPTER NINE

"*I ALWAYS THOUGHT that whole thing about soul mates was just some crap people in love liked to say. Never believed in it. Never believed in faith. And then I met you. And everything changed.*"

Still standing in the bathroom, for the hundredth time, I give my appearance a final look, and... I lose my nerve.

Rushing to my jeans and shirt, I put them back on, over my nightie, and go to look for Sam. So lost in my thoughts of that night, when I believed we were over, I don't see him standing near the bed, taking his clothes off, and I run straight into him.

"Wow," he says, surprised, circling me with his arms to prevent my bounce to the floor.

I shake my head, trying to clear it. "Where'd you come from?"

"I was standing here when you came from the bathroom. Didn't you see me?"

"No," I reply, looking at his bare chest. Once again, I shake my head, this time to clear it from the daze that body of his always puts me in. "I was lost in my head."

"Yeah? What got you so wrapped up?" His hands start to go up and down my back, bringing a delectable little shiver to the surface.

"Um...." Looking into his eyes to try and keep a conscious thought, I can see there's a smirk on his face. "Remember that night, way back when we had our talk—well, you had a talk with me, actually—about if I was in love with you?"

Those hands of his are getting bolder and bolder by the second, now going from my shoulders right down to my ass, giving a squeeze every time.

"Yeah?" He stretches the word.

"Well, I never asked you. What was that about?"

"Offence is the best defense" is his weird answer.

"Huh?" Between his cryptic answer and his hands that are going strong, I'm quickly losing all ability to think, let alone carry on a conversation.

"I needed to know how you felt about me so I'd know what my next play was gonna be."

"Then, why the speech about not being able to have a relationship at that time?"

"You said you weren't in love with me."

I put my hands on his arms, trying to stop them. "Are you saying that if I told the truth we would've been together then?"

But I don't get the answer, because suddenly Sam stills. "What's this?"

In my astonishment of finding out the reason behind the conversation that brought such pain to my very soul, I hadn't realized his hands have gone underneath my shirt. Suddenly unable to look him in the eye any longer, I stare at his ear. "Umm...," I mumble.

"Lace?" he breathes.

In the next second, there are two hands around my waist. In the next, I'm flying through the air. And in the next, I'm bouncing on the bed.

Oh. My. God.

He'd picked me up and thrown me on the bed.

Oh... my God.

That didn't get a shiver. That got a body convulsion.

I look down my body, only to see Sam crawling over me, his eyes fixed on my torso. I try to touch him, to slow him down somehow, but the next thing I know, my arms are flying over my head with the force he's using to tear my shirt off me.

"Lace," he growls, confirming with his sight what his hands found hiding beneath my clothes.

He keeps looking at the nightie like he's afraid it's a mirage and will disappear in the blink of an eye.

"Honey, what're you doing?" I ask, confused by the sudden stop in action.

Taking a deep, rumbling breath, he looks at me. "I'm going to heaven."

And then it's on.

In the next three seconds, I lose my jeans and panties, the area between my legs sticky with my wetness, the nightie only a shred of lace lying forgotten on the floor.

He starts kissing me, but ends up devouring me. I can barely keep up. But, God, I don't want him to stop or slow down.

He pushes my legs apart, falling between them. And in one swift move, he's inside me.

So good. So deep.

Arching my neck, I feel him licking the offered area from base to chin.

Biting on my lower lip, he says between labored breaths, "I missed you."

"I missed you too."

"Wasn't talking to you, baby." He smirks.

"Who were you talking to then?" I put my feet on the back of his thighs and try to move, but his hands stop me.

"I was talking to that heaven you call a pussy," he says, once again biting my lip.

I smile, the expression wonky thanks to the trapped lip. I kiss him, and he starts to move.

Fast.

Hard.

So hard we're moving along the bed and I have to put my hand on the headboard to prevent banging my skull against it and to use the leverage to meet him thrust for thrust.

Two minutes later, I have to stop kissing him. It's coming on fast and strong. But our mouths stay close, our lips connected. Every few seconds, the tips of our tongues touch.

And then it's here. And it rivals the one from that night so long ago in its beauty. But it crushes it in its intensity. Thirty seconds later, Sam plants himself firmly in me, his forehead dropping to mine.

***

Lying in bed, my head on his shoulder, my forehead kissing his cheekbone, I look at the shadows in the moonlight.

"If you'd asked me to, I would've given you all of me that night. I would have said yes," I whisper.

"If you told the truth, I would've taken all of you that night. I would have made you mine."

Slowly, I drag my forehead along his face, stopping by the end of his brow. "You knew I lied?" I ask, surprise evident in my tone.

"Yeah. You've always been shit at hiding your feelings." His body's shaking, a smile on his face.

"Why'd you keep quiet?"

"Because you needed to trust me. And you had to learn how to."

"I trusted you," I argue.

"No, you didn't, baby. But I showed you that you can," he says on a squeeze.

***

Sam

Once again, as was his way the last few months, Sam found himself lying in his bed, on his back, wide awake in the middle of the night.

Only this time, as he was staring at the ceiling, watching shadows play hide-and-seek, he did it with his wife planted firmly by his side.

No.

Not by his side.

She was dead asleep, sprawled half on the bed, half on him. Her leg thrown over one of his, her knee in close proximity to his groin, her head on his shoulder, he could feel her breath whispering across the skin on his chest, her hand at his abs. He had his arm around her, her weight on it like a part of him was lost then found again.

So, once again, he was lying in his bed, on his back, awake in the middle of the night, but only this time, he did it with a smile on his face.

He surprised himself that night. He knew she was finding her way out of the fog her grief had put her in, finding her way back to him. To the *them* they were. But in his wildest dreams, he wouldn't have ever guessed she would finish her journey the way she did.

He didn't understand, at first, why she was so nervous, and why the hell she was talking about that night, but when his fingers touched that first inch of lace underneath her clothes, it all became clear.

In the next three seconds, as he stood there completely still, he fought for and lost all control, throwing her on the bed. And he lost himself in her. Lost, only to be found again when she didn't push him back, didn't say no, but participated fully.

Afterward, as he was lying on top of her, his breath heavy, he braced for her to retreat fully back into the shadows, for him to lose her again, only this time, never to come back. He knew this would happen, because he came on too strong. He should have been gentle; he should have given her what he gave her that night, so many years ago. He should have made love to her instead of fucking her the way he did. But then, instead of pushing him off, she circled him with her arms and quietly, so quietly he could barely hear her over the beat of his heart, she whispered, "I'm home."

Hearing that, he had to get off her or he would start bawling like a five-year-old. So he used an excuse of going to the bathroom to get a washcloth to clean her up, where he splashed his face with ice-cold water, trying to get a grip.

After that delicious task—delicious, because he finally gave that pussy a kiss and a lick, which in turn gave Dani goose bumps—on his way back to bed after taking the washcloth to the bathroom, he grabbed his T-shirt for Dani to wear. She hadn't worn his shirt to bed since she entered the depression stage of her grief, right after the showdown with Brooke. As she took it from him, she gave him a soft smile before she put it on. And that's when it was 100 percent confirmed—she made it through.

Getting in bed, taking his wife in his arms and talking softly about something they both have fond memories of, no matter the beginning of that night, he took a breath. And when he released it, he had the feeling he was holding it for a year the relief was so great. Right then, at that moment, he vowed he would frame the nightie he had ruined, frame it and mount it above their bed to always remind him of what he could have lost.

In a week, they were going to start the IVF. And he knew he could lose her again if it turned out to be unsuccessful. He had no idea what he would do if that happened. How he would bring her back, because he had no idea what brought her back this time. Was it the pictures, her sister, or was it his reaction to her touch? Maybe it was all three. But he knew he couldn't lose her, and he would do anything for her to stay by his side. She was his. And she would always be his. And there was no other possibility.

But he did his research. He read up on the IVF, its success rates. He asked other husbands in the process how the wives were taking it. He had a general idea of what he was facing, and it wasn't good. But he had to win. He had to give Dani her star. He had to somehow make her wish come true. Only problem was, it was out of his hands.

Just then, Dani moves, going to her belly, facing away. And he moves with her, shoving her underneath him, his arm going around her waist.

Once again, Sam lies in his bed, holding his wife, awake as the moon gives way to the sun. Only this time, he does it terrified.

***

Dani

For one whole, glorious week, we were as we had been before this nightmare began. Happy, having fun, living our lives with no looking back or the shadows lurking over our shoulders.

I was in the clear, out of the forest, fully in the meadow, enjoying the sun.

And then, on the morning of the seventh day, my period came.

And the IVF procedure began.

CHAPTER TEN

"***O**F COURSE I want a child, but what I want more is you*," he yells. "*If I don't have you, if I lose you, I can go out, lie down on the track, and wait for the train to run me over. Because if you're not here with me, if I don't have you, then I don't want to breathe anymore. I don't exist anymore.*"

Here we are, sitting in the now familiar waiting room. Waiting for the nurse to call our names so we can finally begin the process of getting our baby.

Leaning my head back against the wall, I expel a huge sigh as my eyes wander around. During this whole process, it seems like most of what we do is wait. And it's starting to wear me down a little. The fear that was absent this past week has come back, and it's growing by the second as I see all the faces here, in the same exact situation as us, hoping, waiting, and most of all, fighting for their dream.

The past week has been the most peaceful, happiest, and, at the same time, the most stressful in a long time.

First thing I decided Monday morning was to take time off work. As it was, I had already taken days off when it was needed to go to my checkups and to get blood work done, and I was getting curious looks from other teachers and the principal, since I hadn't shared with anybody—except my inner circle—what was going on in my life. Not to mention it wasn't easy on my kids, having a substitute at least once a week. I didn't know how all this was going to work. Would I be able to function normally? How often were the checkups going to be? I didn't know anything, so taking the time off seemed like the best thing to do.

Going down the hallway to the principal's office seemed like it took forever. My legs decided to resemble rubber more and more with each step I took closer to the door. That fear that had magically vanished the night before was starting to creep up on me, consuming my body by the second. All that was in my head was Brooke's reaction to the news. She still hadn't called or texted me. I didn't expect her to completely change her mind, but what I did expect from her, being one of my closest friends, was to have my back and support my decision, no matter what. And I was dreading that same reaction, or even worse, from the person inside the office.

Finally getting to it, I raised my hand to knock on the milky glass portion of the panel when I noticed my hand was shaking. Opening and fisting it to try to loosen up a bit, I was startled and even jumped a little when suddenly the door opened, and right in front of me stood Mr. Davenport.

"Oh, Mrs. Hunt," he said, equally surprised at seeing me standing in front of his office making weird hand motions midair as I was by his abrupt appearance before me.

"Hello, Mr. Davenport. I was wondering if I could have a word," I whispered.

"Of course, come in." He widened the opening and stepped aside, giving me enough space to enter his office.

Once inside, he closed his door, gestured for me to take a seat, and then waited for me to begin what I came to say.

Thank God, by the time he leveled his serious and expectant eyes at me, my butt was already in the seat. Otherwise, I would've definitely face-planted on the floor. My knees joined the party and started to shake. I felt like I was in the principal's office as a naughty student, waiting to state my case and receive his ruling.

"What can I do for you, Mrs. Hunt?" He sat at his desk, his hands clasped and lyingon it while he looked at me and waited. I took a deep breath and start telling my story. Once I started, it was impossible for me to stop. It all came out in a rush.

"So, that's about it," I finished, and braced for his reaction. Would it be like Brooke's? Would he start yelling? Would he fire me?

Those were the questions that instantly popped into my mind, and in that single second, I experienced a year's worth of doubt and shame.

It wasn't Brooke's opinion that was the worst thing in all of this. It was that, because of the way she voiced it and the way she acted when I told them, it created a fertile ground for the shame to grow.

Shame over what I'm doing, but most off all, the shame over the fact I'm not woman enough to conceive and have a baby without help. And then there's the doubt. I started questioning and turning in my mind every move and every decision I ever made, looking for the exact mistake I was being punished for.

"I see," he said and looked out the window, not giving me any indication of what he saw.

Seconds then minutes ticked by, while I held my breath and tried to steel myself.

"How much time off will you need?" he finally asked.

"I don't really know. A month, I think."

"Very well. I think we'll call Mrs. Anderson. The children liked her and reacted well when she was here the last time."

"That's it?" I couldn't believe it was going to be that easy.

"No."

Of course not, here we go.

"I would very much like it if you would call and tell us what's going on and how things are progressing. I want you to know you have full support from this school and its faculty. Anything you need, don't hesitate to call."

"Thank you." The tears made my voice watery and shaky. I couldn't believe that was his reaction. Before the lunch with my girls, it never crossed my mind people could react badly to the news that someone was willing to do anything in their power for his or her family, but that day, I was taught differently. And since then, I did the one thing I actively avoided doing, which was judging people, putting them all in the same basket, expecting the worst from them. Obviously, it wasn't only Brooke who had some thinking to do.

At the end of the day, each and every single one of my colleagues sent me away with a hug and a few words of support. And that was it. All that stress for basically nothing.

Yesterday, just as I was dancing on the edge of being awake, cuddling deeper into Sam and trying to decide if I wanted to fully wake up and begin one more day of joy with him, or if I wanted to go back to sleep, I went over the edge into full consciousness. And that was because I got an awful feeling like when you unclog a sink and a sucking noise happens, only this time, the suction came from deep in my belly.

My eyes flew open, my body giving a jerk, and I scrambled across the bed as fast as I could. My target: the bathroom. Because I knew. I knew what that feeling was. My period came.

I closed the door and went to the toilet, mumbling, "Please, please."

At the same time, the door started shaking from Sam's pounding on it, all while he yelled, "Dani. What's wrong?"

I ignored him while I did my business, and when it was confirmed that indeed I got my period, the sensation of such pure joy and happiness washed over me, causing my body to tingle all over.

It's funny. Before, I would lock myself up, mumbling that same word, only it was in despair. Or I would stand in front of a sink, still chanting and not taking my eyes from the white stick.

But now, for the first time, my wishes were granted.

More banging on the door, this time accompanied by the growling sound of "Dani."

"Get the phone, honey. I gotta call my doctor," I yelled.

"Why? What's wrong?" He hadn't moved to do as I said. "Dani, open up or I'm gonna smash this fucking door."

Almost skipping across the bathroom, I opened the door, my face accessorized by the biggest smile in a year. "I got my period. It's time!" I practically squealed.

He looked at me for a few moments, his eyes getting that gentle look, before abruptly turning, going to the nightstand, and then handing me the phone. While I was busy looking at it to be sure I typed the right number in, he cupped the back of my neck, gave me a sweet kiss on my temple, and with his lips still resting there, he said, "I'm gonna make some coffee." Then he left me to do what I needed to get done.

That afternoon, my joy and happiness turned to nerves. I was restless, wandering from room to room, not knowing what to do with myself. My appointment was set up for the following morning. The house was clean, and Sam was at work. Being so nervous and unable to sit in one place long enough to relax, I had no interest in reading. So, I did the stupidest thing I could've possibly done.

Eyeing the computer, I sat in front of it, went to the net, and in the search engine, my fingers typed in **IVF process.**

I knew nothing good could come from it. I mean, whenever there's something wrong, even when it's only a runny nose, my mom always asked the Internet, and surprise, surprise—it was always something serious, leaving her only six months to live.

But, I didn't expect the horrors that awaited me.

From the medical articles, YouTube videos, to the forums, against my better judgment, I clicked on them and got so overwhelmed with the information that I closed down the window and jumped from the computer ten minutes later, deciding to forget all that I saw.

But once seen, it can't go unseen. Those posts were burned into my brain.

From that moment on, the happiness and lightness I felt that morning were long gone, completely forgotten, only to be replaced by fear, which magnified as the hours went by.

"Is this your first time too?" A voice coming from beside me pulls me from my thinking. Turning my head, I see a petite, round-faced woman with big blue eyes sitting next to me.

Giving her a small smile, I say, "Yes."

"Who's the problem between you two? For us, it's my husband. Low count and immobility of the sperm," she explains like she just told me it's sunny outside.

Trying to come up with the answer, I'm saved when the nurse comes out and calls our name. "Sorry," I reply, thankful for the interruption.

"That's okay. Good Luck! I'm sending you lots of baby dust," she singsongs while waving a little.

Weird.

Never once had it crossed my mind, and I certainly have never heard Sam clarify which one of us has the issue between us to *anybody*. I mean, sure, it's me with the problem, but it's *us* who can't have the baby. If he heard me say something like that, he would lose his mind.

Turning and sending one more smile in the direction of the woman, I take Sam's hand, interlock my fingers with his, and follow the nurse into the room.

Entering, I can see it's a lot more lit inside this time. The blinds aren't pulled shut, as there's no need for privacy since she won't do the actual exam today.

"Dani, Sam." The doctor stands from her seat behind her desk, coming to us and shaking our hands. Sam's hand that's still fused with mine sends me a reassuring squeeze.

"Hello, Dr. Sanders," I say, my heart banging in my throat.

"Please, sit down. How are you?" she asks after we are seated.

"Nervous."Sam keeps hold of my hand, bringing it to lay on his thigh, and every word makes his grip get tighter, anchoring me to the room.

"Let's get this show on the road then," she replies, a smile on her face. "The test from this morning came back, and everything looks good. We've created your protocol for you to follow. After we're done here, the nurse will give you your medication, and she'll explain how and when to administer it. Also, on top of your hormone injections, I've decided to put you on steroids, just a small dose, in order to avoid any infections during this time."

As she keeps talking, I bounce between positive excitement and complete horror. How the hell am I supposed to do this right? I turn and look at Sam, but he doesn't even glance at me. The doctor has his total attention.

"Okay," I respond and turn back to look at her.

Her face once again shows understanding of just how out of my element I truly am. "Don't worry, Dani. The nurse will guide you step-by-step, and you can call us with any questions you have at any time. If you're not comfortable with administering the injections by yourself, or if Sam can't give them to you, you can come here and somebody will. We're here every step of the way." Her words bring a small amount of relief, returning the confidence.

"We'll try by ourselves, and if we have any problems, we'll come here." I want to be able to do my part to bring our baby into the world. Maybe it's not a smart decision, but I want to be able to someday tell my child that I did everything in my power to have him or her.

"Then that's settled." She goes on, "I'll see you in four days for your checkup to see how things are progressing. That day, you'll also have to get blood work done again to determine your estrogen levels and to see if we have to change something in the protocol. We'll monitor your estrogen closely so you won't go into hyperstimulation. By the end of the month, you'll resemble a pincushion. Sorry in advance about that." She looks to me from her papers, chuckling. "Any questions?"

When neither Sam nor I make a peep, she continues. "Now, please follow all instructions you'll be given. And again, if there is something that bothers you, don't hesitate to call. But most important, Dani, is you have to stay calm. No stress, no worrying. Surround yourself only with things and people that make you happy. It's crucial for you to be calm and not have stress."

I don't get it. How can she ask me this? Doesn't she see this whole situation is one giant stressor? Come on, I'm here to try to get pregnant. To have a baby. To start my family. Of course I'll be under a great amount of stress, wondering what's going on inside my body. Especially after all I've read on the Internet.

She must see something in my face, because she quickly adds, "I know you think it's impossible, but trust me, it's crucial. Not only will the reactions to the drugs be better, but your blood pressure will stay constant and normal, which we need it to do. Please don't go and read stuff on the net. So many of our patients do, and it only makes things difficult for them."

As she says that, I feel heat inside my cheeks from the guilt of what I did.

"I already did," I confess.

"And did you read anything good or positive about the experiences of the people?" she asks, the displeasure coloring her words.

"No," I whisper. It's like I'm five again, when I went out in my brand-new dress and got grass stains on it after my mom asked me to wait just five more minutes and we'd be ready to go. I can't bear to look at the disappointment in her eyes.

"Has it ever crossed your mind that the reason there are only negative results and experiences written there is because the people who got what they wanted—that being a beautiful and healthy baby—don't have time to write about it? Because either they have their hands full, or they just simply moved on from that part of their lives, enjoying the time with their child."

My head flies back from its downcast position so fast there's a slight pain in my neck, because no. No, it hadn't crossed my mind at all.

"I see it didn't. Think about that. For now, just relax and let us do the worrying." She stands from her chair. "Please follow the nurse, and you'll be given everything you need. See you in four days." And with that, the meeting is over.

***

"Hi, I'm Alyssa, and from today on, I'll be your personal nurse. Here's my contact info, and please do not hesitate to call."

She's about my height, with chocolate brown hair in a braid that goes all the way to the middle of her back. Her blue scrubs only manage to make her blue eyes pop even more, reflecting the color. I take her outstretched hand in mine, feeling her firm and sure grip.

"Hi, I'm Dani, and this is Sam." I gesture to the giant mute by my side.

"Hello," she greets, also shaking Sam's hand. "Dani, first, I'll need to take your blood pressure, and I'll need you to step on that scale over there so we'll know what weight you're starting at." After she's done all that she needs, she instructs us to sit at her desk, writing all the information in my chart. "This is your medication." She picks up a flat, light-blue box sitting at her elbow. "It's called Puregon. Basically, this is the magic potion that will help you grow your eggs."

She smiles at me, opening the box and revealing a pen.

"It's really easy to use. Before, you had to mix the powder with the solution, but now it comes in the form of a pen. Just like insulin. Basically, all you need to do is determine the dosage, stick a needle in you, and press the end, like a pen. Easy."

I wonder if having a bubbly personality is required to work here. Everybody is so overly happy, and it's starting to grate my nerves. I'm so far away from being excited it's not even funny.

"I'll write your daily dosage on the box so you don't get confused and start panicking that you're doing something wrong. But first, let me show you how this works." She pulls the top of the pen out, slowly turning the point and showing us a little window on the pen where there are numbers changing with each twist. "After you find your dosage, you click once, bringing the top back in place."

"Okay," I say with a nod.

"Now, please lift up your shirt." She gestures to my midsection. Doing as she says, I watch her hands as she takes a milky white plastic top off the tip of the pen. "Okay. Sam, please look closely now." She glances at him. "Every afternoon at 5:00, you'll give yourself a dose, Dani. If you like, Sam can do it for you, or you can just come here and I'll do it, but you must learn how. Before you do anything, first, take a cotton ball with alcohol and wipe off the area where you wish to give the injection. Then, you pinch slightly to raise the skin and insert the needle. Once you've done that, just press the top, like a pen. And that's it," she instructs.

"Got it," Sam speaks for the first time today.

"Also, alternate the side of where you administer the drug, so your belly doesn't bruise much," she adds as she indicates my belly button. "Now, the steroids, which are called Decortin, you'll have to pick up at the pharmacy. We don't have them here to give them to you."

"Okay," I nod, getting to my feet. It's the only word I can manage to say today, it seems. The whole morning is so overwhelming my head starts to spin a little.

As she gives me the box, I see she's written the dosage as she promised. "After you take Puregon, stay in bed for about half an hour. Many of our patients say they had some discomfort and lightheadedness if they didn't."

And that's it. We're set to go. We say our goodbyes, the nurse once again ordering me to "Relax. And no stress," which immediately causes my blood pressure to spike high.

In the car on our way home, I set the alarm to go off at five minutes till 5:00, the whole time the drugs burning a hole in my purse.

CHAPTER
ELEVEN

"*I* *CAN'T BEAR* to watch you like this, to fight for us alone. *I'm reduced to a mere bystander with only one job,"* he admits.

"It's a pretty important one." I try to lighten the mood, but he doesn't listen.

"And I hate these," he whispers, gliding his hand over the bruises on my belly, his eyes caressing each and everyone, like he believes that he can heal them. He's healing my heart and soul, but I can't find a way for him to see that. *"But I can't help myself but love them also,"* he admits, his ravaged look coming to my face. *"Because I know, in the end, they'll give us our baby."*

Sitting on the couch, my eyes are glued to the coffee table, where my phone is currently placed. Next to it, there's that blue box I got today, the pen sitting on it with the right dose for today showing in its little window, and beyond it taunts its alcohol and the cotton wipes.

Once again, I push the round button on the bottom half of my phone. It's eight minutes till5:00 p.m. The time drags along, while I mentally try to rush it so I can finally give my body what it craves. I don't even know how it's possible to crave something you've never had, or in this case, even knew it existed, but here I am. My feet are bouncing. I don't know what to do with my hands, so I alternate between twisting my fingers, making my joints pop, and make that God-awful sound of biting my nails. I never bite my nails. The adrenaline currently coursing through my veins is simultaneously reducing me to a freaked-out teenager and causing me to behave like a junkie who's desperately in need of a fix.

One more push of the button on my cell.

It's seven till 5:00 p.m.

Fuck!

"Relax, baby," Sam says quietly, while his hand travels up and down my back. While usually that voice of his—which is like a hot chocolate on a snowy day—soothes me, now it only makes my adrenaline spike even more, grating on my nerves until I can actually feel my pulse thrumming in my temples.

I tear my eyes from the phone to send a death glare his way, and through clenched teeth, I seethe, "You relax." I quickly look back to the object of my obsession, pushing the button to light up the phone.

Still, seven till 5:00 p.m.

Damn, damn, damn!

Why has the time decided to crawl now, when usually it speeds by, leaving me behind, making me late for everything?

"What if we do it now? The drug doesn't know what time it is. And anyway, I doubt five minutes will make such a big difference," Sam suggests.

One more push of the button.

"It's *six* minutes! And we have to do it right. We can't make any mistakes. No matter how insignificant they seem."But while I explain this to Sam for the third time since we sat down to wait, the alarm mercifully goes off, making me jump. "Okay, okay," I chant. "Let's do this. Get the wipes ready with alcohol," I instruct while pulling my shirt up.

I slouch back into the couch and watch Sam as he opens the bottle of alcohol and douses the wipe with it, then turns to me to clean my skin.

The feel of the coldness of the wipe on my heated skin is incredible. It's not something I thought I would ever cherish, but right this second, I know I will remember this moment, the chill on my skin, the freezing breeze of air on that disinfected area on my belly, for the rest of my life.

The sound of that alarm going off was like the sound of the starting gun at the beginning of a race. Only problem is I have to remind myself over and over that we're running a marathon, not a sprint.

"Now what?" Sam asks, the look on his face one of a frightened boy. I've never seen that look on him. He's always so sure of himself—of what he's doing and sometimes of what other people should do—that this look on him is completely foreign and wrong.

"Now, take the pen and give me a shot," I say while pinching the selected area for him to do as I ordered. He goes from the couch to sit on the coffee table in front of me. With the injection in his hand, he looks at my belly like he's waiting for it to reveal some great, big secret to him.

"Sam?"

"What?"

"What're you waiting for?" I'm confused. I lean forward and slightly to the side to check the time, again, thinking maybe he's waiting for the exact time. It reads two till 5:00 p.m.

The time is now.

"Sam!" I snap.

"I'm sorry, baby, but I can't do it."

"What?" I breathe in horror. What does he mean he can't do it? This is the only way for us to have a baby, and he chooses this moment to tell me he can't do it?

Probably seeing the emotion written all over my face, he quickly explains, "I can't stab you with this." Up goes his arm to indicate the magic potion.

"You won't be stabbing me. You'll be giving me medication," I try to reason with him.

"No. I can't cause you any pain. Not even this little bit. If it's in my power, I won't do it," he says firmly.

"Fine!" I snatch the pen out of his hand. I'm not in the mood to try to motivate him. Just as I'm ready to do it myself, in my peripheral vision, I see movement. Looking back to Sam, I can see he's turned his back to me. "What the hell are you doing?" I try not to laugh, only to start coughing from trying to push back the chuckles that threaten to break free.

"I can't watch. Did you do it yet?"

"No!" I snap. He's irritating the hell out of me at the same time as he's making me laugh.

"Just tell me when you pierce the skin, and I'll do the rest."

"Fine!" I repeat. I look back down, still pinching my belly, and in the needle goes. It's funny; sure the needle is tiny, but I still expected some small dose of pain. But all I feel is slight discomfort. "It's in. You can turn now." For some reason, I whisper the words.

We're both quiet as we watch Sam's thumb push the top of the pen down. The whole thing lasts about a second and a half, but I swear every click of the pen lasts a decade, and with every click, the

103

slight burning sensation that appeared with the first one intensifies just a little bit more. "There. Done," Sam says quietly. "How are you feeling?"

"Okay. It burns a little." Taking the wipe that Sam is giving me, I pull the needle out and put pressure on the area.

"Lie down. I'm going to make you some tea. And remember you have to stay lying flat for a half an hour," he commands. Hearing him issue his orders, I chuckle a little while doing as he says, because I know the situation where he was so totally not the strong person I rely on and acted like a complete wuss is over with, and I have my husband back.

I look under the wipe and see there's only a slight redness. Maybe that means there won't be any bruises after all.

***

Today is the day of my first checkup. For the past four days, we've gone through the same routine as with the first shot, camped out on the couch, staring at my phone, waiting for the alarm to blare the countdown on the last five minutes. Every day, Sam turned his back to me, not able to watch the needle pierce my skin, and every day, I thought it was funny how he turned into a complete pussy near the needle. But also, every time, my heart melted with how sweet he was, unable to watch me inflict "pain" on myself. I wasn't lucky after all, and eventually those red areas that were initially the site of the shots became bruises. When Sam sees my belly, he clenches his jaw. And at night, right before sleep, he turns me on my back, pushes my top up, and kisses every single bruise. Only then does he turn me back to my side, puts his arm around me, and lightly caresses my belly, as if his touch can erase the bruises, and he lulls me right to sleep.

We went step by step, exactly how Nurse Alyssa instructed, only yesterday I didn't stay lying flat afterward. Instead, I went back to cleaning the bathroom.

Stupid mistake!

A short time later, I was bent over our bathtub, scrubbing away, when suddenly intense heat started at the top of my head and surged through my whole body, leaving in its wake dizziness so immense that I lost sight of my hands on their task and flashes of light were all I could see. Quickly, I sat on the floor, bent my knees, and put my head on them, all the while deep breathing, hoping it would pass. When this went on with no indication that it would stop, I yelled, "Sam!" the panic coloring my voice.

I could hear his footsteps running down the hall and through the bedroom, but it was like he was running through a tunnel, the echo banging in my ears.

"What's wrong?" He put his hands on my shoulders, and when I didn't move, not in the slightest, just kept deep breathing, he took me in his arms and carried me to our bed, laying me down. "Dani, baby, what's wrong?" he tried again.

I opened my eyes, only to have nausea kick in. I closed them back, taking a huge breath through my nose, and on the exhale, I moaned, "Oh, God," wrapping my arms around my stomach.

"That's it. We're going to the hospital."

"No, we're not. It'll pass. This is because I didn't lie down after the shot."

Sam wasn't convinced it was because of that, and by the time I finally managed to talk him down from going to the hospital or calling the doctor, everything was gone at the half hour mark—the time I should have been resting. It was like someone swept the nausea and dizziness away with a flick of a hand.

Lesson learned.

"Hunt!" Nurse Alyssa's call jolts me back to the present, and I stand and grab my things to go to her. "Hi," she greets with a smile on her pretty face. It kind of irks me a little, because all I want to do right now is sit in some corner and cry. I don't know why that is, since I was okay just a few moments ago, leaning on the happy side of emotions, but for some reason, I've taken a wrong turn and ended up tearful.

"How're you feeling, Dani?" Slight concern colors her tone, but that smile is still present.

"I'm fine. Just a little tired." When the words come out of my mouth, I realize it's the truth. But how can that be? I was fine and rested not even ten minutes ago. What's going on with me?

Alyssa looks at me a little harder. I can see the wheels spinning in her brain while her eyes travel the length of me. "It's the drugs, honey. Don't worry," she assures me on a squeeze of my arm. "Now, let's get this part over with so you can go on with your day."

An hour later, I'm on my way to my parents' house. My eggs are growing nicely, so there were no changes in my medication, and the next dose is sitting on the seat next to me. I have to go back in two days for another checkup. As Alyssa gave me my dose, she also left me with a stern look and demand of "No stress! Just relax." Easy for her to say, she's not the one who has to give herself a shot every day and hope it'll work so she can finally have a baby. I bet the only thing she has to do is lie on her back, and bam! She's pregnant!

***

"Mom!" I yell, entering the house.

"In here!" Her voice comes from within the house, but the smells have already tipped me off.

Walking through the entryway, I can see the queen ruling her kingdom. If there's one room in the house that's completely my mom's, it's the kitchen. Last year, when she finally came to terms that Dad's retirement would not be just as she pictured it, she decided she should find him some work, and that work was to renovate her domain. When she went to him and told him, "I've been thinking," all my dad asked was, "How much?"

After more than thirty years of marriage, he knew what those three words meant. Every time my mom uttered them, it meant there would be some work done on the house. At first when he found out the amount of money he was going to have to spend, he was against it. But then my mom said, "After twenty years, I deserve a new kitchen. One that *I* want. If you don't give it to me, I'll stop cooking, and then we'll see who'll get what they want." Needless to say, Mom won.

At first, I was stunned to see what she chose. Light gray cabinets, so light they were almost white, with white quartz countertops that had midnight blue to black veins throughout the surface, giving the impression of marble. Same with the huge island in the center of the room. The stools at the island were black with white rhinestones decorating the back, creating the cool pleats along the edges of the seats. The range, dishwasher, and the double doors of the fridge were stainless steel. There was no color to be found. And for a person like my mom, who painted the house light blue, it was weird.

But then, her personality started to show. The fridge began collecting magnets all over it. On the magnets, names of places she wanted to go, some places where her friends went and brought them back for her, or a few places she'd actually gone. There are two ceramic pitchers in which she stores her utensils. One green, the other yellow. On the windowsill, above the sink, she put pictures in frames, all in purple. Two of them are of me and my sister, and one is her and Dad. And there is another one, bigger than the rest, which is empty. It awaits a picture of her grandchild. All of her small appliances are one of those three colors, so when she gets one out to use it, the color matches. And on the island, there's a huge crystal vase, and in it are the flowers of the week. Every Monday, she goes to the florist to buy herself something special, as she says. They are never the same, and they are always colorful.

"You've been to the doctor?" I don't know why she asks that question, because I told her this morning I was going and I'd come here afterward. We talk on the phone every day. She calls me just to check "If my daughter's alive, and since that's clearly the case, why hasn't she come to see her mother?" Basically, she guilttrips me to come see her almost every day.

"Yes."

"And?" she asks, the impatience evident in her tone.

"She found eight big follicles, but there're a bunch of small ones, so she kept me on the same dosage since we're so early in the process."

"Is that good?"

"I think so." But really I don't know. I'm hoping it is, since anything else is too heartbreaking to even think about.

"Hmm...." is all she says on the subject, not looking at me. "The food is ready. Let's eat."

After she feeds me a crazy amount of food, consisting of her homemade burgers and salad, she tops it off with cheesecake. We sit in the living room, our coffee cups on the table in front of us. I'm on the couch, starting to enter a food coma, the heavenly embrace of the couch doing nothing to keep me awake, when I hear a light clearing of a throat that is not common from my mom. She usually just tells you what's on her mind.

"What is it, Mom?" I ask, finally looking at her. There are dark circles under her eyes, which have already started to water for some reason.

"How're you really doing?"

"I'm okay. Just tired," I say, looking at my knees. I can't stand to look at her while she's so sad. "It's funny; at first, all I wanted was to miss my period, for that plus sign to finally show. Then, all I wanted was to get my period for us to finally start with this procedure. And now, all I want is for the procedure to be over so I can be pregnant. All I want is to be pregnant. I feel like all I do is wait. Wait for that one moment to come. The sad part is, when that moment comes, there's always the next one, and the next. When will the moment for me to be pregnant come?" I let go of some of the things that have tortured my mind for some time.

But I don't tell her everything. I don't tell her how, for the last few months, every evening I stand in that empty room in our house that was supposed to be the nursery, watching the stars and hoping one will finally pick me. I don't tell her how, for the last four days, I stand in the center of it, decorating it in my head. I don't tell her how, every night, I cry myself to sleep, scared of what I will dream that night.

Along the way, I've picked up the fact that a person dreams their biggest desire or their biggest fear. I don't remember if I read that somewhere or if someone told me, but it's stayed with me. And now I know it's true.

In the first one, I dream I'm pregnant. My belly is big, so big. And I can actually feel my baby kicking inside. The kicks are strong. And all I do in that dream is look at my belly, cooing nonsense to the baby. My hand rests on it protectively. It's like the picture from the doctor's office, of that lady in the pink shirt. And when I wake up, I'm on my side, my knees are bent, almost touching my belly, and my hand is on it. Always mid rub. The pain that comes when reality takes over, and the dream is just a memory, is pure torture.

The second, I'm holding my baby. I don't see its face or know if it's a boy or a girl. All I know to the depths of my soul is that it's my baby. I've finally done it. I gave birth. I'm a mom. The peace and love I feel is something I never thought a person could feel.

And the third is the most excruciating. In sleep and awake. It's of Sam leaving me. Always when it starts, I'm sitting at our table, the papers in front of me. The one I see most clearly is the one that says the IVF was unsuccessful. Then, Sam comes. His face granite, his eyes unforgiving. When he opens his mouth, my world stops. No, not stops. It disappears. There's nothing left for me when he says, "I was wrong. I thought I could do this. But, you're not the woman for me after all, Dani." Then, he turns and leaves. After I wake up from that dream, I'm always drenched in sweat, my hands shaking, my pillow wet with my tears. And then, I feel Sam's arms around me, holding me tight. And I know… I know I've woken him up and he's trying to calm me down. The only problem is that fear doesn't go away. Awake or asleep.

The next morning, when he brought me my coffee in the bathroom, he leaned against the doorframe and asked what it was all about, and when I told him, his face got that granite look from my dream. There was the rumble of stones once again in his voice when he said, "You will not lose me. There's not one thing or person in this world that could ever take me from you." Coming the two steps that separated us, his hand went to the back of my head to pull me to him, and with his lips resting on my forehead, he added, "You're stuck with me, baby. And if you go, then I go with you." Since that first time, we hadn't talked about it anymore. But when I have that dream, I wake up, only to have Sam's arms around me, holding me tight.

My musings vanish when a sniffle breaks the sudden silence in the room. I get off the couch like a shot, going to my mom. I sink to my knees so I can put my arms around her, my head in her lap. As if I'm little again, she silently cries, her hand going to my hair to play with the strands.

"Don't cry, Mommy. It'll be all right," I try to soothe her. I barely have any strength left in me to fight for myself, let alone to give to someone else. But I can't stand to see my mom shed another tear for me. I know she's in pain seeing her daughter fighting like this. To have one thing that for the most is something that just happens, getting pregnant. But for me, it's something that's out of reach.

"I just want to know. What did I do?" she wails.

"What do you mean? You didn't do anything."

"Then why is this happening to me? What did I do? Am I paying for some mistake from my previous life?"

Hearing her say that, the anger that left not long ago comes back instantly. How can she say that? How can she be so blind to think that this has anything to do with her? I know she's hurting. I know it affects her too, me being her daughter and all. But has she stopped for one single second to think about me? How I'm dealing with all of this? And in that moment, I know I have nobody I can talk to, nobody to tell my fears. I'm left all alone. I can't even talk to Sam. That one time I let it slip just a little what's been on my mind, he basically told me to stop. Stop thinking like this and everything'll be just fine. Except it won't.

"I don't know, Mom. Listen, I have to go. It's nearly time for my shot," I say to her, my tone even.

"Dani!" I hear her yell as I rush to the door.

"I have to go." I don't want her to see what her words have done to me. I won't cry in front of her. It'll only make her feel worse, and that also will be because of me, and only about her.

Once I'm in my car, the tears come. I let them. I cry for my parents, for Sam, but most of all, I cry for myself. And when I park my car, all those confusing emotions of the day have left me, leaving me right back where I started, happy and excited. I know that's not normal, but for right now, I don't care.

CHAPTER TWELVE

"*OODNIGHT, MY LOVE.*" *He squeezes me and pulls me closer to him. "I love you," he whispers, on the edge of his dream.*

Feeling the squeeze of my hand that's held tightly in Sam's as it rests on his thigh, my eyes fly to him and abandon my hundredth study of the now familiar waiting room.

"You okay, baby?" he asks, worry evident not only in his voice and face, but his whole body he's holding tight, almost like he's waiting for someone to attack.

I don't answer, because I know I don't have the energy to lie to him right now. So instead, I just nod and send a small smile his way, hoping it'll ease his worry a little bit, and then go back to my aimless perusal of our surroundings. Suddenly, my eyes find a familiar figure.

It's the "baby dust" lady.

I've seen her every time I've come to get a checkup, so it's no surprise she's here today. Looking at her, the feeling that something is off overwhelms me. It takes a couple of seconds, but then it hits me.

She's all made up. From her full-on makeup, perfect—probably done professionally—hair, skinny jeans, and silk blouse, all the way to her thin-heeled pumps. She has a small suitcase with those little wheels so she doesn't have to carry it anywhere, just pull out the handle and, like the lady she is, wheel it wherever she's supposed to go. Compared to her, I look like a hobo. I don't have a stitch of makeup on my face, showcasing my lack of sleep for all to see. My hair's a mess—mostly—contained and unsuccessfully showcased in a weird combo of ponytail and a messy bun on top of my head. I'm in yoga pants and have on a tank top underneath my hoodie that says

I'm a virgin, on the front, and *This is an old shirt,* on the back. On my feet there are flip-flops, on which sits my backpack full of all the things I'll need today from the list Alyssa gave me two days prior, including my Minnie Mouse PJs and a robe with bear ears on it.

I don't get it. This is not like in the movies, where some character in the middle of it says, "I'm going to get my eggs harvested" and off she goes, while planning a shopping spree afterward, like it's no big deal.

It's a very big deal. There are drugs, doctors, OR, and needles involved!

So, why is she dressed to the nines? But, then again, maybe this is not her first time. Maybe she knows how this works, and maybe I'm just a teensy, tiny bit overreacting? If that's the case, I'll kick my ass later for allowing myself to leave the house the way I look, put on some decent clothes, and off I'll go for some shopping spree.

I may look like a sailor looks the morning after he's been allowed to shore after two months at sea, but, again, one of my hands is held tightly in Sam's, resting on his thigh, his arm around me, curling my body slightly into his. My head alternates between resting on his shoulder and rubbing my temple on his chin, breathing him in whenever I feel like bolting and reminding myself why I'm here today. While the "baby dust" lady sits on the chair next to her husband, flipping the pages of a magazine, filling the waiting room with small but, in this silence, loud, crack of thunder-ish noises, since she's doing it roughly and sharply. It reveals her current mood, which is definitely not scared, nor is it the muted excitement that's radiating from two other women waiting with us to get this done. All the while her husband is leaned forward, his legs spread, elbows to his knees, messing around on his phone with a bored expression on his face, not even a glance her way.

Looking at them, I can't help but get the feeling they're worlds apart. I know there're couples who don't touch or kiss in public. It's not like Sam and I do that—much—either, but since this whole nightmare started, if Sam's close to me, his hand is around my waist, shoulders, or just simply holding mine in his. When he has something to say, his hand is always, *always,* at the back of my neck. And if we're standing somewhere, he's behind me, his heat seeping into my back, his arm tightly around my belly or chest. And every few moments, I feel him giving me a sweet kiss on my temple, forehead, neck, or shoulder. It doesn't seem like much, but those touches, kisses, and that heat at my back gives me some relief from the constant simmering fear that's been plaguing me, reassuring me that he's here, he's got me, and it'll all be okay.

It's Saturday, the thirteenth day of our cycle and the day when the doctor is going to harvest my eggs. And for the first time in this long journey, today is the day when I would rather be anywhere else in this world than right here.

After the first four days, the shots became our new daily routine. It's funny how something so life changing can become just a small part of your day. Sam would come home every day, sometimes just to be with me when the clock hit five, and then go back to work. And every day, we danced the same dance of him turning his back when the needle would pierce my skin. It would be reduced to an even smaller thing if not for the bruises. But, as the days have gone by, as the new dosage was pushed into my belly, and as the new needle broke my skin, I would get a new reminder of it. So, by now I looked like a leprechaun has used my belly as a punching bag. I have nine greenish dots on each side of my belly button, which are sore enough that every time my clothes brush that part of my body, I'm once again reminded of what is going on in our lives right now.

Like there was any chance of forgetting it.

On my second checkup, it was decided that the dosage would stay the same till the end of the procedure, since I responded well— or should I say, my eggs did—and also because my estrogen levels were a bit high. So, not to test the luck, we didn't want to change anything.

In addition to the dreams, which were not fun at all, I got to experience all the moods and feelings one person can feel. On the first day of injections, unknowingly I entered the rollercoaster that would, and did, take me from the highest of highs to the lowest of lows. I would be on top of the world, basking in the knowledge that we were going to have a baby, that in about twenty days, there would be a little person growing inside me, that finally my dream would come true and I would be pregnant. Then, something would trigger me, something so small like a dirty coffee mug, or a TV commercial, or a passerby bumping into me on the street, and it would send me into tears. I would cry until I exhausted myself, and then sleep came, only to have one of those dreams that tortured me every time I slept. Also, there were now only two of them—me being pregnant and Sam leaving. And if that didn't happen, every day, I told myself I wouldn't go online and look at the posts of other people's experiences, and day after day, I found myself sitting in front of my laptop, scrolling the posts. When that happened, when those words met my eyes and entered my brain, the fear would strike. Fear so strong it would paralyze me. And on the heels of it, I would lose all my fake bravado and fall into the pits of depression, going straight to bed. At first, Sam tried to get me out of it, and then he tried to prevent me from going anywhere near the laptop. In the end, all he could do was crawl into the bed with me and, holding me tight, softly whisper in my hair until I decided to once again face the world. Through all these times and emotions, I knew my reactions were extreme and weren't natural. I kept thinking that I had to stop, I had to start behaving normally, but I couldn't. Something would happen, and I would go into some new curve of the rollercoaster and have to ride it through. And more often than not, I would decide I wasn't able to do it; I couldn't see it through. There was no way I could finish the procedure. But then every afternoon, I would sit on that couch, looking at my phone, all the paraphernalia neatly placed on the table, waiting for the alarm to start the countdown for the last five minutes until medicine time.

I spent my days in bed watching TV or staring at the wall with no will to ever get up, telling myself that Sam didn't know. If he did, he never mentioned it. On Tuesday, banging on the door made me jump from the bed and run to it. Opening it, I was greeted with fire burning in Marcy's usually warm eyes.

"What the hell?" she muttered right before she shoved me out of the way and bulldozed her way in. I knew this would happen. I'd been dodging her calls and texts since the lunch with the girls. As I shut the door and turned to her, dread pooling in my stomach, her eyes traveled the length of me, her hands dropped from their previous position on her waist, and she repeated, this time with almost no sound at all, barely heard yet it had such profound pain in it that, if it were possible, it would've made my ears bleed. "What the hell?"

Hearing her say those words, and the way she said them, and why she said them, made my knees go weak and I collapsed to the floor. I was fooling no one, and the aftermath of my ride was showing clear on my face. In no time at all, her arms were around me, her ass to the floor, and right there, at my front door, my best friend held me and rocked me like a baby while I sobbed. In broken words and sentences, my face in her neck, my arms around her, holding tight, I told her what had been happening since I last saw her. I didn't know I needed to tell somebody until I spilled it all out.

"You should have called me. You should have told me everything from the beginning. Why haven't you, Dani? Why have you been going through this alone?" Her voice was scratchy from crying.

And then, right there on that floor, I admitted the truth that I was hiding from everyone, including myself."I was embarrassed."

"Of what?"

"Of the fact that I'm a woman, and I can't have children." I took a chance and looked into her eyes and found what I was expecting to find, rage. But strangely, it wasn't directed at me.

"Why the fuck would you be embarrassed because of that?" she snapped.

"Because the definition of a woman is to be able to give birth, and I can't. So what does it make me?"

"It makes you Dani. It makes you my best friend, my sister. It makes you the most beautiful woman in the world, because you're fighting for your future, for your husband, and for your child. That's what it makes you. It makes you a strong woman." She cupped my face, and the devilish little smile started dancing on her lips. "But what it will give you is a tanned ass when I tell your husband the shit that came out of your mouth." I couldn't believe it, but after I heard her words, my head went back, and I laughed out loud.

And when the last of mirth left my mouth, I was again feeling happy, merry, and bright. I knew it wasn't normal; I knew it wouldn't last, but I didn't care. For the first time in days, I could give my husband a genuine smile when he came home.

Afterward, she told me she thought my disappearing act had everything to do with the episode at lunch and she was having none of that. But she knew how I was, she knew I probably retreated into my head, and she planned to give me a few more days until she came banging on my door. But then, she got a call and she could wait no longer. I had my suspicions about the caller, and they were confirmed once Sam got home.

I didn't care. I was happy my friend was with me. I was feeling light from the day spent with her. It was like we were back in college, giggling ourselves stupid, eating and drinking—tea for me—and not once mentioning what the real world held for us.

And then the time came for my shot, and the thin shell of my bubble burst. Sam's back was turned to me and I was positioning the needle at the right angle it was supposed to be, when something made me look up. At what I saw, my heart splintered, making the surrounding tissue inside my chest bleed, and those splinters found a home in those little wounds, which were going to get infected with time and almost ruin everything.

Sam had his head bowed, eyes on his hands, which were held so tightly in one another the knuckles were turning white. And Marcy, looking at him, then his hands, then finally coming to me, one tear slowly going down her face, she sent me a soft smile and a nod.

When Sam cleaned everything up and made sure I would stay lying on the couch for half an hour—not that I would ever make that mistake again—and left back to work, Marcy sat by my hip and held my hand. Leaning into my face, she said, "Anything. Anything you need, you tell me. You need me to find some doctor in Mexico who'll perform a transplant of my uterus to give it to you, I'll find him. Anything."

"My uterus is fine. It's my tubes and ovaries that don't work," I tried to joke.

"Those too," she fired back, squeezing my hand. "Anything, Dani." I knew she would do it, and as crazy as it sounded, hearing her say that, knowing she would stand by me no matter the situation, there was one more small weight lifted from my shoulders. And the light feeling would carry me in a good mood to the next afternoon.

***

The next day, I was sitting on the exam table in the doctor's office. Swinging my legs back and forth, the good mood was still lingering from the day before. When the light knock on the door came, I looked up and saw the doctor enter.

From the look on her face, I knew something was wrong. So, when she opened her mouth and started explaining things, my good mood was a thing of the past.

Turns out, I was responding to the meds so great—or in this case, bad—that I was in danger of hyperstimulation, or OHSS. But, since I wasn't getting a high dose of hormones—as usual with patients doing this procedure—she had hope that, once I get my trigger shot, the OHSS wouldn't happen.

This meant, in the case it did happen, she would postpone the embryo transfer for my next cycle, since it goes away in about a week, if it's not severe. But, if she did the transfer and the pregnancy took, it would make the symptoms worse. It would also likely mean the pregnancy would not survive.

This did not make me happy, for the obvious reasons, but worst of all was the thought I would have to wait a whole month. Not to mention, I'd have to go through the preparation phase all over again, in order to do the embryo transfer and finally get pregnant. Minus the daily shots. The good news was, if that happened, I would only have to take three shots. All the rest were in pill form.

This also meant that the following days, the no stress policy was just a fading memory. I was under so much stress that every time I went to the bathroom to check my body for symptoms, my hands started shaking, a sheen of cold sweat covered me from head to toe, and my breathing became erratic. I was constantly on the verge of a panic attack. From the moment I woke up, till the time I went to bed at night, I was in that bathroom every hour, looking to see if my belly had swollen, stepping on a scale to see if I had gained weight, and deep breathing just to test if it started to get difficult. To say I was freaking out was putting it mildly.

And then, a new fear came.

I was, once again, reading the posts when I came across one that terrified me.

It was from a woman who went through all this torture, but when the time came to have the eggs harvested, there wasn't a single one.

None!

When my brain managed to process that information, I was out of my chair, running to the garage to Sam like a bullet. When I reached it and opened the door so fiercely that it slammed into the wall, I took a step inside and then completely froze.

I saw Sam's head jerking my way at hearing the door slam, and I heard his "What's wrong?" but all I could do was stand there, my hands balled into fists, my eyes filling with tears. I watched him slowly getting up from his seat, after his repeated "What's wrong, baby?"

But I couldn't move.

My eyes stayed glued to the spot where they last saw him. My chest was going up and down harshly, but there wasn't enough air.

My lungs were full of it, but it wasn't enough. I was suffocating. I felt coldness so severe I was freezing. All the terror, the hope of succeeding to get pregnant, the near crippling fear of disappointment of failing in this process, left me immobile.

How I managed to stand on my own two feet was beyond me. I wasn't on the verge of a panic attack. I was there.

Only when Sam's bark of "Danielle!" came at me, did I jump in place. My eyes shot to him, and I finally got enough air in me. Only to choke on it.

And then his arms were around me. The heat came back, but the air still tried to choke me. I was just about to put my arms around his waist and burrow my face in his chest, when my knees gave up and I lost my footing.

The next thing I knew, I was moving through the air, until I was surrounded by Sam. After he had me sitting in his lap, my face still in his chest, he finally murmured, "Baby, what the hell is wrong?"

I pulled my face out of his chest, tried to look at him, but still couldn't because of the tears, and brokenly asked, "What if I don't have any eggs?"

After that, my tears came faster, stronger, the sobs wracking my body.

After a few moments of trying—and failing—to calm me down by whispering softly to me, Sam picked me up, carried me to bed, and put me in it. He got in with me, gathering me in his strong arms, and pulled the covers over us.

Then, in the middle of crying broken statements of "I can't do this," "I'm tired," "I won't have any eggs," and "I'm done!" did the heat from the bed, but most importantly from Sam, start seeping into my body, straight down to my soul. I finally began to calm down.

We stayed in that bed for the rest of the day, and we never mentioned it again.

Also, since the day she showed up at our house, Marcy's been a permanent fixture in it. From the moment I woke up, until the moment Sam came home, she was with me every minute. It was impossibly sweet, made me feel loved beyond reason, but also, it sucked all the energy out of me—what little being freaked out and scared out of my mind had left—because I had to put a brave face on and fake being happy, happy, happy. Because I knew she was worried, and I wanted to ease that worry away. All of that left me drained and tired.

I was done with all that was happening. All I wanted was to be pregnant. But this nightmare's road was nowhere near done, so I faked my way through the day. And only in the pitch black of night, when the nightmares of my sleep woke me up, I would sneak out of bed, tiptoe my way to the empty bedroom, and sit my ass on the floor. In my mind, the room was fully furnished with all things baby, making it the greatest nursery in the universe. Watching them through the window, I would beg the stars, and God or whatever power there might be, to finally just pick me, to come to me, to make my wish come true and help me make Sam's dream come a little bit closer to reality.

***

On Thursday, I was at my final checkup, where I got the go-ahead for the trigger shot—or the oil shot, what patients called it—for 7:00 p.m. that day. Everything was ready; we had come to the middle of the road, entering the last leg of the journey. But I was starting to feel drained, beginning to lose focus, the will, and the drive for it.

All those appointments with the doctor, the injections, and the weight gain that started to happen just three days after I started the injections—but was thankfully still on the normal side of things, so I was not rushing my way to OHSS—were overwhelming me. On top of that was the lack of sleep because of the nightmares that tortured me constantly. Even though one dream was beyond beautiful, every time I woke up from it, I would be reminded it was just a dream and it wasn't real, and the pain that came instantly because it was *just a dream* was almost unbearable. So, in itself, it was a nightmare.

And worst of all were the people. My loved ones and complete strangers. I still haven't talked to my mom, not really. We had our daily chats, but those were not the same. All I ever said was "Yeah" and "Okay."She knew something was up, but unfortunately, she hadn't figured it out on her own. Marcy was trying to cheer me up, expecting near constant excitement radiating from every pore of my being, and Sam had completely shut himself in the garage, only to come in when Marcy would miraculously leave me for five minutes. I would fall in bed, and he would lie with me in total and complete silence, just holding me. People on the street would assume I was pregnant, because my belly had swollen from the hormones, and stop to ask me when I was due, or just send a gentle smile my way. Those were the worst. Brooke's reaction to the news of the IVF triggered something in me, and after the breakdown I had in front of the church, I started feeling ashamed. Ashamed of me, of my body, of being unable to do something so normal, as common as getting pregnant and having a family, and in the end, ashamed of what we were doing.

And, because of that, I was left alone.

I was alone in the sea of people all reaching a hand out to me, trying to pull me to shore, to bask in the sunlight, away from the dark.

But not one of them could help, since all those hands came with advice on how to handle this, and expectations to, in the end, give them—and myself—what they wanted: a pregnancy.

There was no other option in people's minds. The IVF would be successful on the first try.

But somewhere deep inside, I knew there was a big possibility that it would not be.

So, when the doctor took a good look at me, and with gentle voice asked, "How are you, Dani?" I answered, "I'm just tired." Because I was.

I was *just tired.*

Tired of everything. All I wanted to do at this point was give up and sleep.

But every time I thought that was it, I was giving up, that little voice inside, the voice that wouldn't shut up no matter what, would remind me that maybe this was it. Only this one time. Only this once, and it would be successful. I would get pregnant.

And I kept going.

"You're a strong woman, Dani. You can do this" was her answer to that.

That answer and hope that wouldn't stop living and growing inside me was what got me through the last few days.

***

"Danielle Hunt!"

Hearing Nurse Alyssa call my name, I focus back to the room, and surprise washes through me seeing the baby dust lady is gone.

I send a small smile the nurse's way and turn my head toward Sam, squeezing his hand, ready to stand up and go start the next mile in our road. Sam's hand suddenly pulls away, only to gently land on the back of my neck. He hauls me to him until our foreheads touch and, looking deep into my eyes, he says, "You can do this." And he gives me a light kiss.

"*We* can do this," I remind him, as he used to do with me, and I watch his eyes smile. Only then, I stand up, gathering my things, and start following Nurse Alyssa. But, in the middle of the waiting room, I stop, turn back, and find Sam's eyes that had been following my every step.

At the same time, we open our mouths, and "Love you" comes from both sets.

After a final gentle look from him, I softly touch my fingers to my mouth and send him one last kiss, before turning around and going where the nurse is taking me.

CHAPTER THIRTEEN

"**I DON'T THINK** *I can do this," I admit to him. My vision is slightly blurred from the pills they gave me. They hope, if they give me something to relax, I'll be able to go with the pain. But I remember, I remember how much this hurts.*

"Say the word, and I'll take you anywhere you wanna go. Just say the word and all this'll be over," he leans in and whispers, looking deeply into my eyes. "Just say the word and we'll find another way."

Standing almost in the middle of the room, I kept glancing through the open door. And every time I did it, my hands went to needlessly rearrange my nightie, or to push my hair behind my ear only to go back to the nightie when I remembered that my hair was tied up.

After I left Sam in the waiting room, Nurse Alyssa led me to her office, where she took my blood, gave me a shot for my uterus and cervix to "relax," and handed me the pills for the pain—at which point I learned I would be awake the whole time. And after seeing the deer-caught-in-headlights look on my face, she assured me, "Don't worry, honey, it doesn't hurt." Then she instructed me to go to this room and change my clothes.

Upon entering, I could see there were five other women inside, including the baby dust lady, and ducking my head a little, I send a soft and shy "Hi" in the general direction of… well, everybody. I hurried my way to the only bed left and took my clothes off, only to put my gray nightie with the three-quarter sleeves on, which came to my mid thighs. I love this nightie, because it feels like a T-shirt, which due to its length reminds me of Sam's shirts. Everything to do with Sam brings me comfort and a sense of security, which in this moment I needed the most. Putting my robe on the bed, my eyes turned and glued to the open door and, most importantly, what was beyond them.

Here I was, standing and sending glances into the next room, fidgeting and ignoring the soft murmur of voices intermingled with some laughter, when someone whispered beside me, "Shit!"

Looking that way, I could see a woman standing next to me, probably doing the same thing I was, but now her eyes were glued to her phone that she was holding in her hand while typing something into it. She was my height, and compared to other people, she looked like she was on the heavy side. But thanks to my now trained eye, I instantly knew the puffiness of her cheeks —due to steroids—and the roundness of her belly—hormones—wasn't because of food but thanks to this process.

This newfound knowledge that I wasn't the only one going through this made something ease inside me and allowed me to ask, "What's wrong?"

She looked at me, her words coloring her cheeks. "Jake can't... you know."

Confused, I prompted, "Can't what?"

"You know...." She trailed off, only for her fist to come up and moving it up and down, demonstrating what Jake couldn't do.

The instant she did this, the room exploded with laughter.

"What's funny?"

The question coming from Nurse Alyssa sobered the unfortunate Jake's wife up and, hurrying to her, she whispered "My husband can't...."

"Can't what?"

As one, we all formed a fist and started the motion to show what exactly Jake couldn't do.

"Men," Alyssa harrumphed. "Here's what you're going to do. If you think it'll help, take a selfie. Or if you want to give him a little more, there's a bathroom you can use. It's your choice. It works every time."

Expecting her to take a selfie, another round of laughter came when, with a crimson face, not looking at anybody, she hurried to the bathroom.

Through the laughter, Alyssa came my way. "It's time. Let's go."

Giving her a slight nod, I wiped the wetness from under my eyes, and that brings me to the present, as I head toward the door.

123

"Wait!" I turn toward the voice. "We don't know each other, and hopefully we'll never see each other because we won't have to come here anymore, but we have something in common. We share a fight in our lives, and I want you to know I'll never forget you. You'll be with me for the rest of my life. And good luck to all of you."

"And lots of baby dust," one of the other women says, and we all give a small chuckle at that and take a good look at each other. I know what the lady said was true. Never, never in my life will I forget those women. The laugh we shared, breaking the tension and the visible nerves. But most of all, the families each and everyone of us wanted to create. We may be complete strangers, but we formed a bond that'll last us a lifetime. In this journey, in this war we battled, we were made warriors. And that's not something anyone can easily forget.

***

Feeling a light push on my hand, I turn and enter the OR. In the center of it, there's a table, and next to it is an ultrasound machine. Up against the wall are cabinets and trays of instruments. The floor is black, but the stainless steel and glass dominate the room. The only colors around are dots of green and blue. That's all. It makes the coldness on my skin more pronounced as it seeps into my bones from the feel of this room.

"Climb on the table, pull your gown up, and put your legs in the stirrups," Alyssa instructs me.

I do as she says, and lying down, I see the big light above me that's in every hospital show there is. It's on, and the light is blinding me, so when I raise my hand to shield my eyes from it, Alyssa turns it slightly toward my legs and says, "Please state your name and protocol number."

"Danielle Hunt, one-zero-eight-four."

She takes my hand in hers and rests them on my chest. "The doctor is going to start now."

"Okay, Dani. First, I'm going to clean the area, and then we'll start. The nurse is going to hold the ultrasound wand on your belly so I can see what I'm doing. Don't worry. Everything is going to be fine, and try to keep your stomach muscles relaxed." I didn't see when the doctor and another nurse came in, so hearing her voice surprises me. And then, they start.

They clean me, the gel is put on my belly, the wand moving through it, and then, the sound comes.

It sounds like a vacuum cleaner.

"And we're in," the doctor says.

At first, I don't feel anything, and I start to relax. But then it comes.

At first, it's the pressure, and it's so strong that I can feel it in my head. In the next second, there's pain. Such sharp pain, the likes I've never felt in my life. It catches me completely off guard, and in response, I flex my muscles. All of them, not just my stomach.

"Relax. Squeeze my hand. But you have to relax your belly," Alyssa whispers in my ear.

I turn my head her way. "You lied!"

Her look is gentle and understanding, but the pain keeps coming, so I repeat, "You lied."

"Honey," she coos as she caresses my head.

I look in her eyes the entire time, squeezing her hand and trying to focus enough to answer her questions about stupid stuff. I know what she's trying do, asking me about my family, work, my favorite color, every damn thing she can think about, but the pain is so severe I can't concentrate. I can't think of anything but how much it hurts. It's like they're stabbing me over and over at the same place, winding around the wound, making it bigger and bigger, but most of all, more painful.

I don't know how long it lasts. The only thing I know is the whole time, I keep screaming in my head for them to stop.

Just stop!

I can't do this.

Stop!

But not one single word leaves my mouth.

Not one.

Not even a sound.

When the words "We're done" are heard, I relax my lips, let go of Alyssa's hand, and close my eyes.

There's a light touch at my elbow, so I open my eyes again. It's the doctor, and she leans in and whispers, "We have one."

One.

Only one.

I can't keep the tears at bay. They come out in the mix of disappointment that it's such a low count, only one, and relief there's any at all.

"I'm sorry," I cry.

There's a deep understanding coloring the woman's face, and once again, she leans in and, in a firm voice, she says, "Only a mother could do something like this."

Her words stun me. "I'm not a mother. I'm trying to become one."

"Yes, you are! You are a mother, Dani. Only you have to fight *early* for your baby to come to you." She takes my hand from its resting point on my chest. "So, once again, only a mother could do something like this." And she gives me a squeeze.

I look into her eyes, the eyes that are shining with conviction, with assurance, and with the utmost belief of her statement, and I squeeze her hand back, letting her words settle over me like a warm blanket. I've never given it a thought, but she is right. Only a mother could go through something like this. Only a mother would fight for her child with everything she has—even if that child is not here yet. And only a mother could love her future child in this way.

I give her one last look and a small nod when I hear Alyssa instruct, "Slide onto the gurney, honey. But please try not to flex your belly muscles too much." It's not an easy thing to do, and now that the pain is slightly more bearable and the "business" part of the procedure is over, I'm fully aware of the fact I don't have any panties on, my nightie is resting right under my boobs, and my legs are open, giving a flash for everyone to see. But somehow, I manage to do it without flexing my belly too much, cringing, or dying from mortification, and the moment my body hits the gurney, I finally relax.

After sliding my nightie back into place and covering me with a sheet, she takes me back into the room, positioning me into place. "You have to lie here for two hours, and then you can be on your way to go home, honey." And then she's gone, calling another woman's name. One by one, they go in, and one by one, they're all wheeled back here. The whole time, I just stare at the wall on my right, and the only thing in my head is the number of my eggs.

One.

Only one.

I didn't expect to have some crazy number of them, but the fact there's only one is crushing. I try to remind myself that one is enough, and there was a real possibility there could have been none. But still.

It's just one.

And as that thought keeps popping into my head, the tears start to slowly leak from the corner of my eyes, gaining momentum, and soon my body starts bucking in my effort to contain my sobs.

"Are you okay, Dani?" There's a light hand on my shoulder, and when I look around, I see it's Alyssa standing by my bed. I don't answer her, but the look on my face must be enough of an answer, since she takes a quick look around the room, and leans in to whisper, "I'll go get your husband."

Not even one minute later, the door is opened and Sam marches through them with a hard look on his face. The moment my eyes drink him in, my sobs become audible, the tremble of my body turns much worse, almost painful in its intensity, and I can't keep in anything anymore, as it all comes out.

"Sam," I sob. "I'm so sorry. I tried."

"Hush, baby." He tries to soothe me, but it doesn't work.

"I promise, I tried."

"Tried what? What's wrong?" he asks, the worry and confusion evident in his voice.

"We have only one egg," I whisper, looking into his eyes, afraid of his reaction.

His eyes close, his forehead coming to mine in slow motion, and once it's there, he releases such a huge amount of air his whole body sags. He stands there, hunched over my bed, his forehead on mine, silent. After a few seconds, he pulls back. Framing my face with his hands, his thumbs going under my eyes to wipe the tears away, his eyes are open and the love shining in them is enough to blind me. "Thank God," he whispers.

His response stuns me enough that my tears stop coming, but his thumbs still go back and forth, now caressing my face. "What?"

"You did it, Dani. We have one."

"But we have *only* one." Every time I think of my failure, my heart squeezes.

"No, baby, we have *one*. That means that we're one step closer to our star coming to us. You did it. You went through something horrible. But you did it, baby. And now, we have a chance."

His words hit me somewhere deep inside, and they bring such relief that even lying down, I feel my knees giving out, making my legs jerk. I close my eyes, bring my hand to his neck, and, holding onto him, I turn my head to fully experience the magical feeling of being released from the chains. I don't even know when it happened, or who made it happen. Was it me? Or the words Brooke hurled at me, judging me, making me spiral into darkness? Maybe they bound me tight every time I looked to Sam and saw the pain lurking deep in his eyes. Pain he was trying to hide from me. I don't know. But, with my every heartbeat, those chains rattle and break one by one.

We have one.
Snap.
We're one step closer.
Snap.
We have a chance.
Snap.
Only a mother could do something like this.
Snap.
Free.

***

"Ladies, you can get dressed and go home!" Alyssa yells, coming into the room.

Still feeling the lightness from earlier, I gingerly roll to my side and slowly sit up in bed, my legs dangling from it. Now that the time has passed since the harvest, the pain is coming back stronger.

"You need to take the rest of the day off. Rest as much as possible, and take something for the pain. Also, it's possible you could bleed a little, but that's normal. If you have any questions, call me." She gives instructions going from one person to another, making sure we're all right. Coming to me, she takes me by my forearms and lightly tugs me to my feet, steadying me. "Dani, you have to watch for any sign of OHSS. If your breathing starts to become labored, you have to come back. For now, everything looks good, we got your blood tests back, and the hormone levels are fine. But still, we have to be careful." Once she's sure I won't fall down, she turns back to the room. "That's it, ladies, your job today is done. Your eggs and your husband's sperm are at the lab being mixed together as we speak. And hopefully, the magic of conception will happen and dividing of cells will start. Tomorrow, you have to call the number I've given to your husbands and you'll be given the time of your embryo transfer."

The light murmur of sleepy voices fills the room as I go to my bag. Thankfully, while Sam was here earlier, he put my panties on me under the covers, making a joke that that's a first for him since his job is taking them off. I try to put on my yoga pants, but the pain is getting worse, so I just slide my feet into my shoes and keep my stuff in my hands, deciding I'll ask Sam to help me change.

"I'll help you, honey." Alyssa appears by my side and takes my clothes from me, dumping them on the bed. She squats before me, holding my pants for me to slide my legs into them.

"Thank you." I put one hand on her shoulder and the other to the bed for support.

"Where are you?" I look up and see the baby-dust lady talking on the phone. "What do you mean you went to get the car? Come right back here. You need to take my bag." She takes the phone from her ear, angrily stabbing it and ending the call. "If it wasn't for you, I wouldn't even be here," she mutters.

Hearing her words, I curl my fingers into Alyssa's shoulder, my eyes going from the baby-dust lady to glance around the room, and finally land on Alyssa. Her eyes are wide and filled with horror—much like mine are probably. I can't believe she said that. How could she say something so insensitive? It's not like her husband wanted this to happen. But, thanks to her comment, there's now a seed of doubt, of new fear planted in me, and I hope with all I am that Sam doesn't share her opinion. He never once gave any indication that he might. But still, I heard of couples splitting because of the inability to have a baby, or because the pressure of IVF was too much to bear.

I uncurl my fingers and finish getting dressed. Thanking Alyssa, I go out to meet my husband, who is waiting right outside the door so we can go home. And through it all, I hope we won't become one of the couples who are a statistic of failing under pressure.

***

Only a mother could do something like this.

I open my eyes, the words echoing in my brain, and see my mom standing beside the bed, a soft look on her face.

Once we got home, Sam gave me some pain pills and put me to bed. I thought I couldn't sleep, but turns out I was wrong.

"Hi, Mom." I stretch and put my hand on my swollen belly. It started to swell about an hour after the harvest, and before we went home, Sam hunted down the doctor and asked if that was normal. Turns out, after your insides have been dug through, it's normal. I would have laughed if I weren't in pain.

"Oh, my baby." Mom's eyes go back and forth from my belly to my face.

"I'm okay." I try to reassure her, but I can see she's not hearing me.Her eyes are filling with tears. We haven't seen each other since that afternoon at her house. I haven't had the energy to be the strong one. I still don't.

I get out of bed and hug her. "I'm fine."

She puts her hands on my shoulders and moves me back a little to do her mom inspection. "You're pale." It comes out as an accusation.

"Mom, I'm fine," I stress. And I am. The pain is finally gone, there are no more injections, and the worst is over. All that's left now is waiting.

"You're awake." I look toward the door. Sam stands there, his shoulder resting against the frame, his arms crossed on his chest, and he's giving my mom a hard look.

Uh-oh.

What now?

"I didn't wake her up," she says quickly, letting me go. I look between them, biting my lips so I won't laugh. Mom's standing with her hands planted on her hips, giving a death glare to Sam, only for him to completely ignore it and come to me.

Once he reaches me, his arms instantly curve around me and he shoves his face into my neck, where I feel his puffs of air as he tries to swallow down his laugh.

"I'll be waiting in the living room." And with one final glare Sam's way, she storms out.

"I didn't want her to wake you," he murmurs into my neck.

"I think I got that."

"Your dad's here."

"Then let's go out there." I try to take a step back.

"In a minute." He pulls me back the step I didn't take. "You okay?" he asks.

"I'm fine." The words have barely left my mouth when there's a hand at the back of my neck, pulling me up and closer to him. I don't have to go far; he meets me halfway. And then he's kissing me, his tongue entering my mouth. The rush of lust hits me instantly, but on the heels of it comes a painful realization that it's been a long time since we kissed like this. So long, I can't even remember when it was. All that we've had were lip touches and careful caresses. I've done that to him. To us.

Throwing my arms around his neck, I bring us closer, determined to show how much I love this man, and I give it my all.

Suddenly, I'm pushed back by Sam's hands on my ribs, holding me from him. His breath is heavy, his eyes hungry. "*Now* you're fine," he rumbles, and then turns and goes out the door.

Looking at where he was standing a few moments before, a small smile starts to stretch my face, and with a new spring in my step, I follow him.

CHAPTER FOURTEEN

"**THEY SAID YOU** *need to rest and to relax, so you'll goddamn relax,*" *he yells, and slams the door shut.*

The next morning, I get out of the shower, only to stop with one foot on the bathroom rug and the other still in the tub, and stare at the coffee mug that's sitting next to the sink.

Yesterday, after my parents were assured I was doing fine, the swelling stopped and actually started to go down. Since all I did was lie on the couch, the only thing I lifted all day was my mug or a glass, when what I really wanted to do was go back to that kiss. But, as we got ready for bed and then got in bed, Sam did nothing, and I was too scared to try to start anything.

In this process, I've lost all my confidence. I was sure he could see as much as I did all the changes in my body that the drugs have caused. My belly has never been flat, but now it looked like there was a balloon stuffed inside it. Every time I even thought of touching him, the nerves would start eating me away. I was convinced he didn't find me attractive anymore. What with the changes and the fact that I couldn't give him a child. So I stopped doing it completely. That was why I just waited for him to initiate. But he didn't. He just turned me so my back was to him, put an arm around me, pulled me to him so much he was almost lying on top of me, pinning me to the bed, and whispered into my hair, "Love you," and that was it.

And now, looking at the mug, I realize that, for the past two weeks, there wasn't any waiting for me when I got out of the shower. Sam didn't bring me my morning coffee. I always thought that if something like that happened, if he stopped doing those little things that carried such a big meaning, then I would see it instantly. I would feel the void they would leave behind. But for those two weeks, I hadn't seen a thing. I was so absorbed with what was happening in our lives, what I was feeling, that I was blind to all the rest. And I missed the most important thing of all. My husband's pain.

I get out of the shower, dry off, and pull my underwear on. Taking the mug carefully, I wrap both of my hands around it and bring it under my nose. With eyes closed, I take a deep breath, inhaling the aroma of my favorite substance, but in it, I get my husband back.

He was there for me every step of the way, the only way I let him be, and that was left out, not actually letting him do anything except help me with the injections. I didn't talk to him or include him in any other way. He knew when my appointments were, but I only gave him the bare minimum of information. He kept waiting for me to open the door, to take his hand so we could go through this together. But I didn't. And I wasn't there for him in any way, shape, or form. All this time, I was convinced I was the only one suffering, that I was alone. And I abandoned him. It's no wonder he spent so much time in the garage, all by himself, losing his time, burying himself in work.

After I finish with all my business in the bathroom, I go in search of my husband. I find him sitting at the table, looking at his phone that's sitting among the papers scattered in front of him. Coming to stand behind his chair, I lean down and rest my chin on his shoulder. I can see they're my discharge papers from yesterday. On them in red ink is the phone number we're supposed to call to find out if all our efforts have worked and if we'll get to do the transfer.

I turn my head, stuff my face into his neck, and breath deep, inhaling the smell of him. "Morning," I whisper contentedly, for a second forgetting all my fears that he doesn't want me anymore. But then, like a bear trap, those fears snap back into place and my body goes tense. I start letting him go, pulling my face out of his neck, when his hand closes around my wrist that's traveling across his chest in its escape.

"Morning, baby. You sleep okay?"

With the news we're about to get in just a few moments, you would expect me not to sleep a wink, but strangely, each night, when he reminded me he loved me with his words, I slept like a baby. "Yeah," I sigh.

"Good."

After a few moments of silence, he shifts a little, moving my arm with him and bringing my body closer. "It's almost time," he muses, tapping the papers with his index finger.

"Could you call them?" I ask, my voice small. "I'm too nervous to do it."

"Sure," he agrees readily, kissing my hand as he stands, dislodging me from him. He takes the phone from the table then, turning to me, he kisses me. It's not like the kiss from yesterday; it's not so desperate, but it's still an effective one. By the time I'm completely lost in him, the feeling of him surrounding me, he breaks it, leaving me in a daze. He pushes his forehead to mine almost painfully, and in this proximity, I can see I'm not the only one affected. His chest is rising and falling rapidly, his harsh breath making his words almost like an order. "Whatever happens in the next half an hour, remember, I *chose* you. I want *you*. No other but you. I love you. You're my sole purpose for being on this earth. You're my whole life, Dani. Please, remember that. Please, God, no matter what, don't forget that." And then he's out the door in a flash.

Ten minutes later, hearing the door opening and closing, I look up and wait for him to come into my line of sight as the nerves start to shift, waking up and making my body vibrate. I try to read his face, but I can't. His stoic expression causes the flutters of anxiety in my belly to intensify. Oh, God, it didn't work! I open my mouth to say something, anything, but nothing comes out. My throat is clogged with the tears that have started to fall. I put my shaking hands on the table to try to stand up.

"Tomorrow morning at eight, we have to be at the clinic to do the transfer," he says matter-of-factly.

"What?" I breathe.

"She said that the cells are dividing as they should. She mentioned there are no cracks, but I don't know what that means. She didn't explain. And we are good to go for the transfer," he finishes in that businesslike tone. And then it shows. The smile on his face is something I've only seen once before. And that was the moment I said the words "I do" at our wedding. It portrays the man who bested the beast.

And seeing the victory dancing in his eyes, I fall to my knees and cry the anxiety right out of me.

***

"For the next two weeks, rest as much as possible. Don't lift any heavy objects. Take short walks every day to get your circulation going. And try to avoid the stairs as much as you can. On the fourteenth day, you need to come back here so we can do the blood work and see what your betaHCG levels are. Hopefully, they will be sky high. But basically, that's it. You did all you can do. And now we have to wait to see if you hit the jackpot." I listen to Alyssa's instructions on what to do next.

Only a mother can do something like this.

I let the words that have been my lifeline for the past three days filter through my brain, giving me strength once again. "Thank you."

The transfer was done two hours before, and thankfully, it wasn't painful like the harvest had been. I mean, sure, it was uncomfortable, but nothing I couldn't handle.

I can't believe there's something inside me. Something that has the potential to grow and get strong and become my baby. I refuse at this point to acknowledge it's our child, who right now is trying to find a home for the next nine months inside me. What I gathered of this whole process and from the things Alyssa just pointed out is that this part of IVF is the same as if I had gone out and bought myself a lottery ticket. It's a fifty-fifty chance. Either I'll win or I won't.

"I know you don't like it when I say it, and you think it's impossible to do, but Dani, you need to relax. Stay away from stress as much as possible. Don't spend your days fretting with what's going on inside. Just stay positive, and it'll all work out." She smiles and waits for me to agree.

I nod, even though it's a complete and utter lie, because right now, all I'm picturing inside my head is what the embryo is doing and wondering if it's nesting.

"I mean it."

"I know," I confirm.

I say goodbye to Alyssa and gather my things. With one more quick glance to the good, kind nurse, I go out to my husband, knowing this is the moment the waiting game begins.

CHAPTER FIFTEEN

"**D**ON'T YOU DARE *leave me!" he shouts, but I can't look at him. I've come to the point that looking at my husband brings me pain, so instead, I look at the wall and wait for him to say what he has to say, so we can move on and do what I know is the best for us. The best for him.*

I scroll down the forum, reading the post of the path an embryo goes through after the transfer. I know I shouldn't do it, but I tricked myself into thinking that reading it helps me stay calm. When in all reality, all I'm left doing after the daily read is stressing if my embryo is doing as it should. Feeling the pressure my full-to-the-max bladder is creating, I groan and get on my feet to go to the bathroom. I started to hate going in there. Every time I sit on the toilet, I inspect my panties for the tiniest drops of blood. I put to shame every criminal show ever made with the intensity of my search.

I'm on day twelve. In three days, we're gonna find out if the IVF worked. For the past almost two weeks, I did nothing more than veg on the couch and take one very short walk when Sam got home from work. I was too terrified to do one single thing. Whenever I had a mind to do something, that post would pop into my mind and leave me immobile in the fear of doing something that would screw up the embryo's task. So, I stayed put. The only thing I did was "listen" to my body and try to catch any signal it sent my way of me being pregnant. All that listening managed to do is convince me that every single emotion, every single twitch in my body, is saying something to me. In the end, for almost two weeks, I've been doing the last thing I was supposed to do. Stressing.

I go into the bathroom and pull my panties down, ready to do my inspection and at the same time send good vibes to the embryo, when I see them.

Two drops.

Right there in the middle of my panties.

One is watery in its redness, almost pink. But the other, the bigger one, it's full-on horror movie red. Immediately, I take some paper and wipe, and on it, more redness. I wipe again. And again, there's blood. With every swipe and wipe, my hands are shaking more and more. The panic is setting in. Doubling over, I can see that every few seconds there's a drop of blood coming out of me. And I know. It's over. And just like that, there's no more fear, no more panic. There's nothing.

Feeling numb, I finish up in the bathroom then go look for my phone so I can call Sam. I find it on the bed next to the laptop with the posts showing on the screen. Not bearing to look at them for one single second, I snap the laptop shut, and then I call my husband.

He answers on the second ring, as he's been doing ever since the transfer. "Everything all right, baby?"

"Sam," I whisper.

"What's wrong?"

"There's blood."

"I'm on my way home." And he disconnects.

***

Twenty minutes later, I'm sitting on the couch, looking at the wall across from it, not seeing anything but those two spots, and not hearing anything. And then Sam's worried face fills my vision.

"Dani?" He's on his knees before me, his arms resting on my legs. I was so out of it I didn't hear him come in or feel his hands on me. All I feel is nothing. There's hollowness in my stomach, creeping its way up toward my heart.

"It's over. I started my period," I say in an even tone.

"I'm so sorry, Dani." I can see the sorrow marring his green eyes. "What can I do?"

"Could you please call the clinic for me and let them know?"

"Sure, baby." His gentle voice tries to penetrate the wall of pain that's surrounding me, to shed some light into the darkness that is invading. But nothing can help me now. There is no hope, no chance. There is nothing left.

"Okay, thank you."

I'm startled by the sound of Sam's voice coming from the front of the house. When did he leave? Confused, I look around me, but I can see nothing that will give me some kind of clue how much time has passed. Looking at Sam as he walks back to me, his eyes downcast to his phone, I try to hide my discomfort from losing the time.

"What did they say?" I ask, even though I know what was said. They probably told him that I should rest for a few days and then come in to start the preparations for another try. In time for my hormones to be evaluated again, for the treatment to be adjusted if needed, for the endless examinations and ultrasounds to be done, and then when my next cycle starts, we can be ready. Ready to start with the injections, ready to start another IVF process. That's how it goes, right? You try. You fail. Then you try again. But I don't want to do it all over again. I want to be pregnant now. I want to have a baby growing inside me *now*. I want to feel the excitement and plan how our nursery will look. I want to go from store to store and buy cute baby outfits. I don't want to feel like I do now, hollow.

He crouches back in front of me and puts his hands on my thighs. Their warmth spreads through my whole body. "Alyssa said that, sometimes, the bleeding is normal. That it doesn't have to mean anything. It can be residual blood from the transfer that is just now getting out. You have to continue with the medications you have been using since the transfer. And you have to come in two days for blood work to be done, as scheduled."

And just like that, the hope I can hear in his tone invades the blackness that has consumed me, firing a candle and spreading the light inside me, keeping at bay the nothingness that lurks and waits to take me away.

***

Hour by hour, the bleeding gets worse, and with every trip to the bathroom, the winds of doubt are getting stronger, threatening to extinguish the flickering light of the candle that's burning within me.

***

Two days later, I'm standing at the nurses' station, waiting for Alyssa to come back with my results.

My nerves are a wreck; I keep folding and refolding the flyers lying on the counter. My feet dance across the floor, taking my weight with them one at a time. I probably look like I have to pee really badly. Right next to me stands the "baby dust" lady, the picture of calm. Once again, there's not a hair on her head out of place, her makeup done perfectly, her hands folded in front of her, gently placed on the counter. The two of us paint the picture of exact opposites.

Looking from her and in the direction where Alyssa went, I see the nurse coming back. I try to read her face, but I can't. She's a closed book. That is, until she places the folded paper on the counter in front of me and looks me in the eyes. "I'm sorry, Dani. Your HCG levels are a zero," she says quietly. And in one sentence, she blows out the candle, extinguishing the light. And all that is left of me is the thin line of smoke after the flame. But try as I might, I can't catch it. It just flows into nothing between my fingers. And then, I'm lost. I'm lost in the dark.

CHAPTER SIXTEEN

"*YOU'RE THE ONLY person on this earth with whom I can be just me. I can be the real me. With everyone else, I have a role I have to play, but not with you.*"
"*And why is that?*" I ask.
"*Because with you, I'm safe.*"

Two months later

The sound of the door closing makes me jump and look around. I'm on the couch, the room around me a disaster. There are dirty clothes covering every surface. On the coffee table are the five mugs from my five trips to the kitchen to get the said coffee. The layer of dust is so thick it's become visible. I stopped doing anything. I spend my days sitting on this damn couch, and the only time I get up is to get another mug or go to the bathroom. All I do is stare at the wall. All I feel is pain.

Hearing the footstep nearing me, I try to gather some will to get to my feet to do…something. Anything. But by the time he's near me, I don't move a muscle, and I don't look away from the wall.

"Dani?" That voice. The sound of gravel moving down a hill. The sound that used to bring butterflies and the dull ache in my body that would only be soothed when his hands were ghosting in the barest of touches or exploring me or playing with my body. The sound that used to fill me with joy and bring me to life, now only makes the pain worse.

"Hey," I say, my voice hoarse from not using it. I don't look at him. I can't. That would only worsen the pain. It's bad enough as it is, but looking at him might just destroy me. I'm scared to see all the things I already know all written across that handsome face.

He stands there a few moments, his eyes burning the side of my face, until he gives up and walks away. Only then do I relax my tense body. Every day, we do this dance, and every day, he walks away. For the first month, he tried touching me, talking to me; he even once tackled me when I was standing near the bed. I guess he hoped if he cornered me, he would give me no choice. But all he got were false promises and disappointments. And now he waits, and then he gives up.

I used to wake up and say to myself, *This is the day I will go back to the old me. This is the day I will clean my house, make dinner, and start taking care of my husband.* And every day, I would stay on the couch. Every night, I would wait until he's fallen asleep before I went to bed. But I can't go on like this anymore. I know what I have to do.

"Sam?" I call.

"Yeah?" By the sound of it, he's running down the hall, probably freaked out that I willingly called out him. He comes into the living room and scans me from head to toe. "Are you okay? Do you need anything?"

I tear my eyes from the damnation of my existence and look to my husband. "We need to talk."

I can see the relief washing the worries from his face. "Yeah, we do."

Before I can start with my speech I have been practicing over and over in my head, he sits by me and takes my face in his hands. "What are we going to do, baby? You can't go on like this. *We* can't go on like this."

"I know." The image of him starts swimming, the tears gathering, the pain intensifying from the knowledge of what I'm about to do.

"Tell me, baby. What do you need? What do you want? I'll do and give you anything you want."

I put my hands on his wrists, and for one last time, I savor his touch, his love. "I want a divorce," I whisper.

It's like I slapped him across the face. But on the heels of shock, the anger starts leaking in. "What the hell?" he growls.

I stay quiet, those rehearsed words now long forgotten.

He lets my face go and stands with jerky movements. Turning back to me, he crosses his arms and, with authority, declares, "No."

"Sam—"

141

"No."

"It's for the best."

"For the best? Best for who?"

"For you!" I shout.

He comes back to me and, sitting down, he says, "We are not getting a divorce."

"Yes, we are," I argue. "I want you to have everything. I want your dream to come tru—"

"Quiet, Dani. We are not talking about this anymore," he interrupts me. I look into his angry eyes and don't say anything. I just wait for him to say more, but he doesn't. He just looks back at me. Eventually, I look back to the wall, losing myself into the darkness once again. When he puts his arm around me, trying to pull me into him, I can't stand it. I can't stand the realization that I'm standing between him and his dream. That I'm the one who's taking the possibility of a child from him. The warmth that's seeping into my shoulders is burning my soul, so I stand, and, not looking in his direction, I mutter, "I'm going to take a shower." And I run. I run away from my salvation.

***

Sam

"I want a divorce."

Those words, said in that quiet voice of hers, the sound he cherished most of all in this world, were spinning in an endless loop, torturing his mind, heart, and soul.

When he said he would give her anything she asked for, he was prepared to do just that. Break his bones, work himself to the ground to find a solution, to shake her out of her grief. He was prepared to go to war to slay those demons that wouldn't let go of her, even in her sleep. To steal her from the clutches of the depression that had such a firm hold on her.

He was prepared to do anything, give her absolutely anything she had set her mind on.

Anything, but that.

"I want a divorce."

He sat there for half an hour, looking at her, not believing what he heard. Assuring himself that he heard her wrong. But just like the last two months, she said what she needed to say and calmly went back to staring at the wall across from her.

She spent her days sitting on that couch, looking surprised when he would come home from work, finding her in the same spot he left her. He could see in her eyes the discomfort of calculating where the hours went. And just as he stood there, waiting for her to snap out of it, hoping she would come back, he could see the dull look seeping back into her once vibrant brown eyes, her spirit dying once again as she averted her eyes, back to it. Back to the wall.

"I want a divorce."

For the past two months, she's been lost. The pain is written all over her, and she is so far gone he can't reach her. He's tried everything, but still, she focuses on that wall like it's her lifeline. But enough is enough. It's time. And he will stop at nothing to get his wife back.

"I want a divorce."

Before, he had to win a fight with himself to have her. And he promised himself that no one was going to take Dani from him. No one. Not even her.

Listening to the shower going, he closes his eyes, takes a deep breath, and, gathering all his strength, he stands up.

"I want a divorce."

Walking to the bathroom, he makes a promise.

He is going to make sure those words never cross her mind again. And especially not those lips.

Past
Dani

The hallway is dark, so dark I have the fingertips of my right hand lightly sliding along the wall so I won't bump into something as I walk. Or is it because of the foul sensation in the pit of my belly? Because I know with every fiber in my being that I will need the support the wall promises?

With every step of the way, the beat coming from somewhere in the darkness vibrates through my whole system.

Step. *Thump.*

Step. *Thump.*

Even my heartbeat is mimicking the beat of the music.

The sliver of light shyly pouring into the darkness from the slightly ajar door is getting closer and closer. It's Sam's apartment.

I knew the instant I entered the building and heard the music that it was coming from here. But still, I had hope. And now, with every step I get closer, the hope in me is dying a slow, agonizing death. I come right in front of the door, but I don't go in. I can't. Instead, my fingertips become my palm against the wall, then the length of my arm. Until, I'm resting my whole side against it. My eyes are glued to that door. I can see the shadows of people moving inside. And then it comes.

"Sam!" A girl's giggle pierces the music and my soul. My knees lose all their power tokeep me up, and like in some movie, I slowly sink to the floor. I rest my back against the wall and close my eyes. The tears trail down my face as I listen to the nonstop giggles and some girl crying out Sam's name in obvious delight.

Listening to all this, I try to list in my head all the reasons why I stayed this long. But for the life of me, I can't come up with a valid one. There're a hundred and one reasons why I should have ran in the opposite direction and not in his.

After the night I thought was our goodbye, everything changed. But then again, nothing did. The next weekend, I was at the bar again. Determined for a fresh start. For new adventures. Then, he walked in, and all that determination to move on evaporated. I kept sneaking looks his way. My hands were shaking so badly I could barely bring the glass to my lips to take a drink, and my insides decided to mimic the motion of jelly on a plate. Fifteen minutes later, he planted his sculpted ass in the booth next to me and, throwing his arm the length of the seat, he turned his head my way, opened his mouth, and casually said, "Hey."

I don't know what I expected when I saw him again, but this casual greeting was not it. If I were honest with myself—which I was not, because that would mean I still held some hope—I would expect him to fall down on his knees, kiss my boots, and declare his undying love for me. Or something small like that. But this, no. No way! Acting like it didn't bother me in the slightest, I gave him a small smile and greeted him back, saying, "Hey."

The whole night, he kept his seat next to me, and the whole night, I was a mess—aware of his every movement, of every breath. I finally started to relax when he turned his head my way and asked, "You ready to go?"

Before my brain could fully process what he was asking me, and the fact he asked that question in front of everybody and not just sent me a text, "Yes!" flew out of my mouth like a bird from an opened cage. I was, once again, back at his apartment and in his bed. And the next night. And the next, and next. Then, the texts started coming, then the calls. By the end of the month, we would see each other almost daily, sometimes just the two of us, most of the time with friends around. But still, the Saturdays were reserved for just us.

He stopped hiding his touches and would be right next to me, wherever I was.

For two months, I walked on clouds.

Sure, everyone was wondering what was going on between us. Were we a couple or not? But that didn't matter. We were just... us.

Then, his birthday came. Marcy and I were waiting for him along with his guys to have a drink or two, and then we were going to his place. I don't know why, but I was a nervous wreck. I kept fidgeting and rearranging the purple bow we tied on the on his birthday present. When his foot crossed the threshold, the whistles and cheering started. Everyone rushed to him to wish him happy birthday, but I stayed put. Not because I didn't want to wish him the best, but because my feet couldn't support me and take me to him. I could see from a distance that his eyes were searching for something in between receiving well wishes and kisses on the cheeks from girls, but still, I stayed put. When they found what they were looking for, spotting me there, a devastatingly beautiful smile graced his face, transforming his features from breathtaking to out-of-this-world gorgeous, with a hint of wicked when he spied the bow.

One second, he was across the room; the next, he stood right in front of me. Feeling like a complete dork, I lifted my arms and, with jazz hands, screamed, "Happy Birthday!"

"That's it? No kiss for the birthday boy?" he asked through a chuckle.

"Umm... sure." I got up on my toes and planted a fast, shy one on his cheek.

"I think we can do better than that," he teased. "Prepare yourself, we're about to kiss in public."

He didn't give me time to even blink before he did what he said. He hauled my body into his and, fisting the hair on the back of my neck, planted a hot and heavy one on me. I'm sure there was some reaction to this from everyone else, but I was so lost in him that I couldn't hear it. All that existed in this moment was Sam and what he made me feel. I was instantly ready for this night to be over and to be just the two of us in his apartment in our little bubble.

Then time for presents came. I didn't give him mine, because I wanted him to open it when we were alone. It was nothing big or special, but still, I wanted to be alone with him.

There was a lot of silly stuff he got, but when he opened Marcy's gift, he froze. He started to grind his jaw so hard I was afraid he would turn all his teeth to dust. Peeking over his shoulder, I saw what held him spellbound.

It was a two-picture frame. In both pictures, it was only the two of us.

In the first, I was sitting on his lap, my head thrown back from laughing. And Sam's forehead was resting against my exposed neck, his eyes closed, and a small, secret smile playing peekaboo on his lips.

The second was a close up of our faces. I actually think it was the selfie that Sam took using Marcy's phone. My face was sideways; my eyes were turned upward from looking at somebody who was standing by my side, a smile gracing my face. Through the hair that cascaded down my shoulders, Sam's eyes were peeking through. You couldn't see much of anything else but his eyes. And in the depth of them, the truth was hiding. He was happy, content. And if I'm not mistaken, there was love buried deep in them, behind all the shields and walls, behind the mask he put on for people surrounding him, shyly waving to the onlookers. They were the eyes of a man in love.

We looked like a couple. Not just any couple, but one that was in love. Happy to be together, to be with the person who gave them the freedom to be themselves. Not just like… what-ever-the-hell we were.

That was a week ago.

And now, here I am, sitting on this dirty floor in the dark, watching the shadows moving in his apartment through the crack. With every tear that slides down my face, a piece of my fractured heart comes out. If it were visible, you could actually see it all scattered around me, leaving a bloody trail in their wake. For the life of me, I can't figure out what changed. Why is he suddenly pulling away from me, when we were just starting to get closer? Why is he doing this to me? To bring a bunch of girls to his apartment and throw a party on a Saturday night, when he knew I was coming over. He left me waiting for him in that bar for over an hour, when he said he would come pick me up. And why the hell did I come here? Why torture myself, when I knew as the seconds ticked by he wasn't coming…when I knew he was doing something like this?

Hope. That bitch, hope, drove me here. But what have I hoped for? For him to be lying in bed too sick to text or call me? I don't know. I only know some force deep within me brought me here. And now I know. I know we can never be together. This time, it's the end. The end of us.

Hearing the voices getting closer and seeing the shadows growing, I jump to my feet. How long was I sitting on this floor, lost in my own misery? From the numb feeling in my butt and the shooting, sharp pain radiating along my spine and the backs of my legs, it's obvious I was there for quite some time. Now thankful for the darkness of the hallway, I wipe the tears from my face with the dash of my hands, just in time as the door fully opens. The bright, harsh light pouring out suddenly in the hallway, cutting the darkness that enveloped me firm in its embrace, blinds me. Blinking rapidly to dash the stars dancing in my eyes, all I'm left seeing are two figures standing frozen in the doorway.

"Da-Dani!" the male voice stutters.

I put my fingers against my closed lids, trying to help my vision come back, only to make the stars worse for an instant. But then, opening my eyes, I can see who's standing in front of me.

"Hi, Nate." I wave like a dork, but he doesn't see me. He's too busy casting nervous glances over his shoulder. I don't know if he's nervous because he has Brooke draped all over him when he has a girlfriend and he's scared I'll go find her and tell her about that fact right this instant. Or is it because Sam's in there doing the exact same thing as he is, only much worse. I don't know, and honestly, at this moment, I don't actually care. Okay, that's a lie. I do care, but I don't want him to know that. "Brooke," I greet the girl who I've seen a couple of times trying to get Nate's attention.

"Dani," she mutters through her cat-who-ate-the-canary smile.

"Would you like to come in?"

"No, Nate. Thanks. I didn't know you guys had a party. I was bored out of my mind, and I didn't know where Marcy was, so I thought to come look for her here." Lie, lie, *lie*. I know where she is.

She's sound asleep, snuggling her boyfriend since he went to her house for dinner and decided to stay.

"She's not here. I think Jake went to her place. But you can come in and have some fun."

"Umm… no, thanks. But could you please ask Sam to come out? I just need to tell him something, and then I'll leave you to enjoy your night." No way in hell I'm stepping a foot into that hellhole. It's been bad enough listening to what was happening; I don't need to feed my pain with actually witnessing it. I'm positive it would break me even more than it already has.

He looks over his shoulder again. "Uh…sure!"

It doesn't take long for Sam to come out. I don't know what I expect him to look like, but this is not it. His hair is a mess, like he's been running his hand through it all night, or like someone else did. I know how good it feels having my hand go back and forth through his hair, soft and prickly at the same time. He has a beer in one hand, and in the other is a cigarette. I've never seen him smoke. And his eyes are bloodshot. From alcohol or smoke, I don't know, but this is not the Sam I know. The mask he puts on for his friends is firmly in place.

"Hey, babe," he says without a care in the world.

"Hi, Sam." I look pointedly to the couple standing in the hall with us. They're probably waiting for the show to start. *Sorry to disappoint, guys, but there won't be any showcase of jealous rage.* I'm not that kind of a girl. I'm just here to calmly say it's over. And when I get home, that's when the real show can start, in the comfort of my solitude, when I can freely let loose, cry my eyes out, and let the remaining splinters of my heart bleed out. Taking a hint, they turn and walk away in the dark, probably to find some dark corner where they can do what they came out to do in the first place.

"Dan—" He starts to say something, but he stops when my hand shoots up.

"Don't," I whisper, hating the fact I don't have the strength to at least pretend this doesn't affect me.

"I—" He tries again. But, again, I don't let him.

"I know I don't have any right to say anything here. I know that. But why would you do something like this? I don't understand what's changed. We were good. More than good. So what the hell happened?" I wipe the traitorous tear that snuck its way from the corner of my eye.

"I can't do this."

"Do what?"

"This." He gestures with his hand between us. "Us."

"Yeah. I figured that out." I clear my throat to try to give my voice strength for what I'm about to say. "It's okay, honey. You don't have to do this anymore. We were just having some fun, right? It's not like we were in a relationship. And now the fun is over. It started to feel like something completely different than just casual fun, so you can go and have that elsewhere. It's okay."

"But that's the thing. I don't want to have fun elsewhere or with anyone else."

"What? But you just said you can't do this anymore. That you don't want us anymore." I'm confused. Maybe I should have waited until tomorrow morning to have this conversation. He's evidently drunker than I thought, speaking in circles like this.

"Yeah, I know." He sighs, looking away from me. "I like to spend time with you, when we're at the bar or just hanging out, and I also like the way we are when it's just the two of us. More than I should," he mumbles the last part.

"So, what? You want us to be together? Like a real couple, holding hands and skipping through the forest?" I joke, trying to lighten the mood and squish the hope that's once again bubbling inside me.

"No," he almost barks at me.

Ouch, that hurt. "Then, that's it. It's over."

"No. I don't want that either."

"Then what do you want, Sam? Because you know we can't go on like this any longer. We've been dancing this dance for six months now, and I'm sorry, honey, but I can't do that anymore. Every time I have to leave you after our night is over, I feel like I'm tearing myself apart. I can't keep doing that to myself. I just can't. And if you didn't have feelings for me, you wouldn't be this torn up. So, I think it's best to call it quits while we're still standing and each go our own way, so when we see one other, we could actually look at each other without wanting to tear our faces off." I'm winded from this speech, hurling the words his way so this torture will be over quickly. "It's over."

"No!" he barks.

"What do you mean no?"

"I don't know." He sighs and sits on the floor. His head is down, the long-forgotten cigarette almost burning his fingers. In his other hand, the neck of the beer bottle almost slips through his fingers. I go to him and take the cigarette, stubbing it out on the floor, and then I steal the bottle, putting it next to his leg. The moment he realizes his hands are free, he pushes them into his hair. So maybe he did make his hair the wild mess that it is.

Looking at him like this, I want to put my arms around him and just hold him, giving my comfort to him, to ease whatever problem that's making him like this. But I don't. I go to the other wall of the hall, sit down right across him, and I wait. For what, I don't know. All I know is I can't leave him like this.

"If I tell them to go, would you stay with me?" he asks, still looking at the floor between his feet.

"No," I whisper, but even with the music spilling out of the apartment, I know he hears me, because I can see his head nodding through the shadows.

"The fuck?" I look up when the rumbling sound reaches my ears and see Mark standing in the doorway. "What the fuck are you doing here?" Not giving me even a chance to open my mouth tosay something—not that I know what I would have said—he looks to Sam and demands, "Why have you brought her here, man? I thought you two were done. Why do you keep letting her twist you into knots? You should just scrape her off, so you can be yourself again."

"He didn't bring me here, Mark. And don't worry, I won't be staying long," I interrupt, stopping his awful and hurtful words. I can take the verbal punches he throws at me, but what I can't stand for is what he's doing to Sam.

"Well, just like you strutted your ass in here, you can take the same path and go the fuck away. And leave my brother alone. He doesn't need you to torture him. Taking away his Saturdays wasn't enough; you wanted it all. Well, he's with his friends again, partying at his house, as it should be. So, get the fuck on your way."

"Hmm..." I hum in response, looking between Sam and Mark. Something's going on here, and I don't know if it has anything to do with me. I mean, I've seen Mark a couple of times. Three, if we count this charming encounter.

He turns around after not getting any response from me, mumbling something under his breath. Then he takes a swig of his drink and enters the belly of hell for tonight that is Sam's apartment.

I look back at Sam. He's still looking at the spot where Mark was standing a few moments ago, a wrinkle marring his usually relaxed and carefree forehead.

"Sam," I call to get his full attention. "What's going on?" I can see he's putting the mask firmly back into its place. "No. Don't do this. Be who you are."

"I'm always who I am, Dani." He shakes his head a little, trying to give me a look of confusion.

"Don't bullshit me, Sam. We've spent a little too much time together for you to successfully do that. I want to know why you are one person with me, and when you are with your friends, you turn into a completely different one. And only in the past few weeks did you let the mask slip in public." I say the last part with a smile, not wanting to scare him away. I'm genuinely interested in the answer, and scared a little that it's actually the other way around. That he was playing a part, a new persona, when he was with me.

He sighs. The sound heavy, like it came from somewhere deep within him. "They wouldn't understand," he replies, almost to himself, his head turning to look at the entrance of the party zone.

"Understand what?"

"For them, it's always about the next party, about the next great, legendary time we can have. About the next pussy they can fuck. Did you know that most of our talks revolve around fucking, drinking, or passing out from said fucking or drinking? They refuse to grow up. And I'm getting tired of that crap. You must know I was never like them, not to their level anyway. Since you can see me so clearly." He chuckles a little. "With you, I don't need to pretend. I can be who I am, and you take me the way I am. You don't demand to go out, to have a good time, to seek the next big adventure. We can just stay in and watch a movie, or stay in bed, lying in the darkness and talking. Or not talking." He winks. "And you never say a word. You're here for me. You're here to *be with me*. And not because of what I can do for you. What I can give you. In their case, they want a place to crash with no questions asked." He trails off. His eyes once again study the tiles on the floor. "Maybe that's the reason I can't let you go," he says more to himself than me.

"But you have to," I answer him anyway.

We stay seated across from each other for a long time. Neither of us moves, his mask long forgotten in this illusion of privacy this dark hall has to offer. For the first time ever, he shows me all that is him. I can see all the way to the hidden corners of his soul. I can see the loneliness he feels. He's constantly surrounded by people, yet he's like a man alone in the desert, with nothing and nobody in sight. If only he would open his eyes and see what all the people around him are able to see. He's not the one who has to pretend to be someone else, to fit in the little boxes people tend to create for others. He's the one we all gravitate to and are willing to do absolutely anything to stay on the edge of his world. Without him in our lives, we would all just be pawns in this game of life. Searching for that burst of light he gives us.

I wish I could say or do something that would make him see the truth. But I can't—not only because I know he wouldn't listen to me, but also because I have no right to. If he were mine, truly mine, I wouldn't stop until he saw what I can so clearly see. But he isn't. He doesn't want to be.

For the last time, I drink him in. I take the strength I need to get up and go home.

"See you around, Sam." My voice is scratchy from being silent for so long and from the tears that are gathering in my throat on their way up to my eyes.

He doesn't say anything, just blinks at me a couple of times.

I don't know what I expected him to do, but the last thing on my mind is the firm hand holding my wrist as I try to pass him by. He tugs to prevent me from even taking a step. I look at him seated in the same position. Before I have the chance to open my mouth, he opens his.

"Stay," he pleads.

CHAPTER SEVENTEEN

*"**D**O YOU WANT to know why we work as a couple?" he asks, the look on his face indicating he's done with this conversation, but he still carries on. "It's because we listen to one another. It's because we love each other. We didn't get married because we had to, or because you were pregnant and we were scared what people would say. We got married because we wanted to, because we couldn't imagine life without each other. But, most of all, we work because we have respect for one another. And I for one respect and love you too much to just give up on us and walk away."*

And with that, he turns and walks away, but I know he won't go far.

Past

Standing on the blade between consciousness and sleep, I turn around in bed. It's Sunday, the only day of the week I get to stay in bed and just be lazy all day. Burrowing my cheek deeper into the soft pillow, I throw my arm to the side, only to find the sheets empty and cold. Momentarily, my eyes spring open. Blinking away the assault the harsh morning light waged on my vision, I turn my head and confirm that yes, the spot next to me in bed is, indeed, empty.

Confused, I look around and see I'm not in my parents' house in my old bedroom. But instead, I'm in Sam's room and in his bed. So, it wasn't all a dream. I'm not sure if I'm relieved because of that fact, or disappointed. Yesterday was brutal. Until the last second, I didn't know if I would get out of that conversation and situation sane. And until that last possible moment, until I looked in Sam's eyes and witnessed the hope written all over his face, I was, once again, sure it was over. We were done. But I was wrong. And I stayed. And now, he's not here.

There's a beeping sound coming from somewhere in the room, and it takes a moment to realize that it's the sound of my phone, more specifically, an incoming text. When the hamster in my brain finally starts spinning its wheel for the light bulb to start blinking, I spring into motion and try to detangle myself from the sheets.

"Get off me, you death trap," I mutter to the sheet playing octopus and yank it from my body. After almost hitting my head on the nightstand, since the sheet suddenly decided to listenand release me from its grip by surprise, I shakily stand next to the bed and send a death glare in its direction. "Stupid sheet."

Thankfully, the beeping starts again, so I'm distracted from my morning wrestling match. Unfortunately, it turns out my phone is buried somewhere beneath the retched fabric, since I went to sleep last night in my clothes and it was in my back pocket. It must have wormed itself out in the middle of the night. So now, a new battle begins as I try to find my phone in the sheet.

"Ha, I win!" I shout triumphantly, waving my hands in the air. After my little victory dance is over, I look at my phone and see there are three messages and two missed calls from Julie.

Where R U?

Answer your phone!

I can't believe you're not here. It's my last day!

The wave of guilt instantly washes through me when I see her texts. I can't believe I managed to forget my little sister is moving to Denver, and it's her last full day here. I begged her not to go, not to leave me and all her friends and family, but after her last breakup, she said she was done. She needed a fresh start. And who could blame her? After all that has happened, I would probably do the same. But still....

Taking a quick look at the shut door, I bite my lip and glance back at my phone. I know I have to go and spend the day with my sister, and I really, truly want to spend every last moment we have together doing fun stuff and cram all we can into this one day so it can last us a long time. But, on the other hand, I want to stay here and spend time with Sam, and maybe we'll finally figure out what the hell we're gonna do. Because one thing I know for certain is that I can't go on like this any longer. I give and give all I have to him, but I get only scraps in return. I'm scared that if I go on like this, there'll be nothing left of me. And when he's done, when he decides it's finally truly over, then what?

Taking a deep breath, I shove my phone in the back pocket of my jeans and go to the door. I don't even know if he's out there, or if he woke up, saw me sleeping beside him, and ran the hell away from here just so he wouldn't have to face me. Does he want me to take a hint from that and go away for good?

Trembling, I pull the door open slowly and peek through the crack. Instantly, I see him sitting on a stool. His denim-clad legs are spread wide, his bare heels resting on the stool's rails. His black T-shirt-covered back is bowed, dark head bent, and his elbows rest on the breakfast bar. A cup of coffee sits in front of him, and both of his hands squeeze the back of his neck. I can't see his face, since he's sitting sideways to me, but he's a picture of a man who's been tortured. My first reaction is to rush to him, put my arms around him, and try to soothe all his pain and anguish away. But I can't. I can't keep sending him signals and giving him the green light for him to keep treating me the way he is. I have to stand up for myself.

Knowing that nothing will be resolved right now, either because he doesn't know what the hell he wants—despite his pleading last night—or he's not brave enough to take my hand and go down the uncertain road of a relationship with me, I lean my shoulder against the doorjamb and take my phone back out.

I'll be there in an hour.

I send the text to my sister, put my phone back in the pocket, and clear my throat. "Hey."

The muscles in his back bunch, and when I look up, I see he's facing me. "Hey," he murmurs after looking me up and down.

"Do you mind if I use your bathroom?" I ask, hitching my thumb in its direction.

"No. Go ahead." He still speaks in that quiet voice that's freaking me the fuck out.

I send him a nervous smile over my shoulder while hurrying to the bathroom. Upon seeing the state I'm in, mainly my hair, a scream tries to come out, but I successfully force it down. My God, I look like a homeless person.

I'm wiping under my eyes with some wet toilet paper, trying to get rid of the smears of mascara, when there's a light tap on the door. "Yeah?" I call, not looking away from the mirror.

"Here, I thought you'd like some," Sam says, and when I look down, I see it's a mug filled with coffee.

"Thanks," I whisper, suddenly feeling shy. And when I take a sip, it's just the way I like it. "Oh, God." I moan, throwing my head back, fully enjoying the feel of the caffeine going down and spreading through my whole body and soul. There's a slight movement to my right, reminding me that Sam is still in here with me. Feeling self-conscious, I take a quick peek in the mirror to assess the damage and breathe a silent sigh of relief when I see the makeup smears are gone.

I don't know why I'm feeling so awkward and fidgety this morning. It's not like I just met him yesterday. But then again, it's the first time I've spent the whole night with him. When I look back at Sam, I see he's shifting from foot to foot.

Oh my God, he's nervous too!

For some reason, that calms me right away, and taking one more sip, I send him a small smile. "It's perfect. Thank you."

"No problem." And with that, he turns and leaves the bathroom.

Finishing up, I take one final look. Satisfied I no longer look like a wet cat, I walk back to the kitchen. Drinking the final sip of the morning goodness, I rinse the mug and put it in the dishwasher. Through all of that, I can feel Sam's eyes touching my back, neck, the side of my face, but I don't let him see how much he affects me. I'm ready to get what was denied to me last night. With each movement from his eyes, the part of my body where they land starts to tingle. My stomach is turning in on itself, my hands start to shake, and when his eyes fix on my lips, my knees go weak and I have to put a hand on the counter so the throbbing between my legs doesn't send me to the floor, begging for him to ease the magnificent pain. It's like my body knows what day it is. And it knows that we skipped a day, and it's demanding its fill.

Clearing my throat, I summon the strength from somewhere deep inside. "I have to go. Thanks for the coffee."

"What?" The confused expression on his face makes him look almost adolescent—in other words, adorable.

Tilting my head a little, I repeat, "I have to go."

"Go where?"

"To meet my sister. It's her last full day here." I start to go to his room to get my purse, but then I remember I didn't have one last night. I pat my butt to make sure my phone is still in my pocket and then look at Sam, ready to say goodbye and go spend the day with my sister. The only problem is… I don't know how to do that.

"But—"

Something is different about him. I can't put my finger on it, but with his fidgeting, his nervousness, and now, his inability to finish sentences, something is definitely off. He's not the loud, confident guy I know.

"But what?" I ask, trying to figure out what the hell is wrong with him.

"Nothing," he mumbles, getting up from the stool, and he goes into the kitchen to rinse his mug.

"Sam?" I call to get his attention. "But what?"

He takes a deep breath then turns and pins me with his stare. "We need to talk."

"I'm sorry, but I can't right now. I have to go." I take the excuse provided to me, thankful for it. I would much rather live in this limbo of our relationship for a little bit longer and try to prepare for the worst, than be crushed and sent to brokenhearted hell when he removes himself from my life.

"Okay, but I want you here tonight." The way he says it is like a command. He stands with his arms crossed over his chest, legs spread wide, and looking at him, I know I don't have any say. I have to be here tonight. I have to come here and let him rip me apart. Tear my heart out, leave it with him, and go away.

I swallow, pushing said heart down, trying to hold on to it for a little while longer before I give it up, and whisper, "Okay. I'll see you tonight." And I run to the door.

***

"So, what do you think?" I ask Jules.

We're on my bed. After the morning of trolling through the mall, drinking way too much coffee, and buying stuff we didn't need but sure as hell wanted, we decided it was time for a movie marathon. Mom joined us for a while, but then suddenly her sinuses started to get all funny—her explanation for her tears—and she ran out of my room. Ten minutes after that, we could hear her banging away in the kitchen. And now, the credits from the last movie we watched are scrolling on the screen, the debris from our junk-food binge scattered all around us. Jules's bags are packed. Mom is downstairs in the kitchen making Jules's lunch for tomorrow, which will translate into a week's worth of lunches. Dad is closed off in his study. And I just shared everything that happened with Sam, from the beginning right until this morning, with my sister.

"I think you should go back to his place, get laid, and strut your ass out of his life." She wiggles her eyebrows up and down. As she's looking at me, the smile on her face that started to grow slowly melts away. "And whatever you do, don't let him run you out of town."

"Oh, Jules," I whisper. I knew from the moment she said she's leaving that I would miss her, but it's at this second that I know just how much. I can't believe my crazy, brave—sometimes *too* brave—fun-loving, full-of-life sister is letting some douchebag control her life.

"You don't have to go." I lean over and hug her. It's probably the last time I'll hug her for a long time.

"Yeah, I do." I can feel her tears wetting my neck where she hid her face. "I can't deal with all the drama." Sniffing one last time, she pulls her face out of my neck and, wiping her tears away, she gives me a false bright smile. "And anyway, if that happens, if you decide you have to move from here, you can always come and stay with me."

I cup her face and trail my thumb under her eye. "Thank you, honey."

"Always."

"I'm gonna miss you, you little shit."

"I'm gonna miss you, you big shit," she teases me back. "Now, go and get laid."

Watching her leave my room, my heart hurts. This is the last time she'll bounce off my bed after spending girl time together, the last time she'll tease me in here, and the last night she'll spend in the room right next to mine. I know we'll see each other, but hopefully by the time she comes to visit, I'll have a place of my own and not still be living with our parents. And it hurts, because I just said goodbye to one important person in my life. Now, I have to go and say it to another.

***

With my heart in my throat, I raise my hand and lightly knock on the door. Not even half a minute later, the door swings open and here he stands. Wearing jeans, a white tee, and no shoes, his hair all messed up like he spent the day running his hand through it, he's my dream personified.

I open my mouth to say something, so I'm not just standing there drooling like a dork, but the hand that is wrapping around my wrist stops me. And then, I'm pulled inside, the door closing with a bang behind me as I'm marched to the couch while Sam drags me with him.

"What's going on?" I'm confused. I don't know what I expected to happen, but in the scenarios I had in my head, this was not one of them.

"Shut up," he growls.

I press my lips together to stop the questions that are trying to surface, at the same time wondering what I did wrong.

He stops, and since I wasn't paying attention—and if I'm being totally honest, I was checking him out—I walk right into him. "Oh, sorry." The words are not completely out of my mouth when suddenly I'm sailing through the air and bouncing on the couch.

He just threw me on the couch.

Threw. Me.

I stare at him looming over me, my mouth hanging open, and then in the next moment, he's bending down, taking off my shoes and pulling my legs up on the couch. In the time it takes me to stupidly blink at my feet, I lose sight of them because I'm lying down, and Sam is on top of me.

"What the hell is going on?" I yell in his face.

"We need to talk." He squirms a little, dislodging my hands that were on his chest. "So, I made it so we could talk."

"You didn't think we could do it sitting up?"

"Nope," he says through a smile, popping the P.

"And why is that?" The sarcasm in my voice can't be ignored, or so I think, because he has no problem letting it go, nor does he let me up.

"Because something will happen, or someone will call or text you, and you won't listen to what I have to say."

"So, you're basically telling me that you'll be the only one who gets to talk." I try to put my hands back on his chest, either to push him away or to feel him up. I'm not sure which just yet, since I don't know if I want to laugh or slap him silly.

"Yep." Again with the P. "Now, stop talking and listen."

"I—" I start, but don't get to finish, since his palm is covering half of my face.

Finally managing to push my hands back between us, I shove at his chest and stammer, "I ca-can't breathe."

He quickly pulls his palm away, and after a quick peck to my lips, he mutters, "Sorry."

Now, that kiss is a sure thing to shut me up, since it was so unexpected and so out of character. We don't kiss or cuddle if it's not leading to sex. What is going on?

Looking into my eyes, he announces, "We can't do this anymore. I can't keep going on like this."

The hollow feeling and the pain that's coming right on its heels starts to spread through my blood, feeding every cell in my body, threatening to devour me. I knew it would be painful, but somehow I didn't think it would be this much. "Okay," I whisper. Unable to look at his grass-green eyes for a second longer, I focus on his mouth, on those beautiful lips that are allowing such awful words to come out.

His hand glides into my hair, his fingers following the shape of my head, his fingertips pressing slightly, and I know he wants me to look at him, but I can't. I can't let him see how much this is costing me, how much I will leave behind when I walk out that door tonight.

"Fuck, I don't know how to say this."

The frustration in his tone makes me flinch. I want to say it's okay. I want to frame his face, the face I know will haunt my dreams for the rest of my life, and tell him I understand. But I don't. I don't do anything, just keep lying under him, his warmth seeping into my body, and wait for him to shatter my heart.

"I want us to be official. I want everybody to know you're my girl. I want to kiss you as many times as I want, whenever I want, and I want you to hold my hand and touch me whenever you feel like it. And I want you to stop murdering that desire that shines so bright in your eyes whenever you see me."As he speaks, his body gets tighter and tighter. The hand in my hair puts more and more pressure on my scalp, and the pain that was circling inside me transforms into something beautiful. If it weren't made of bone, my ribcage wouldn't be able to contain my heart wanting to fly around the room.

In the face of his obvious unease, I can't resist and ask, "Are you asking me to be your girlfriend?"

"Yes!" he barks at me.

That beautiful feeling steadily builds inside me, and at his ferocity, it starts bubbling until it spills out for the world to witness my happiness, and I chuckle. He's lying on top of me, his weight pushing me into to the couch cushions, but I feel weightless. I actually feel like I could get up and fly. I put my hand on the side of his face, my thumb grazing his five o'clock shadow, and with so much going on inside me, all I can do is whisper, "Oh, Sam." But that's enough for him, because his look goes gentle, and where his eyes land, it's almost as if he's touching me there.

Slowly, his head starts to descend, until his lips are a whisper on mine. "Are you sure?"

"Yeah." I nod.

"You have to think about it, Dani. Really think about it, because I think this could go till the end."

I tilt my head up. "The end?"

"To the altar." He moves back a little, his eyes going from gentle to serious. "I could marry you someday, Dani." I don't know what I expected my reaction to be, but judging by the scowl on his face when I laugh, that wasn't it. "Dani, I'm serious," he growls.

Sobering, I look at him, and moving my thumb back and forth, enjoying the prickling sensation that's somehow radiating through my whole body from my thumb, I swallow. In a clear voice, I say, "Yes, Sam."

Hearing my words, his eyes close slowly, and once again his head comes forward until his forehead is resting on mine. From this close, I can see each and every eyelash that's resting on the edges of his cheekbones. His breath comes in bursts of air, slamming into my face so intensely that I have difficulty breathing. I turn my face a little, but when I do, his eyes spring open as he moves toward me, bringing his lips to rest on mine, and there is a whisper so forceful it could move mountains.

"You're mine."

***

161

Hours later, we're still lying on the couch, only now, Sam's back is to it and he has molded himself along my back, his arm draped over my waist. For the first time since this whole thing between us started, I feel relaxed and free, free to just be myself, no hiding, and most importantly, no lying about my feelings.

It's funny, when I woke up this morning, the day seemed gray and sad, and I was facing the loss of two people who I love most in the world. How Sam ended up on that short list is still confusing to me, but I can't deny it—he's there. And now, I said goodbye to my sister, sending her on her adventure in a new city, building her new life, and then fully welcomed another into my life. I guess it's true what they say—for every loss, there is another gain.

A loud banging on the door snaps me back to reality.

"Sammy boy, open up and let's get this party started!" the familiar voice shouts.

His arm tensing on my waist, Sam growls, "You've got to be shitting me."

Next thing I know, I'm on my feet, swaying, and can still feel the heat and the squeeze Sam gave my hips after standing me up before turning around to stalk to the door, grumbling under his breath.

He pulls the door open, cutting off yet another round of banging, and barks in Mark's face, "What?" It's so ferocious that I look around, trying to figure out which corner of the room is the closest, so I can go there and hide, pretending nobody can see me.

Fury emanates from every cell in Sam's body. Unfazed, Mark pats him on the shoulder and, with the last pat, pushes him slightly so he can bulldoze his way in. Spreading his arms like he's the king of the castle, he turns and, in a pompous voice, tells the crowd that has started to spill into the apartment, "Ladies, welcome to Fuckland!" He turns and his eyes land on me. "This is a place to come and have a good time. A place where the alcohol flows like a river, where there's new pussy available every night. A place where there are no limits. Where your every sexy dream comes to life. A place where most of you will enter only this one time. Some of you will be granted a repeated entrance. And some of you have overstayed their welcome," he finishes with a snarl, the venom dripping from his last words burning my flesh.

I stand there, frozen in place, my soul dying, not knowing what to do. No one has ever been so mean to me. No one has ever, in my whole life, disliked me so much it was evident in their every single look and every word that left their mouth. I can't take my eyes off him, can't sever this trance he holds on me, and when I feel tears gathering in my eyes, making my vision blurry, like I'm looking through the bottom of a glass, he smirks. And unfortunately, that smirk is the last thing I see clearly as one lone tear escapes and betrays my hurt feelings.

"Shut the fuck up!" The roar comes from the door, and I jump from its fury. I look in the direction it came from, but Sam is already standing in front of Mark, his shoulders rising and falling rapidly. The muscles in his back show off their perfection in his tense stance, ready for action. If I look closely enough, I'm sure I could actually see steam rising from his body.

"What?" Mark whispers incredulously.

"Shut the fuck *up!*" Sam ends on yet another roar.

Every normal person would be at a safe house somewhere by now, but not Mark. No. His mouth slowly forms an easy smile, and in a carefree voice, he says, "Sam, brother, calm down. We're here to have a good time."

I watch fascinated as Sam's hands form into fists and his shoulders stop their path up and down, staying up all the way to his ears. "HP."

In this situation, those two whispered letters don't make any sense to me, but hearing them, Mark loses his smile and takes a step back. "What?"

"HP," Sam repeats.

"What's that mean?" someone voices my thoughts.

"Home, people," Mark explains, still looking at Sam like he suddenly replaced his nose with a doorknob. "Buddy, why are you saying the code? It's only in case of an emergency. We don't ever say that aloud. Ever!"

"This is an emergency, because if you don't walk out that door in the next five seconds, you won't be able to walk at all."

Mark's eyes fly briefly to me then back to Sam. "What?"

"That is my girl you were spouting shit at. You don't *ever* do that. I'll give you this one pass since you didn't know and you don't think past how to get your dick wet. But you are looking at my future wife. And from now on, only she has unlimited access to this place. Only she can come unannounced. From now on, this place or wherever I will live and be in the future is hers and hers alone. And if you don't become one with the program, apologize, and give her the respect she deserves, you'll be banished and eventually forgotten, *brother*."

As he listens to Sam, Mark's face gets increasingly redder, and with squinty eyes, he looks at me. "You—"

"Careful," Sam interrupts him, crossing his arms on his chest. He's standing between Mark and me, like a guard protecting his queen from harm. Once Mark takes in his posture, he closes his mouth and gives me a look so full of malice that it burns my skin. Obviously done with this, Sam repeats for the third time, "HP."

Indecision written all over his face, Mark only keeps looking between the two of us, and just as Sam takes a step forward, a small, delicate hand appears on Mark's wrist. "Let's go," a girl whispers, looking up at him with big brown eyes. He glances down at her, ready to say something, and by the look on his face, it won't be pretty. But then his eyes go huge and his frame turns to stone.

"We're sorry for the interruption. It won't happen again. Bye," she tells Sam, not looking at him but instead his shoulder. It's obvious she's scared and wants to get out of here.

When Mark still doesn't move, she tugs on his wrist, looks at him once again, and in a firm tone says, "Move."Then she turns around and drags him out. The funny thing is, she doesn'thave to pull too much. As soon as she starts to leave and the distance begins stretching their arms, threatening to sever the connection between them, he immediately starts walking, still wearing that dazed look all over his face.

Watching him follow her like a lost puppy, I can't help but chuckle a little, which quickly morphs into a surprised yelp when two hands push me back onto the couch.

"I'm sorry all that happened, honey. I promise I'll talk to him."

The remorseful look on his face tugs at my heart. I know he's sorry, but most importantly, he's in pain that his friend won't let him carry on with his life. Mark's still stuck in that space every guy is at some point in his life; the only thing on his mind is when and where he can have a good time. The thing is, Sam is past that point and is now looking at his future.

"I have a feeling he'll come around," I whisper, even though the look on Mark's face when he finally stopped being an ass long enough to see who was holding him was priceless and made my stomach hurt from holding in laughter.

"You don't know Mark. He's like a baby that refuses to grow up," Sam states.

I put a hand on the side of his face and watch my thumb gliding over his five o'clock shadow right to the corner of his lips, enjoying the prickling sensation. I can't believe after all this time, after the pain and the unbelievable happiness this man caused, he's mine. I can do this, I can lie underneath him and touch him without fear of rejection. I don't have to calculate if it'll expose my feelings for him and be unwelcomed by him. Because now I know everything is welcome. He wants this as much as I do; he finally tore down those walls that were surrounding him and let me see all that's inside him. And because of that, I can see his friend's behavior hurt him.

"Trust me, he's going to come around," I stress, bringing his face closer to mine.

"How can you be so sure?"

I can't help but smile a little. I've never seen this side of him—the insecure little boy who is afraid he'll lose his best friend. "Didn't you see his expression when he finally had a good look at the girl next to him?"

"What girl?"

"Clearly, you didn't see her, but trust me. He's going to learn his lesson, and soon."

"What are you up to?" The suspicion and amusement battles on his face, but he starts to relax.

"Me? Nothing. But Mark, he's about to go on the ride of his life," I say, letting out an evil little chuckle. It's going to be fun watching him try to get the girl who won't give him the time of day.

"No, tell me. You know something."

"Yes, I do," I confirm. "Every person who saw his face knows. But I have another important question." I take his face in my hands, and, holding his head steady, I ask in a mock seriousness, "Fuckland?"

Groaning, he closes his eyes and tries to drop his head to hide his face in my neck, but I don't let him. Sighing, he opens his eyes and quietly admits, "I told you they only had one thing in mind. And since I'm the only one not living with parents, this place was free rein." With every word leaving his mouth, his face is getting more embarrassed, and by the time the last word becomes audible, he's not looking at me anymore. Instead, he's looking at the armrest of the couch near my head.

"Maybe we should put a sign above your door and let everybody know what the kingdom is called," I tease. I can't help it; his face is priceless right now.

"No, those days are over," he proclaims with all seriousness.

"What?" I gasp. "Are you trying to tell me there will be no sex in here anymore?" Pushing him off me, I sit up and keep with my stern and serious play. Pointing my finger in his face, I move it closer with my every word. "No! I didn't sign up for this. You are not trying to tell me that now, when I finally have unlimited access to your cock whenever and however I want, you decide there's not going to be any sex here. No, that is unacceptable." By the time I'm finished with my little speech, Sam's eyes are turned inward, looking at my finger nearly touching the tip of his nose. "In fact, I want it right now."

"You want it right now?" he repeats, looking so adorably confused.

Swallowing my laughter, I lean into him. "No, I demand it."

"You demand it?"

His bewilderment is starting to become less adorable and more irritating, since this whole playing with him is kind of turning me on and he needs to get with the program. "Yes, since I am the queen of Fuckland, I demand it."

The light of understanding finally sparks in his green eyes, and with a slight smirk, he teases me back. "You may be the queen, baby, but that is only because I am the king."

Putting my lips near his ear, I whisper, "That's true, but we all know the queen has the king's ear, and in the end, he does whatever she wishes." And with that, I kiss the king of my heart. And a little while later, the queen's wish comes true.

Present
Sam

He stands in their room listening to the shower going.

I want a divorce.

Those words circle in an endless loop in his head, torturing him.

I want a divorce.

166

He looks to their bed, the same bed he left her in this morning, giving her a sweet kiss before going to make their morning coffee. She'd given him a tender smile when he'd handed her the mug.

I want a divorce.

Looking at their nightstands, he can see the picture frames standing proudly on them, exposing their love. He looks back to the bed, trying to trace back to the last time they were actually together. The last time they had sex, made love. He can't recall. Or at least, he can't remember the time when Dani was his Dani. Sure of herself, knowing what she wanted and needed. Going so far as to sometimes—when she was so into it, so into what they were doing—demand it. She's trying to pull away from him. He thought that, because of the changes in her body, she was shy and, for some insane reason, insecure, shutting down his every attempt to connect with his wife, and avoiding his touch. But that's not it. She's pulling back so she can break away completely.

I want a divorce.

His eyes going back to the bathroom door, he doesn't see it. Instead, he sees his wife. He can picture her standing under the shower, the water cascading down on her beautiful, naked body. He can't remember how long it'd been since he had his hands on that body. How long it's been since he had his lips on it, his tongue and his cock inside her.

Christ, just thinking about it gets him hard. To actually have all of that again?

It would be a dream come true.

I want a divorce.

Years ago, he had to win a war with himself. He thought he didn't want what she was promising to be. What that promise had the capacity to become. His wife, the mother of his children, his *life.* And, just like her, he was prepared to push her away, to set her on the path *he* thought was right for *her.* But he was wrong. And now, Dani was wrong. He didn't want a divorce. He didn't want to find another woman, to try to start building a life with her, a family. The mere thought turned his stomach; it was so repulsing.

No one could, nor ever would, replace Dani.

She's his. And now, he has to remind her of that.

Silently, he goes to the bathroom. After taking his clothes off, he stands there watching her.

She has her back to him. She either didn't hear him or she's too far in her head to even acknowledge him. Looking at her, he feels anger coursing through his veins. How could she try to tear them apart? How could she deny him her body, mind, everything that is her?

How could she question his attraction to her?

Looking at her naked form, he sees the changes in her body, the changes that stand as evidence of the hell she's gone through. And those changes are the most beautiful thing he's ever seen, and he feels pride in knowing she's his. His to touch, his to love.

The psychological changes are the ones he has to conquer.

And standing here, looking at her body, that body of what dreams are made of, he decides he has to fuck his wife. He's going to fuck her until that foul word—*divorce*—is erased from his mind. And he's going to fuck her until it never again enters her brain.

He walks to the shower and, opening the glass door, he gets in with her. As she looks at him over her left shoulder, he sees her eyes get big, her body tensing, and her arms flying up to cover her breasts. Her much fuller breasts, which, since it all started, she's never let him explore. He's going to change that now. "Don't move." He comes closer to her, his front hitting her wet back, his arms taking hers and forcing them down.

"W-what?" she whispers.

"I said, do not move," he growls.

He entwines his fingers with hers, bringing her closer still, and looks over her shoulder and down her body, taking his fill.

"What are you doing?" she murmurs.

His eyes slowly making their way up, he looks into her eyes, saying, "I'm taking back what's mine."

Swallowing, she repeats, "What?"

Turning her to face him, he can't help it; his eyes swept her again from head to toe, enjoying the view immensely, and his hard cock grows rock-solid. His eyes coming back to hers, he takes a deep breath, and in a firm tone, one that makes his statement sound like a command, he says, "We are not getting a divorce."

Hearing his words, her breath hitches, causing her chest to pause on the upward glide of her inhale. She stares at him like he suddenly has two heads, and she whispers, "You can't decide that."

He puts his hands on her hips, and squeezing, he holds her firmly. "Yes, I can. Just like you tried to decide all on your own that we are."

She doesn't say anything, just keeps blinking, the water from the shower falling down her face.

He moves her to get out from under the spray and kisses her forehead. With his lips there, he says, "We're not perfect, but we're perfect for each other. And I'll be damned if I let anyone take you away from me. And that includes you." Her body jolts at his words, and he leans away to look at her face. Seeing the tears there, he swipes them with his thumb. "So get this stupid idea out of your head. And don't repeat it. Don't even think about it." He pauses, looking into her eyes to ensure that what he's saying penetrates. "Ever."

CHAPTER EIGHTEEN

*"**I VOW TO** you that you will have all of my love and devotion, in the good times and the bad, in sickness and in health, until forever."*

Dani

"Ever." The word still ringing in my head, I feel his hands squeezing my waist, his thumbs making circles on my hipbones.

"What're you doing?" I breathe when his hands start wandering all over my body, his eyes following their movement.

"Claiming my wife back," he says, his tone harsh and firm, like it's coming from somewhere deep inside. His eyes stop following the movement of his hands and start traveling up my body, and just as they came to mine, his hand slides between my legs, his finger hitting the perfect spot. Then, it starts moving, and I stop thinking. My arms move on their own, enveloping him in them, my fingers caressing the skin of his back. The moment my fingertips touch him, the muscles on his back contract and goose bumps rise, following the shiver that goes through him.

"You okay, baby?" I whisper, putting my lips at his ear, my breath hitching, my whole body shuddering from the wicked movement of his finger.

"Oh, yeah," he murmurs, and gliding his lips from my neck and down my chest, when I shudder one more time, the movement makes my chest tip up to meet his lips. "Fuck, yeah." He takes my nipple into his mouth, sucking deep.

The added feel of him doing that, when his finger never stops making little circles and figure eights on my clit, it's so glorious that I arch my back more, and moan, "Oh, God." My fingertips become palms on his back, gliding through the wetness on his skin, up to his hair, where they become fists, and I push his head to me more, so the pull will be deeper.

Suddenly, he releases my nipple and puts his hand on the back of my neck, looking deep in my eyes. The look in his is feral. Then I lose his finger, and just as I open my mouth to demand it back, he slides two inside me. My muscles contract, trying to pull them deeper. Little stars start dancing at the edge of my vision, and I know it's coming, and it's gonna be huge.

I make the mistake of sliding one of my hands down his chest and belly and taking him in my hand. At the feel of his hardness, I have a brief vision of taking him into my mouth, and it makes me whimper, "Sam."

I don't get more than one pump before his hand wraps around my wrist and dislodges it, and I'm turned around, the cold tiles hitting my back.

"Hey!" I snap, but it comes out breathy.

"Hey, baby," he murmurs, a small smile dancing on his lips.

"Give it back," I demand, trying to evade his arms, which are blocking my access to him, since they're sliding from my waist to my ass.

"In a sec," he says. And then I'm up, my legs around him, and he's inside me.

Feeling him deep in my core, I arch my back again and throw my head back, hitting his palm that's preventing my head from colliding with the tiles, and I moan, "Sam."

"Here, Dani," he mutters, putting pressure on the back of my head, tipping my face down, and he takes my mouth in a deep, long kiss.

He starts moving, fast and hard, going deep. Not being able to breathe, the thrusts coming faster, making my head swim, I break the kiss and press my cheek to his.

Opening my eyes, I see us in the mirror through the foggy glass. I can see the muscles in his back, ass, and thighs contracting with his intense movement, with his every hard thrust. The dance they make is mesmerizing, beyond erotic. The paleness of the skin on my legs wrapped around his waist is in stark contrast to the tan of his. His dark head is next to mine, and when I move one of my hands into his hair, it glides to my neck.

Then, I look at the reflection of my eyes, and for the first time after a long time, in them I can see the girl I was when I married this man peeking through. The woman I was before we started this journey and got on the road of IVF. There're no shadows in them, no pain, just the hooded look of a woman climbing up, up, until she reaches the peek and then shatters into a million extraordinary pieces, only to be put back together by her lover.

Entranced by all that is displayed in the mirror, I slide my hand down between our bodies and touch myself. And that's it. I shatter once again. I close my eyes and throw my head back, opening my mouth in a silent scream.

Coming down, I feel his hands squeezing me almost painfully, his thrusts going faster and harder. I take one more peek at the mirror, and seeing the image is still as beautiful as it was a few minutes ago, I start to glide my hands along his back, watching them in the mirror. Then I open my mouth, and with the tip of my tongue, I start collecting the drops on his shoulder. The taste of the water mixed with his sweat makes me tremble in the hot shower. His mouth opens on my neck, and he bites it, and with the final drive, he groans, pulling my hips into his.

We don't move. Just breathe, recovering. With me still wrapped around him, he looks at me, and with steel in his voice, he says, "You're mine."

He doesn't give me the chance to say anything. He gently slides out and puts me on my feet. Then he guides me under the spray and washes me. The feel of his hands massaging my scalp and the glide of them over my body takes me deeper into the mellow zone the climax put me in. When he's satisfied that the job is done, he gently pushes me out of the spray and steps under it. After washing himself, he turns off the water, gets out of the shower, taking me with him, and after drying me with the towel, he takes my hand and guides me into the bedroom and to the bed.

Once in it, he flicks the covers over us, and with the hand over my waist, he pulls me into him and rolls halfway on top of me, giving me his weight.

After he has us positioned, he sighs and murmurs, "Sleep, honey."

I don't say a word, just lie there and enjoy the feel of my husband's comforting embrace and the heat seeping into my body. And before I know it, I'm nearly asleep, so I barely hear it when he whispers, "Don't ever try to leave me again." And with one last kiss in my hair, he follows me to sleep.

CHAPTER NINETEEN

"*I* *LOVE YOU in the good times, but my love for you in the bad is endless. You're everything to me. You're my whole world. Everything I'm doing is to make our lives better, so you can breathe easier. The day begins and ends with you. You're the light at the end of the tunnel.*"

I wake up confused.

Naked and confused.

There's something pushing me down into the mattress, and the drowsiness of sleep flies only for the panic to set in. My body tenses in preparation to throw the covers off me and run. But then that weight shifts, and I'm pulled deeper into something.

Something warm.

Then, that something sighs, the breath stirring the hair at my nape, and I realize it isn't something, but someone. Someone important.

My husband.

At first, I relax, soaking in his warmth, but then the events from the night before start floating in, and the fact that, after so long, he's holding me in his arms. So, when the words that left my mouth the day before start echoing in my brain, and the warmth seeping into my body, reminding me of just how much I missed being held by Sam, I feel ashamed.

I feel ashamed because my first thought wasn't that my husband was holding me, but that someone came in while I was sleeping and was holding me hostage. I completely forgot my husband, and in my mind, I've already left him.

It's also because, even though I miss our connection and our closeness terribly, I still want a divorce.

And I'm ashamed, because in order for Sam to see reason and accept the fact that he has to let me go to find someone to make his dreams come true, I'll have to hurt him.

The only problem is, I don't know how, and I don't know if I have it in me to do something to hurt him badly enough to leave me behind.

So, suddenly uncomfortable, I gently scoot to the edge of the bed and run.

I flee from my own room, and I leave my husband behind.

Later, I'm standing at the kitchen counter, putting the finishing touches on breakfast and mentally going over my speech, which I plan to calmly but firmly deliver to Sam to make him see that we have to get a divorce, when I sense I'm not alone.

I look over my shoulder and see Sam standing at the bottom of the steps, his arms crossed over his chest, glaring at the couch in our living room. After a few seconds, his eyes find me in the kitchen, and deep surprise washes over his face before, quickly, he hides it.

"Morning, baby," he says quietly, like he's nervous anything louder than that willscare me and send me running.

The sad thing is, he's right. Hearing his words, every cell in my muscles starts vibrating, making them burn from the battle between fleeing and standing still.

I close my eyes, reminding myself I have to do this, and once again repeat my speech in my mind. I manage to beat down the urge to run, and, looking at our meal, I whisper, "Hey." Putting the plates on the breakfast bar, I summon all my courage and ask, "You want breakfast?"

The surprise that was on Sam's face a few moments ago makes a brief appearance, and then it's gone just as fast. "Yeah," he can't hide the gravel in his voice, but he tries to mask it with a cough, making my heart split in two since I know now is the time to deliver the killing blow to our marriage. The only problem is, I'm not sure I can manage it. But I sure as hell am going to try. For him. For his chance at happiness and making his dreams come true one way or the other. Walking to the bar, he throws one more nasty look to the couch before he takes a seat.

"I need to tell you something. And I need you to listen to me. Really listen," I start my speech.

"Sure, but first, come here and say good morning," he interrupts, even before I can properly start.

"I already did."

"Not the way I want you to." He looks at me, his green eyes boring into my brown ones, and in them I see curiosity with amusement swimming around.

"Huh?" I ask, confused. What the hell does that mean? And then, as the images from our night, of our life before this road started, come pouring in, the light dawns, and I look away. "Umm…," I mumble, feeling shy for some reason. How could I feel shy? This is the man I spent the last six years with, the man who has seen me in every embarrassing situation, and judging by last night, he still wants me. But then, freed from the magic of his eyes, I remember the talk I have in mind, and even though I want to give him what he's asking for, I know I can't.

"Damn, you're cute." He chuckles.

"What?" I look back at him.

"Nothing, come here." He turns sideways on the stool, spreading his legs. And just like that, I'm under his spell again, so I go without a peep.

When I'm within reaching distance, his arms come around my waist, and he hauls me into him, plastering me all over him.

Then he kisses me.

And it's not a peck on the lips. It's not a kiss with a little touch of the tongue. It's a full-blown make-out, foreplay, I'll-get-you-naked-in-thirty-seconds kiss. His tongue touches my lips, extending the same invitation he gave so many years ago—to come out and play—and just like then, I open my mouth almost on instinct. I know better; I vividly remember what that invitation means. Hell, until recently, I lived the beautiful aftermath of it. And still, I open my mouth and welcome everything he's offering.

Once he gains access, he doesn't wait for me to meet him halfway. He doesn't lightly or slowly enter my mouth. He surges in.

The moment his tongue touches mine, a moan flows from my mouth and into his, and his hands start moving. One goes up my back to my neck, leaving goosebumps in its trail, spanning it with his palm, and his thumb puts pressure at the spot behind my ear to tilt my head, positioning it how he wants it. Just a tilt to the right angle so he can get better access. The other travels the short path from the small of my back to my ass, and it squeezes.

That gets another, louder moan.

The night before, I knew I missed him, but right in this moment, I realize I've really missed him.

That's why my hand goes into his hair, the other across his back, and I squeeze him in my arms with all the strength in me. Taking a deep breath, I savor the return of my favorite smell in the world. My husband.

Too soon, I feel his hands at my sides as they gently push me away. With his mouth still on mine, he says, "I love what we're doing, baby, and where this is heading, but we have to stop or else we're never gonna do what we have to do today."

"What do we have to do today?" I ask, confused since it's Sunday.

"First, we have to throw out that couch, and then we're going to the park to meet Mark and Amy."

Hearing his plans, I clear my throat and take a step back. "Sam—" I try to restart my speech, the fog from the kiss clearing, but he interrupts me once again.

"Eat your breakfast, baby. We don't have much time."

I can see hope in his eyes. Hope and happiness. And that is why I decide I will give him today, the last day of us being an us, and that I'd talk to him in the evening. So, all I say is "Okay, Sam."

***

Throughout the day, he's constantly touching or kissing me. He's never too far away from me. And when we're at the park, watching the guys goof around, I keep stealing glances at Amy, wishing I'm the one who was pregnant. Wishing I'm the one who, every once in a while, looks down at my swollen belly with a dreamy sigh leaving my mouth. And wishing I'm the one who starts giggling and rubbing a spot on my belly, murmuring, "That was a good kick."

On the way home, my resolve only gets stronger, because I know Sam deserves that. I know he deserves the quiet moments of looking at his wife doing all those things Amy did, with the look of endless gentleness on his face, like the one Mark was wearing when he looked at her.

But when we get home, instead of making dinner or just turning on the TV and ordering takeout, Sam takes my hand and guides me to the bedroom. And after he's done with me, I'm too exhausted and too satisfied to talk, so I promise myself that I'll do it the next morning, and promptly go to sleep.

***

The next morning, I'm in the shower, nervous about my first day back to work after all this time, and the fact I still have to go over my speech and make Sam listen to reason, when I hear the glass door open. I look up, and there is Sam standing in front of me. He has his hand wrapped around his hard shaft, pumping. I become entranced with the upward and downward movement, so when he says, "Turn around and spread your legs, baby," I do as he demands without a peep.

By the time he lets me get out of the shower, the coffee that is waiting for me by the sink is cold. It's only after I go to work and put my purse in the desk drawer that I remember, once again, I didn't deliver my rehearsed speech. So, I decide that night I'll do it, and nothing in the world is going to stop me.

***

Sitting in my car, my hand holding the key ready to start my car and get home, I look up and see a man exiting the building. I pause and think back to the surprise meeting with the principal. He came before the last period and asked me to come talk to him after the kids were gone. I've been back to work for three weeks now, and for the life of me, I couldn't understand what had I done wrong in that time that would require a talk with my boss.

When I knocked on his office door, I was a nervous wreck. It's never good when you have to report to the principal, no matter what age you are. But when he said, "We're concerned, Dani. Maybe you came back to work too soon." I was thankful he offered me a seat. "The kids told their parents that you're sad most of the time, and quite often you look out the window and it takes them several tries to get your attention. As you can imagine, the parents came to me and are demanding we resolve whatever is going on with you."

"What?" I whispered, shocked. I never knew I was losing focus at work.

"Maybe it would be better if, for the time being, we transfer you to the library, just until you get better."

"No, I promise I won't do that anymore," I said, putting my hand on his desk and leaning into it. "Please, don't take my kids away from me."

"Dani—"he started, an uncomfortable look on his face.

"Please, I'll talk to the parents, explain things. And you can sit in on my classes for some time, until you're sure I won't do it again."

He looked at me for a moment, assessing me, and then he cleared his throat. "All right, until the end of this week, I'll pop in from time to time just to check that everything is as it should be. And if everything is good, I'll talk to the parents and assure them there's nothing to worry about."

"Thank you," I said, ready to fall to my knees and kiss the man's feet.

My phone ringing startles me back to the present. I fish the cell out of my purse, and seeing it's Sam calling, I answer with "Hey, honey."

"Where are you?" He sounds irritated.

"I'm at the school parking lot. I'm just about to head home."

"Is everything okay?"

"I had a meeting with the principal," I reply.

"Why?" Concern laces his voice.

"The parents contacted him about my behavior lately. Apparently, I space out a lot, and it started freaking out the kids." I still can't believe it was happening. Sure, I've lost time when I was home, but I didn't think it spilled over into work.

"Baby" is all Sam says.

"It'll be okay. He decided to give me one more chance."

"I know it will be all right. We'll have you back to you in no time," he assures me. "Now, come home. We have a couch to buy."

"We wouldn't if you hadn't decided to throw out our perfectly good one," I chide.

"I couldn't stand the look of it for a second longer. Now, hurry up." And with that, he hangs up.

* * *

That night, after the fun at the furniture store, the belly full of Chinese food, and three gin and tonics, all I do is pass out, my speech once again, as it has been for the last three weeks, forgotten.

***

And for the next two weeks, I keep putting it off. It feels like we are discovering one another all over again. Falling in love with each other once more. Every morning, he comes into the shower with me, and every night, he makes love to me. But whenever I start talking to him, he either touches me or kisses me, or does both of those things, which then leads to other, more fun activities. Or he puts me in the car and takes me to dinner, movies, or some other place I mentioned in passing. He keeps me on the move so much that I don't have time to be locked in my head.

And then, I'm not putting it off anymore. I forget all about it.

Until I bump into Brooke.

***

Two months after Sam forbid me to divorce him, I'm walking down the street, phone to my ear, listening to Marcy try to avoid meeting me, when I bump into someone. "Oh! I'm sorry!" I say, lifting my hand to steady the person. My hand freezes midair as I get a look at them.

"Dani, are you okay?" Marcy asks in my ear at the same time Brooke breathes, "Dani."

"Brooke," I whisper. I haven't seen her since that lunch. It seems like it was a lifetime ago, since so much has happened, but then again, it has been six months.

"That bitch!" Marcy screeches in my ear, making me jump. "Where are you? I'm coming."

"Marcy, I have to go," I speak into the phone.

"No, don't you dare. I have some hair to pull out. Just tell me where you are!" is the last thing I hear before I end the call.

"How are you?" Brooke asks.

"Okay. And you?" I ask back, even though I don't want to know. I don't want to be standing here in the middle of the street with her. She was once one of my best friends, and now, I can't stand looking at her.

"I'm fine." The tears in her eyes tell a different story.

"Are you sure?" I ask.

"Yeah." Taking a deep breath, she rushes out, "I'm so sorry, Dani. I miss you."

"I miss you too." And it's the truth. She hurt me deeply, and for right now, I can't be anywhere near her, can't stand looking at her since it reminds me of the last time we were together. Of the words that came out of her mouth. But I still miss my friend.

"Can we go back?" The hope in her tone is blinding.

"I hope so," I admit, but still unable or ready to. I want to go home, to be with my husband, but the moment my eyes landed on Brooke, the doubts and questions started to pour back in. "I have to go. I'm sorry. But... yeah... I have to go," I finish lamely and walk by her.

"I'll talk to you soon," she calls to my back, her hope still lingering.

I turn around, and unable to stop myself, ask her, "Do you remember what I asked you to think about?" When that hope vanishes from her face, I have my answer, but I still ask after she nods, "What would you do?"

"I don't know," she admits.

"And from the bottom of my heart, I honestly hope you never have to find out." Then I turn around and walk to my car, her look of shock burned into my brain.

***

Later, sitting in my car, I look at the fairy-tale picture the church makes in the evening, thinking about everything and nothing, when the door opens.

"How did you know where to find me?" I ask Sam when he's settled in.

"Marcy called."

I can feel him facing me, looking me over, worry radiating from him.

"I wanted to talk to you for so long," I say toward the church.

He chuckles. "I know."

"But you kept distracting me." I turn to him and see he's wearing a mischievous little grin.

"You weren't hard to distract."

"I know," I whisper, smiling in return.

"What are you thinking?"

"Nothing much," I admit. "But then again, everything."

"I don't get it."

"You will," I assure him. I know he isn't ready to hear what I want to do next. I know he fought hard to get me back to me, and the smallest possibility of me going back to that dark place could make him refuse to even talk about my decision. But I need him to be on the same page as me because I can't do it alone. And seeing Brooke today made the desire come back full force.

"What do you want to do now?" he asks when I take his hand in mine.

Placing a kiss on it, with my lips on his skin, I whisper, "I want to go home."

***

I answer the phone, excited to hear all about Jules's adventures, since the situation in Denver is heating up, but when I hear the hitching sound followed by the broken "Dani," all the excitement is momentarily replaced with dread.

"What's wrong?" The panic coursing through my body makes me tremble, and I run to the garage to find my suitcase, so I can start packing and get on the first flight to Denver.

"He-he-he proposed!" she wails.

Pulling the sheet from the mountain of stuff that it was hiding, I ask, "Who?"

"He proposed to that awful woman."

I don't comment. Don't ask for clarification. I'm too shocked with the sight that is in front of me. Instead of all the things that I expected to find under the sheet, there is a crib. It's a work of art. Painted a deep chocolate brown, it has swirls carved in it. It is everything I want a crib to be, and more. It looks exactly like the one from my vision. The one I described to Sam, down to the very last detail. And I finally have my answer what Sam was doing, cooped up in the garage all those months ago. And that is why I whisper brokenly, "Sam."

"No, don't tell Sam!" Jules screams in my ear. "He'll come here and make everything worse. It's going to be okay. I just have to move to a different city."

"Oh, Jules. Don't do that. First, you have to calm down." After one last look, I pull the sheet back over it, making sure the whole crib is covered so nothing can damage its magnificence.

"I can't calm down. He proposed." She goes back to crying.

"Come home for a weekend, and we'll figure everything out. Just please, stop crying, since I can't hug you or feed you or pour liquor in you," I try to joke, still looking at the crib, now covered under a sheet, longing filling me. "Just don't do anything rash."

"Yeah, okay." She says the words, but I have a feeling she won't do as I asked. And time will tell I was right.

***

Later that evening, with my discovery in mind, I tell Sam about my decision. "I want to try again."

"Try what?"

"I want to try the IVF again," I clarify.

The only thing he says is "No," and he gets up from the table and walks away.

I wait for him to come back, and then first thing I ask him is "Did you finish the crib?" Once the words leave my mouth, I know I did the wrong thing. I never should have let him know I knew it even existed. The look on his face goes so dark it's scary. But, not being very smart, I don't back down. I keep asking the same questions over and over. "Why did you build the crib? Why, if you're not going to let us try again?" But he just keeps standing at the threshold, looking at me, his jaw ticking. So, after going at it for over an hour, with no answer from Sam, I can't take it anymore. And once again, I am the one who storms out of the house and, for the hundredth time, leave my husband behind. I go to my mom, and with my head in her lap, I tell her everything.

***

After I'm done, she keeps playing with my hair, making my eyes cross it feels so good. "Aren't you gonna say anything?" I ask. My mother has an opinion on everything, and she isn't afraid to let you know it. So for her to be silent is beyond strange.

"About your fight? No. About how to make Sam see reason and go your way? No, he's your husband, and you're the one who has to

183

make him bend." She pats my head. "But I will tell you one thing. There's no possible way on this earth for you not to be a mother." I turn, my head still in her lap, to look up at her. "Since you were a little girl, at that age when adults ask kids what they want to be when they grow up, you always said you wanted to be a mom. And when I asked you if you'll stay with me forever and ever, you always said no, because you were gonna find yourself a good husband, but not to worry, you'd visit me and bring all your babies with you."

I keep looking up at her. This is the first time I'm hearing about this, and I have no memory of it. I remember saying I would grow up and be a teacher, but I don't remember this part. Good news is, at least some of my wishes came true.

"So you see, I know it has to happen, because you were born to be a mother. And if I know one thing about my daughter, it's that, when she wants something, she never gives up." Her thumb catches the tears that are leaking silently from my eyes, down the side of my face, and into my hair. "When in doubt, just remember the whole start of your relationship with Sam," she whispers, letting me know she knows it all.

***

After my mom made everything better and filled my belly with delicious food, I go home and don't say a word to Sam about any of it. Neither do I mention the crib again. I can feel him watching me, night after night, as I stand in the empty space of our nursery looking out at the stars. I know he stands in the hallway, waiting for me beyond the open door. We don't talk about him not coming in, and we never speak a word about my gazing at the sky. But I know my husband's soul, and I know the need for a baby is growing, the wish for it almost as strong as mine. And it won't be long before he gets on board.

***

Phone calls in the middle of the night are never good news. Every person on this planet knows this. So when my phone starts playing a current favorite of mine, "The Story" by Brandi Carlile, Sam all but rolls over me, trying to get to it. He knows I'm able to have an entire conversation and still turn around and go right back to sleep, with no memory of said conversation or the fact that somewhere, there's a person waiting for me as I agreed to meet with them. More than once, I've gotten an angry call from Marcy, my mom, or Jules, yelling at me about how they'd been waiting for over two hours, coffee cold and the breakfast eaten, and I was a no-show. You would think, since these are the people closest to me, they would have learned by now, but no. They swear I sound alert enough to think I have been awake for at least an hour. That is why, any time I'm in bed or taking a nap, Sam's quick to answer the call, as he's this time, in the middle of the night, since he knows any information relayed is probably important but I'll likely just go back to sleep, not even knowing I answered the phone.

"Yeah?" Sam mumbles, still on top of me, his lips pressing into my hair as he listens. I feel his body getting tenser by the second, but all I can think of right now is the fact that, for the last two months, I've had his weight pressing down on me, deeper into the bed, giving me warmth, and once again making me feel loved.

In the beginning, I was sure I would notice if that weight went away, if he was no longer holding me throughout the night. I would miss it so much; it would be like someone cut off my limb, and I would not be able to sleep or function until I did everything in my power to get it back. Then, it went away. As the IVF started and I lost myself in the process, he stopped holding meand doing countless little things that mean the world to me. And I didn't notice. But now, thankfully, I have it back.

And it was completely my fault he stopped.

I pushed repeatedly, until I shoved him far enough that he couldn't reach me anymore. And then, two months ago, I pushed him over the limit, and he was determined to break down all the walls that I spent so much time building. The sad fact is, I didn't even know I was doing it; I was so lost in despair.

My breakthrough and comeback to my old self didn't come over night. It took me weeks, and I still carry the pain with me. There are still instances that it shines through and blinds me in its intensity, but those moments are further and further apart, and now I have ways to cope.

But the worst of all was I didn't know how to act toward Sam, especially the morning after I said those hideous words.

I shouldn't have to worry.

After all, this is Sam.

His body wound tight on top of mine, he shouts into the phone, "Right! We're on our way." Sam ends the call and throws the phone back on the nightstand.

"Who was it?" I ask drowsily, coming out of my memory of the past two months.

"Mark. We have to meet them at the hospital. Amy's in labor." At the first mention of Mark, I started to wiggle my way out from under my husband, and when the last word left his mouth, I'm on the floor, on all fours, tapping the carpet, trying to find the clothes Sam took off me last night when we went to bed.

"Baby, what're you doing?" he asks, perplexed.

"Trying to get dressed!" I snap. "But you threw my clothes all over the room, and I can't find them."

I can hear him moving around the bedroom, and then the light comes on, blinding me. "Will this help?" His body is vibrating, and it takes me a minute to figure out he's trying to swallow down his laughter.

"Are you laughing?"

"No." He turns his back to me to put on his own clothes, but I see the movement in his shoulders and back.

"Stop laughing!" I demand, peeking under the bed and fishing my bra out.

He turns and puts his shirt on. "As much as I like the view, I can't do anything about it now, so quit goofing around and let's go."

Five minutes later, we're in our car and on the way to the hospital to meet the new addition to our family.

CHAPTER
TWENTY

"_**T**_**HERE'RE ONLY TWO** things a man chooses in life. His best man and the woman he's going to marry." He removes his right hand from the wheel and, taking mine, he briefly looks at me. "And I chose you." Looking back at the road, he turns the blinker on. "I love you." And turning right, he drives us home._

We meet Mark and Amy at the entrance to the ER.

I rush to her and take her free had in mine. Her other one is held tightly in Mark's. "Are you okay?"

"Oh yeah, I'm fi—" But then her response turns into a loud, painful moan as she takes our hands, pushes them to her stomach, and squats a little. A few seconds after, she stands up straight, smiles at me, and finishes, "Fine."

"We should probably take you inside," I say, giving her my other hand to hold onto, as I shake out the one she was holding when the contraction started.

"Give me that," Sam demands, and takes the bag from Mark. Throwing it over his shoulder, he turns around and marches in, leaving us behind.

"Sam!" I yell after him. "Where are you going?"

"To the delivery room. Where else?" he asks me, confused.

"Umm…honey, you're not the one in labor," I tell him, tipping my head to Amy.

"Oh, right!" Rushing back, he pushes me out of the way, takes Amy's hand, and he and Mark then carry her into the ER, her legs trying to walk on air.

After she's all settled into the room, the baby monitor whooshing the heartbeats throughout the space, I look down and see

Mark has his shoes on the wrong feet. "What happened there?" I indicate to his feet.

"He couldn't find his shoes," Amy mumbles between crunches of ice. "And then, when I told him he was holding them in his hand, he was shaking too hard to put them on his feet. So, being the darling I am, I helped him."

At the sound of our laughter, he asks, "What?"

"Bud, you put them on wrong. Switch them and you're good." I'm laughing so hard I can't stand up straight, but when the whooshing starts to go faster and a moan spills from Amy's mouth, we all go quiet. Watching that line on the monitor reaching its peak then slowly going down is pure torture, since there's nothing we can do to make this easier for her. We can only stand there and watch.

***

It's been hours, ten of them to be exact. And still no baby.

After hearing the screams, the crying, and the swearing, Amy threw Mark out and called him back in seven times. But this last time, I think is the one, since we can clearly hear her scream, "You did this to me, you fucker! I'm never doing this again. If you want another child, you have to give birth to it yourself!" Then, nothing, until a small cry pierces the air.

I look at Sam, and whisper, "She did it."

Looking at me, he swallows. "Yeah, she did."

"It's a girl!" Mark bellows, standing in the open door. And seeing him, all the fatigue, the hunger, the pain that Amy has inflicted on our hands and arms is forgotten. All that is left is pure joy.

***

"Guys, meet Emma," Amy whispers, not looking away from the precious bundle in her arms. She's in the hospital bed, and even though she's visibly exhausted, there's a light shining from her. And I realize she's glowing from satisfaction, from happiness, from knowing that, right at this moment, she found the reason for her being on this earth, living the life she leads, and it is all summed up in one tiny little being. Her baby daughter. And as much as it shames me, I can't help the hot wave of jealousy that spikes through my body.

Leaning over, I take a peek at the chubby face. "She's beautiful!"

"Do you want to hold her?" Amy extends her arms to me.

Carefully, I fold my hands under hers. For the first time in my life, I have the weight of a baby pressing down on my arms. I can feel the fragility of her, and smell the most perfect scent in the whole universe. And I know it's time for us to try again.

I want so badly to give Sam this moment, to give *us* this moment. To give us the future that lays before our friends, the joy of raising a child.

"We wanted to ask you something." I look at Amy when she speaks, and I catch a nervous glance she sends Mark's way.

"Uh…" Mark clears his throat. Scratching his neck, he twists his head and, without looking at any of us, asks, "Would you be her godparents?"

"What?" I ask, stunned. I didn't expect this in a million years, and I look at Amy with eyes wide. "Are you sure?"

"There's no one else we would rather have," she says, tears streaming down her face. I know what she's doing. And I feel my face get soft. She knows we're having a hard time. She knows we're on a rough road. And she knows there's a good possibility that we're never going to have our own child. So, she's doing all she can to somehow give me one. And I couldn't love her more. "Of course we will," I reply, my own tears dripping from my lashes.

I look at Sam, only to see the ravaged look on his face. I know he's struggling with wanting a child and his instinct of protecting me from any harm, including the pain of IVF. But, as he looks at the newborn baby in my arms, I know his refusal to try again will soon change. So I just give him a small smile and mouth to him, "I love you," and then I look down to the baby girl in my arms, my *goddaughter,* and I lose myself in the beauty that is her.

***

Sam

It's late. It was a long day, and he's happy it's coming to its end. All the pains from the day of sitting in the waiting room, running out to get something to eat or coffee to drink, all the squeezes Dani did to his hand as she stood by Amy's bed, enduring the pain in her hand that was held by Amy, is letting itself known. And as much as he wants to go, to take his wife home and sleep for a week, he doesn't move from his position.

He's standing with his shoulders against the wall, his arms crossed on his chest, looking at his wife.

She's never been more beautiful than she is right at this moment, holding that baby in her arms. Amy is in bed, trying to stay awake and losing the battle. Every few seconds, her eyes fly open, checking on her daughter who is sleeping soundly in Dani's arms.

There is a movement at his right side, but he doesn't stop looking at her. He can't. In this moment, he knows what he has to do. And that knowledge burns in his gut.

He's finally got his wife back. After everything they've been through, she came back to him. And with what he's about to do, he will, once again, set her on that hard and dark path, possibly losing her again in the process. Probably forever.

But, looking at her, at the joy written all over her face, he has no choice. It's the right thing to do. When she admitted she's seen the crib, he knew it was coming. He wanted to make something for their baby, something they could both cherish, and something strong enough where their grandchildren could lay their little heads at night. At that moment, when she brought it up, he couldn't stomach the idea of them trying again, of her disappointment when it didn't take, of her pain. The sight that is in front of him gives him strength. He wants that. But he wants that baby girl she's so adoringly looking at to be *their* child. One they made together.

Feeling a hand squeezing his shoulder, he glances to his right. "Look at her. Isn't she a beauty, or what?" Mark's eyes go from his wife to his baby girl, not staying on either for long. Like he isn't quite sure which one he means.

After that scene so many years ago in his first shithole of an apartment—a shithole that Dani treated and acted like it was a mansion—it was tough staying friends with the man. He knew his priority was Dani, and he had absolutely no intention of speaking with him ever again. But, after a week, Dani forced his hand. She texted Mark from his phone, saying that they were broken up and that he should come and bring the gang. Surprisingly, he came alone.

And when he saw Dani standing at the counter, putting finishing touches on the snacks she made—"No reason for the people who come under this false pretenses to go hungry," she explained when he asked what in the hell she was doing—the first thing out of his mouth was, "Dani, I'm so sorry. Would you please forgive me?"

Hearing Mark's words, she turned to Sam and confusingly said, "I told you so." Then with a teasing glint in her eye, asked Mark, "Is she a miracle worker? And does she give you a hard time, playing hard to get?"

"Yeah," Mark answered to both questions, red-faced and scratching the back of his neck.

"That's my girl. I wanna meet her soon," she demanded. Then seeing Mark's embarrassment, she walked to him on her bare feet, put her hand on his chest, and whispered, "Don't worry, tiger, you'll get her."

And that was it. From that moment on, they were inseparable.

"Happy for you, brother. Down to my soul, happy for you," he says to Mark, sincerity dripping from every syllable. "But jealous of you. Down to my bones." With a slap on Mark's chest, he mutters, "Congratulations."

Sighing, he pushes from the wall and walks the five steps that took him across the room to his wife. Putting his arm around her waist, he molds his body against her back and buries his face in her neck, inhaling her scent.

"She's perfect," Dani whispers.

Hearing the longing in her voice, the pain pierces his chest. Squeezing her, he whispers back, "Yeah."

Turning her head, she puts her lips to his ear. "You okay?"

He pulls his face from her neck and looks into her eyes. For a while now, she's been after him to try again. But he can't put her through it. He can't watch the grief and depression eat away at her. The day the results came in, even though they knew before that it didn't work, was the worst day of his life. To watch that amount of sorrow mar her whole being was pure torture. And the worst part was, he was helpless. There was not one thing he could have done to make it better. To make the pain go away. All he had left to do was watch. Watch her get lost completely. And now, he's going to set her on that path once again, when he said he wouldn't, couldn't do that again. But, he has to. She wants this, and with every fiber of his being, he wants her to have it.

"Set the appointment" is his answer.

Hearing that, there's a spark in her eyes, and she gives him her weight. She doesn't need more explanation. She knows what he means. Looking back down to the precious baby she hold in her arms, she smiles and says, "I'll call the doctor in the morning."

EPILOGUE

"*I KNEW WE would make a beautiful baby, but this.*" *He shakes his head like he can't believe his own words and looks to the baby next to him on the bed. "He's more than perfect." He leans down and kisses his small cheek. His lips there, he says to the baby boy, "And it only took a team of ten doctors to make you." Hearing that, I throw my head back and laugh.*

Standing in the middle of the room, I look through the window to the night sky. There are no clouds in the sky, so the moon and the stars are shining in all their glory, cascading the bluish light into the room. After so long, I can look at them and feel at peace, for once not wandering which one would choose me.

Turning from the nightly canvas, I look to my vision come true. "You know you do us no good by holding him while he's asleep," I pretend to scold him.

"Yep," Sam says, popping the P. But still his ass stays planted in the rocking chair next to the crib, our baby boy sound asleep with his diapered tush high in the air, as he lies on his daddy's chest.

It took us three years and four tries, but we finally did it. We finally got our star.

"You have to put him down." I try to be firm, but the humor is peeking through, because I know I'm fighting a losing battle. Every single night since we came home from the hospital, bringing our little prince, we have this conversation. And every single night, I give in and leave them be.

A long time ago, Sam told me there was not one person in this whole world he could love more than me. I knew he was wrong, and I tried to tell him that; he just wouldn't listen. Even now, when I gave him someone to love more, he's still firm we hold an equal measure of his love. I know he's full of shit, and I'm happy beyond reason because of that. Then again, I love my husband and my son more and more each day that passes, so what the hell do I know?

Looking back at those three years, all I can see is gray and black. There is no color, no sparkle. No joy. Nothing. It was such a hard road that I'm amazed we made it through. After the third time, Sam wanted to stop, but I promised him, only one more try. Only one. And if it didn't work, we'd stop. He said he was losing me and he didn't know how to reach me anymore, how to bring me back. I never once stayed planted on that couch, losing the hours, doing nothing, but the process did change me. He said I stopped smiling, stopped living, just went through the motions of everyday life, there but far away from him. My behavior got so bad that Marcy kept her pregnancy from me for four months, and when I asked her why she didn't tell me, she said she was scared of hurting me. And Jules went through her drama all on her own, because she didn't want to add the burden of her hectic love life to my pain. That was the moment I knew we had to stop and find another way. But me being me, I couldn't just say, *"Hey, it didn't work. Time to move on."* I had to give it another go.

Since the beginning of the last try, everything felt different. Even the doctors and nurses said so. All of us just knew this was the one. This one would succeed. So, when the betaHCG confirmed the pregnancy, no one was surprised.

From that moment on, Sam kept saying it was a girl. He wanted one with blonde hair and big blue eyes. He even tried to order it from the lab technician when we came for the transfer.

He got the opposite.

He got a boy with brown hair, and from the moment he opened his almond-shaped eyes, they were deep, chocolate brown. Sam says he got perfection.

Moving from the middle of the room, I go to my boys and do what I do every night. I bend deep and put my palm on my son's back. Closing my eyes, I feel his heart beating and the rising and falling of his back with each breath he takes. His first cry aside, there is no more beautiful sound than thatof his breathing.

I open my eyes and look at the green ones of my husband. "Five more minutes."

"Ten." He grins.

"I'm gonna go and get ready for bed."

Kissing the miracle that is my baby, I stand up and kiss my husband then turn around to go do just that. Stopping at the door, I glance at the night sky one more time. "Sam?"

"Hmm?" He hums against our son's head.

"There's another one waiting for us." I don't look at him, just keep looking at the stars.

"I know," he whispers.

Sending them one last smile, I go get ready for bed.

The End

Little star,

There will come a time when you will ask me how you came to this world. I will tell you then that the stork brought you to us.

Then, more time will pass, and once again, you will come to me and ask that same question. I will tell you then that Mommy and Daddy loved each other very much and wanted to have a baby, and one day we found you in a cabbage. By that time, you will know I'm full of shit, so I'll try to bullshit you some more and tell you that you were made in a workshop. It won't be a total lie, since you were made in a lab.

Then, the time will come for you to learn some facts of this life we have on this earth and how we all are created and born. And after what I'm sure is going to be an extremely horrifying talk with your father (for the both of you), I will give you this book.

This is not the story of your daddy and me, my star, although the words at the beginning of each chapter are the ones he told me throughout the years we've been together. But, it represents the love we had for each other and the love we had for you, even before you were born.

And then, the time will come when you'll be standing in the room, holding the hand of the woman you chose to spend your life with, of the woman you will love beyond measure, that you'll think nothing can compare to, and you will understand. That will be the day you will make your daddy's dream come true. The day you will make him a grandfather.

I want you to know how much we loved you, and how much more we love you now. For five years, you were the only thing moving us forward. Our only focus. We were willing to move heaven and earth to get you. So, I want to thank you.

Thank you for coming to us. Thank you for choosing us to be your parents.

We dreamed of you, but you turned out to be so much more than we could possibly ever imagine.

I was maybe five months pregnant when you woke me up in the middle of the night, kicking. It was the first time you kicked more than a couple of times in a short period of time. I put my hand on my belly, and the more you kicked, the more my smile grew. It lasted for two minutes, tops, but by the end, I was giggling so much the bed shook, and I ended up waking your father. I was so happy, and my happiness just grows as you do. I will remember that night and the feel of you for the rest of my life. So, thank you for that.

Every morning, you give us a gift of your sleepy smile peeking through your crib, or when we don't act fast enough, you throw you pacifier at our heads. That smile is something I took millions of pictures and videos of. I don't know if there will ever be anything as beautiful as each and every morning you give us. Thank you for that.

Thank you for when you see that Mommy and Daddy are still sleeping, so you play in your crib quietly, as rare as it is.

It took me six days to tell you that I love you. Six days after you were born was the first time. I couldn't understand what was wrong with me. Why I didn't feel that wave of love the instant the midwife put you on my chest. And then, on the sixth day, it came to me. That wave couldn't come. It couldn't, because I loved you from the very moment you were conceived, from the moment the transfer was done and the doctor gave me an ultrasound picture of you. Hell, I loved you even before that. And on the sixth day, you opened your eyes and looked right at me. And I knew the answer. Thank you for that.

Thank you for your unconditional love that shines through your eyes when you look at me. For the faith you have in me.

Thank you for every word you learn, most especially the word "mama," and that you know who it represents.

Thank you for the three most beautiful sounds I've heard in my life.

Your first cry. It was so quiet but so persistent. I laughed and cried with you at the same time.

The sound of your breathing when you are sleeping.

And the sound of your laughter. It's so very rich and warm. Like when you shake a bag full of walnuts. I think that one is my favorite.

Thank you for teaching me new things and showing me the beauty in the world. Your reaction to the leaves rustling and your facial expression when you first touched the grass is something I will cherish forever.

Thank you for each and every day you give me.

I could tell you that I love you as much as there are grains of sand in the desert, but that wouldn't be enough.

I could tell you that I love you as much as there are the stars in the sky, but even that wouldn't be enough.

So all I can tell you is...

One day will come when you'll hold something precious in your arms, and you'll know. You will know how much I love you.

All I want for you is to be happy and healthy.

That's it.

However that comes.

Nothing is more important to me.

So, thank you.

Thank you for taking me on this journey.

But, most of all...

Thank you, my little star.

Thank you,

for choosing me.

Love always,
Mama Ana

ACKNOWLEDGMENTS

For the last couple of weeks I keep listing in my mind all the people I need to say thank you to, and all the ways I'm going to do it.

And now, sitting in front of my computer, my fingers at the ready... and I forget everything.

So I'll just start and if I forget someone, please forgive me, and know that I'm deeply thankful!

First, thank you to all the lovely woman behind the Hot Tree Editing! Becky, Donna, Kayla... You did wonders transforming my story (full of mistakes, grammatical and some other) to the perfection that it is now. I can't say thank you enough for that small miracle (there're were that many problems with it!) and for the fact that you managed to pull me back from the edge I was standing at, and not letting me give up. (Kayla especially.)

Next, a huge thank you to JM Walker for creating a breathtaking cover. All I took was describing the mere idea, and you managed to capture it to the smallest detail. (I suppose now is the time to come clean, and confess; it wasn't mine, it was my husbands' idea. Where did he come up with it, I still don't know, but as he was describing it, I stopped breathing from the beauty of it, and new, it was it!)

I would like to say thank you to my beta readers, Randie, Rebecca, Paula, you were the first ones to read the story. So, thank you for giving it a chance, and thank you for not running away after you did!

Now, these two were mention earlier, but they did so much for me, answering all the questions I threw their way, always having patience for me, it just needs to be done. Kayla Robichaux and JM Walker, thank you! Thank you for everything. Without you, this day would never come!

Thank you to my sister, Dora. I don't have enough time to list all the reasons why I am thankful to you, so I'll just say, thank you for being my sister.

As every woman in love, I'll also say thanks to my husband, Sven.

I was at work today, when you went out of your way and brought me lunch. As I asked my co-worker to bring it back, she looked at me with surprise in her eyes, and asked disbelievingly, "Your husband brought you this?"

"Yes," I answered, looking closely as she kept glancing between the food in my hands and my face.

"You have such a good husband," she whispered and took the food to the kitchen.

All I could think at that moment was, you don't know the half of it.

To you, Sven, it not may seem much this little moment of my work day. But to me, it's everything. It perfectly describes the man you are.

Thank you. Thank you for being that man, and thank you for choosing me.

And last, I WANT TO SAY THANK YOU TO EACH AND EVERY PERSON WHO GAVE DANI AND SAM'S STORY A CHANCE! From the bottom of my hart... HVALA!

ABOUT

Ana Balen was born in Zagreb, Croatia, where she still lives with her husband, their son (read boss!) and the son's pet rabbit named Shhh! (or some other gibberish that's the favorite of their son for the day.)

She spends her days driving her husband up the wall (when he can't get her ass up from the bed in the mornings), reading and daydreaming, or following orders from a two-year old. In the hectic life she leads (and loves every second of it), she never thought about writing. But, then one day a name popped in her head, then, the snippets of things, and she sat down and started typing. Next thing, she wrote a book. And now, she's trying to write another one ;)